AUTUMN DAFFODILS

CHARLIE'S STORY

Peter Turnham

Cover design and interior formatting by JD Smith Design

Copyright © 2019 Peter Turnham

All rights reserved.

ISBN: 978-1-9160979-0-2 (ebook)
978-1-9160979-1-9 (paperback)

Dedication

To my old friend Rex Hudson,
the inspiration for the character Stanley.

Stanley's exploits throughout the book
are entirely fictitious, but anyone who knew Rex
will recognise him in Stanley immediately.

A Note from the Author

First of all, thank you for deciding to read Autumn Daffodils. I hope you will enjoy reading it as much as I have enjoyed writing it. The story is written in first person dialogue, narrated by Charles (later known as Charlie). This enables us to share his inner thoughts, and you will gradually come to realise that Charles doesn't just narrate the story; he is the story. I can assure the reader that Charles is not based upon me but, as the story progressed, he knew what I was thinking before I did! This was when I realised that something wonderful had happened. My characters were not just believable; I became conscious of sharing these people's lives. The story then unfolded quite spontaneously through them. I lived every emotion with them and hope you will too.

There is a common link between the characters. They have each suffered a traumatic event in their lives, which is what brings them together. They have all been left with a legacy from their troubled past; it may be guilt, shame, or denial. In the case of Charles, it's his broken heart. In other words, Autumn Daffodils is a study of the human condition. You are not just invited to be an observer. I invite you to be a part of it, just as I was. It will be a roller-coaster ride. You will laugh and you will cry but, above all, enjoy the ride!

Peter Turnham

April 2019

Table of Contents

Acknowledgments

To my wife Carol,
my spell- and grammar-check
my editor and IT consultant,
my indispensable other half.

Chapter One
THE NEW BOY ARRIVES

I was enjoying a cup of tea that Lizzy had kindly brought over to me (my trousers were nearly dry where she had spilled the contents of the saucer into my lap). Charlotte appeared, escorting someone who was obviously a new boy. Being the end of the tour, she introduced him to one or two people and then left the poor sod to get on with it. I was a new boy just a few months ago, so I knew exactly how he felt. I watched with interest. Audrey was the first to comment.

"Do you see the new boy? At least this one has the grace to wear a jacket and tie; perhaps there's hope for him!"

I smiled at what Audrey had said.

"Let's be fair to the chap. It can be a bit daunting entering a community like this."

"What do you mean? What's not to like about this place?"

"Nothing," I said. "No, it's not that, it's not entering this place. It's leaving your last place that's daunting."

"Oh dear. Shall I take him a cup of tea?" Lizzy asked.

Harold raised his eyes toward the heavens.

"For God's sake, don't soak the poor chap in tea before we even know his name! Anyway, what's wrong with leaving your past life behind? I thought that was the point of coming here."

Bill's attention remained focused on the new boy and he has an eye for detail.

"You're right about the tie, Audrey. Have you noticed the motif? Country sporting man, I would say."

My coping strategy when I arrived here was to be reactive, never proactive. In other words, keep your head down and smile when appropriate. The usual procedure would be for some kind soul to engage the new person in conversation and ask them the usual questions: where you lived before you came here, do you have any family, you know the kind of thing? I was beginning to think that the new boy had adopted my time-honoured strategy and was keeping his head down. It certainly worked for me. I like to adhere to the old maxim that it's always better that people think you have little to say, rather than opening your mouth and confirming their worst fears. Not so the new boy. He did no less than walk right up to one of the couples and engage them in conversation.

"Can you hear what they're saying?" asked Audrey.

"Don't be ridiculous," replied Harold. "I can only just hear you, Audrey, and you're sat right next to me."

"What did he say, Harold? I can't quite hear you," said Lizzy.

"I didn't say, Lizzy, that's the point. We're too far away so none of us can hear what's going on. Just pretend you're at some sort of sporting event. You don't want to take part, do you? You just want to be a spectator."

"I don't like sport, Harold."

"Oh, for pity's sake, will someone save me from this?"

Harold's exasperation was quite entertaining, but then we watched with increasing interest as another couple joined in the conversation with the new boy. The next thing we knew he was quite the centre of attention. They were all beaming from ear to ear. It was as if the new boy had brought his own little carnival with him.

Audrey looked on in disbelief.

"What on earth are they finding to talk about?"

"I can't really hear," I said, "but the new boy is obviously asking them questions about themselves and everyone's smiling."

Audrey couldn't understand it.

"We don't talk about ourselves, not to perfect strangers. What on earth are those people thinking of?"

She was quite right. We don't talk about ourselves. They asked me the usual questions when I arrived, to which I replied with the usual answers. We probably spent at least two minutes on the subject. From then on, it seems to be inappropriate to delve any further. This is exactly what happened when I met Audrey. In fact, this is what happened with all my little group of friends.

"I suppose you're right, Audrey," I said. "Perhaps this is our version of polite society."

"And what on earth is wrong with polite society? That's exactly what's lacking these days!"

Bill seemed to be keen to avoid that subject, drawing our attention back to the new boy.

"Do you notice his shoes? I bet they were a first-class pair of brogues twenty years ago but look at the condition of them!"

Harold put his cup of tea down, and those of us facing the wrong way turned in our chairs, staring in unison at the ancient brogues. Even from some distance away we could see they were badly cracked with age, but still polished to perfection.

"You can learn a lot from a man's shoes," proclaimed Bill. "He appreciates quality and derives great pleasure from owning and maintaining them. They are old friends for whom he feels a duty of care. This is a man you can rely on."

At that precise moment the lounge wall clock struck twelve. It was as if Bill was a television news presenter and, having made a profound statement, 'Big Ben' had chimed to add gravitas to his words. We all smiled and waited for his next observation.

"What do you notice about his jacket?"

Once again, we all stared in unison, but by now the new boy had moved slightly out of view, so we all raised ourselves up in our chairs. We must have looked like a gang of alarmed meerkats.

"I see what you mean," I said. "The jacket and trousers are the same vintage as the shoes, and those leather hems on the cuffs and the elbow patches are later additions."

"He might take care of his kit," Harold said, "but I bet it's donkeys' years since the buttons on that tweed jacket met with the buttonholes. The fellow looks like Humpty Dumpty."

I'm not sure I would have expressed it quite like that, but Harold was right. The new boy did carry a fair bit of excess weight, and it was entirely around his middle. I commented that he also sported a very rosy face.

"High blood pressure, I expect," said Bill.

"Are you sure I shouldn't take him a nice cup of tea?" Lizzy said, obviously immediately alarmed.

Audrey pretended to look indignant.

"I think you're very rude, Harold. He looks charming in that yellow waistcoat. He has the air of a gentleman about him, unlike some of you."

"That's good coming from you, Audrey. You think any man who doesn't wear trainers is a gentleman."

"Quite right, Harold, trainers on a man of a certain age are an abomination."

Lunch time was rapidly approaching. I concluded that we had probably deduced as much about the new boy as we were going to. In all probability, he would now fade into a genteel state of anonymity, rather like the rest of us really. We sat down for lunch and the new boy was not even mentioned.

Audrey looked very thoughtful.

"What you said, Charles, about leaving your last place behind. Did you mean that?"

This wasn't the kind of thing we normally talked about, especially Audrey, so she caught me a bit unawares. I hesitated for a moment, and Bill stepped in to answer the question.

"As you said, Audrey, 'What's not to like here?' The thing is, before we came here, we were all surrounded by those things that identify us, job, home, all that memorabilia. When we came here, for most of us the apartments are smaller than the homes we left behind, so we're effectively downsizing. It simply means that you leave a lot of your 'stuff' behind. You don't have to bring any of that identity with you if you don't want to. It could be used as an opportunity for a fresh start."

It's noticeable that, when Bill says something, it's quite often followed by silence from the rest of us. This was one of those occasions, as we exchanged glances around the table. I had certainly left behind a lot of 'stuff' and talking about it was the last thing I wanted to do. It was quite out of character for Audrey to talk about such things, and so I was even more surprised when she continued with the subject.

"You said it was daunting, Charles. What did you mean?"

"Well, it's what Bill said about leaving your 'stuff' behind. It's all about the world we create for ourselves, it becomes our identity, it's who we are. When you join a community like this you automatically leave that past behind. There's a sense of finality about it; that's what makes it a bit daunting."

"Can't see the problem," said Harold. "Pleased to dump my 'stuff'."

My possessions were in storage, so I suppose, really, I was being a bit disingenuous, not that I was about to admit it. A quick change of subject was required.

"How's your lunch, Audrey?" I asked.

-oOo-

That evening, we all arrived for pre-dinner drinks as arranged. This place is rather like a sprawling resort hotel; you could easily imagine you were in some exotic holiday location except, of course, you're not. We're near Cambridge! Alternatively, you could even convince yourself this is a small village, which is why it's known by everyone as 'The Village'. If you overlook the bland mix of harmonized neutral colours and the contract carpet, the apartments and most of the reception rooms do have a nice feel to them.

The bar is no exception, it has a welcoming atmosphere. Perhaps it's simply that it's too posh to smell of beer! We pulled a couple of additional leather chairs round a table, not an easy task, as they're heavy with little to get hold of. Finally, we all sat back to enjoy the start of our evening. No sooner had we settled ourselves down than the new boy appeared.

"Whisky drinker," I said to Audrey. "Any man who enjoys a single malt must be a good egg."

At that point the new boy made a beeline for one of the other ladies and we could overhear what was being said.

"May I introduce myself? Stanley Hudson at your service, madam. May I say what a great pleasure it is to meet you?"

The unsuspecting lady appeared to be taken aback. She hastily babbled a reply.

"Vera. I mean I'm Vera. That's my name, Vera."

"And may I say what a charming name for such a charming lady. Now, tell me, my dear, where did you live before you came here?" continued Stanley.

I was just a little surprised. The new boy was supposed to keep his head down and wait to be asked questions. The lady seemed almost anxious to respond and she gave the name of a small village in Suffolk.

"Oh yes," said Stanley. "And what is your family name?"

"Jennings," she replied.

"Did your family own the grocer's shop there?"

"How on earth did you know that?"

Stanley responded by saying that he had sold a house in the village and remembered the shop. It gradually came to light that Stanley was an estate agent. Later, a conversation with one of the gentlemen once again started with Stanley's favourite first line.

"Now, tell me dear boy, where did you live before you came here?"

Would you believe it. He knew all about the place, even though it was halfway across the country! Later in the same conversation, the gentleman was telling Stanley about his preoccupation with showing dogs. Stanley immediately responded.

"Tell me old chap, did you ever show any of your dogs at Crufts? I may well have judged them!"

Over the next couple of weeks these revelations simply continued at an extraordinary rate. Everyone was talking about Stanley. Knowledge about furniture, dogs, heavy horses, poultry, rabbits, you name it, Stanley appeared to be an expert. He said he played cricket for his county and was a member of the MCC. He was an estate agent, a land agent, a valuer and auctioneer, not to mention various judging and commentary roles. He was also involved in just about every country sport you can think of. If all this sounds a little far-fetched, it pales into insignificance compared with the fact that he seemed to know something about almost everyone who had ever lived!

"He's a Walter Mitty character. Either that or he's a kind of con artist," said Harold, unconvinced.

"I'm not sure about that," I said. "Have you noticed how he puts people at ease and gets them to talk about themselves?"

I had quickly noticed that when Stanley engaged with someone, however briefly, he seemed to leave that person happier for the experience. Bill, as always, made one of his erudite observations.

"Stanley's one of those charismatic personalities who consumes all the oxygen in a room simply by walking into it. The innocent bystander, who's left gasping for breath, ends up blurting out their life story like a drowning man gasping for air."

It would have been very appropriate had the clock struck ten at that precise moment. Instead there was a long silence. No-one said anything, until Lizzy became very concerned.

"Oh dear, who did you say was gasping for air?"

Harold said something which was almost funny.

"Audrey will have to take care. The air's thin enough from where she talks down to me!"

Chapter Two
AUDREY'S STORY

Secretly we were all looking forward to meeting Stanley. Our opportunity came the following day. We were sitting together enjoying our afternoon tea when Stanley appeared.

"Oh, my goodness, I do believe he's coming over to us," said a very alarmed Audrey.

"Don't panic," I replied, "and no blurting."

"And watch out for the lack of oxygen," said Harold.

Stanley duly presented himself and warmly shook everyone's hand, saving Audrey until last. He held Audrey's hand and then cupped his other hand on top of it.

"May I say, my dear, I have been so looking forward to meeting you. In so many ways, I feel I have saved the best until last."

"Oh good heavens, oh dear, I mean I'm surprised you noticed me!" Audrey immediately blurted out.

Stanley maintained his hold upon her hand.

"How could I not notice beauty such as yours my dear, you light up the room!"

In one sentence the oxygen was gone, and Audrey was left gasping for air. Harold whispered into my ear.

"Bullshit, he must be after something."

Stanley was not wrong about Audrey, she does light up any room. I just wish I had said it. Stanley could do no wrong from this point on as he continued his invasion of our little group.

"Now, why don't we sit down so that I can get to know you all," he said.

Whereupon everyone duly did as we were told. Audrey had completely capitulated. Harold was the only one of us who was resisting.

"You look parched Stanley," he said mischievously. "Perhaps you'd get Stanley a cup of tea, Lizzy."

Everyone smiled at the prospect except Audrey, who was still gasping for oxygen. Lizzy eventually staggered back with her stick in one hand, while the cup and saucer in the other hand were held at an even more alarming angle than usual. She passed the cup of tea to Stanley, whereupon the contents of the saucer duly poured into his lap.

"Good plan," I whispered to Harold.

"Oh how silly of me to spill my tea like that, after you've gone to so much trouble, Lizzy," said Stanley immediately, "but it's no bad thing. I've been meaning to have these trousers cleaned for ages."

He then seamlessly continued the conversation.

"Let me tell you why I have been so looking forward to meeting you all. I hope you don't mind me saying, but you're the enigmatic group that no-one seems to know much about. That tells me that you're the most interesting people here."

"Well, I don't know about that," said Harold, "but tell me Stanley, why are you here?"

"Oh, that's easy, old boy. The bar."

"What's so special about the bar?" growled Harold.

"Hang on, Harold," I said. "You're not a whisky drinker, but I can tell you this place has got one of the finest collections of malt whisky you're likely to find. It all started some years ago with one of the residents, and it's simply grown ever since. Place has quite a reputation for it."

"Oh, dear boy, do I detect a kindred spirit?" said Stanley, looking very pleased.

I smiled in acknowledgement. I'm not sure I wanted to admit it, but let's just say the bar's reputation was a contributory factor when I made my decision to join the community.

"Now this is the interesting thing about you all," said Stanley, "you must be among the youngest people here." (He was being very diplomatic to include Lizzy in that observation). "So, I'm wondering what's drawn you together as a group, and what made you each decide to come here? Forgive my presumptuousness, but I'm guessing that you must all be keen golfers or tennis players?"

"Oh, good heavens no," said Audrey. "I can't abide the game."

"It's the footwear, you see, Stanley," said Harold. "Audrey couldn't possibly wear trainers!"

Audrey gave Harold one of her condescending looks but declined to comment further. I looked at the others and they looked at me, but no-one spoke. Stanley in one question had gone straight to the point, and his satisfaction was self-evident.

"I'm usually right about these things, you are the most interesting group here!"

Our silence about our reasons for being there was all grist to the mill for Stanley. He smiled at us like I might smile at the cover of an interesting book. He made himself comfortable in his chair, adjusted the buttons of his waistcoat and turned towards Audrey.

"Now, tell me Audrey, where does such a beautiful lady originally come from?"

It was perfectly clear that Audrey, having been both flattered and starved of oxygen, was in no condition to resist, so we all sat back to follow the outcome.

"This will be interesting! He's not going to get much out of Dippy, is he?" whispered Harold, leaning across to me.

I had to agree. Audrey avoided conversation about herself

most assiduously, though she's anything but dippy. This is a misconception about Audrey that Harold started. When she says she can't remember or doesn't know something, she can give the impression of being dippy. I suspect the others are not seeing the sparkle in her eyes that I see. Nevertheless, we sat smiling, waiting for what we assumed would be the inevitable rebuff of Stanley's question.

"Well," Audrey said. She paused and then started again. "Like my parents, I was born near Oxford."

"Delightful county," said Stanley smiling broadly, "I know the area well. Whereabouts exactly?"

"We lived just on the edge of Oxford, in a country house called Belmont."

"Belmont, Belmont," Stanley repeated the name to himself. "It does sound familiar. Would you describe it to me?"

Audrey appeared to be very thoughtful as she mentally recalled the house of her childhood, and we were all amazed at the detail she could remember; it was as if she had only recently left there. The reason for this soon became evident. Belmont was Audrey's ancestral home, occupied by her family for over two hundred years. It was a wonderful house, built in the seventeenth century. There were eight bedrooms, four bathrooms, a grand dining room, library and music rooms, as well as various other reception rooms. Outside there were several outbuildings and staff quarters. The house sat in the middle of a large estate and enjoyed a magnificent vista towards the south.

None of us had heard anything about Audrey's childhood, much less a description of this magnificent house. I was left to wonder why she had not told us about it before. It did answer one question. I had often wondered if Audrey's aristocratic demeanour was genuine, or an adopted affectation. In less than a few minutes, Stanley had extracted this information with effortless ease. He continued with his probing questions, except that they didn't in any way appear to be probing.

The next thing we learned was that Audrey had a brother, John, and a nanny called Pam. It was immediately clear that Pam was a very significant figure in Audrey's life. Her father's name was George and he had been a stockbroker. As soon as she mentioned him, it was clear from her expression that they were very close. Audrey went on to describe her school days, first the local village school then a private day boarding. These early memories were always associated with Pam the nanny. There was no mention of her mother.

Stanley sat back in his chair, adjusted the next tight button of his waistcoat, and drew a long, relaxed breath. All of this was no doubt designed to put Audrey at ease; indeed, she did appear to be strangely compliant.

"Do tell us, my dear, about your mother," Stanley said making the apparent compliance quickly change. Suddenly Audrey looked like a rabbit caught in the headlamps. I thought it might be a kindness to stop Stanley's flow for a moment.

"It's a bit early, but what about a gin and tonic, Audrey?" I asked.

It was as if I'd thrown her a lifeline. She replied with obvious relief.

"Oh Charles, what a good idea! Make it a large one."

"Oh! How terribly kind of you, old boy. I'll have a single malt," said Stanley, his eyes lighting up.

I proceeded to the bar, with Harold and Bill close behind me. It quickly became apparent that we were all thinking the same thing, but it was Harold who was the first to put it into words.

"How on earth has Stanley got Audrey to reveal her past like this?"

"I've never heard Audrey talking about her past," said Bill, looking bemused.

"I know what you mean," said Harold. "Perhaps there's more to Dippy than she lets on."

Bill, as an emeritus professor, usually has something erudite to say, and this occasion was no exception. "Maybe Audrey's here to get away from her past; it's the nature of a place like this."

"Lizzy might not agree, Bill," I said. "She's convinced you're a psychic, not a physicist, she wants you to communicate with her dead husband."

We returned to the others, laughing about Bill's psychic abilities. Audrey drank her gin and tonic like a woman who had just trekked across the Atacama Desert, whereupon Harold displayed a moment of unaccustomed empathy.

"Sorry, Audrey, that bloody stupid barman has given you a piddling little gin and tonic. We asked for a double, I'll get you another one."

"I'll have another single malt," Stanley shouted after Harold as he sped away.

Audrey consumed the second gin and tonic with equal urgency, and slumped back into her chair, altogether lacking her usual poise.

"I've never spoken about these matters to anyone before," she said. "It's all so difficult." Stanley was quick to ease her fears.

"Difficult my dear? Nonsense! It's not forming the words that worries you, it's how those words will be received. Now let me reassure you, my dear. You've offered us the privilege of sharing a part of your life. We in our turn embrace that privilege and welcome you into our lives. The bond that we share is in the present, not in the past."

We all sat looking at each other. I'd assumed Audrey was telling us a little about her childhood, not that she was entering a confessional and baring her soul with us as her priestly confidantes. There was, however, something about Stanley and his way of approaching people. If he said that Audrey was offering us the privilege of sharing a part of her life, then suddenly that was a reality. No-one contradicted Stanley, so we had all effectively agreed to welcome Audrey into our lives.

How Stanley did it was a mystery but, in an instant, the bond he described between us sprang into existence. No-one said a word.

I was not sure if it was Stanley's hypnotic charm or the gin and tonic, but Audrey did relax a little. However, Stanley's question about her mother still hung in the air.

"I can't remember my mother before things went wrong," she said. "I can only ever remember her in a perpetual state of depression."

Audrey described her childhood relationship with her mother, Isabelle. At first, she recalled images of her mother, where she stood, where she sat. Her mother's voice was talking to her, she could see the empty look in her eyes.

Finally, as she allowed these long-suppressed memories to return, her mother was no longer just a face or a voice. Audrey was back there with her, a little girl who felt rejected and unloved. It was an extremely uncomfortable moment; this was obviously a great sadness in Audrey's life.

It transpired that Audrey's mother suffered from a kind of lifelong clinical depression. The unfortunate part was that her father, George, was discovered to have had a brief affair while Audrey was still only a child. Isabelle blamed her condition entirely upon George's indiscretion which, although untrue, cast a permanent cloud over their relationship.

"The affair was totally out of character for the father that I grew up knowing. He always bitterly regretted it. He referred to the affair as his 'deplorable moment of weakness'."

"I see now, this is why your nanny was such an important part of your life," Stanley said.

"Oh yes," replied Audrey. "She was the wonderful mother I never had."

We all sat in silence. I couldn't think of an appropriate thing to say and obviously neither could anyone else, until, that is, Lizzy spoke up.

"I'm sorry about your father's deplorable weakness, was it

arthritis?" Audrey was trying to be considerate and answered in a loud voice so that Lizzy could hear.

"No, Lizzy, it wasn't his body, it was his mind that suffered."

Lizzy appeared shocked. "Oh dear, I've not heard of arthritis of the mind. Do you think that might be why I can't remember things so well?"

"God help us!" said Harold.

Bill laughed and excused himself as he regularly does, saying, "I'll just pop off for a moment."

Why he can't just say he has to go to the loo, I have no idea. However, Stanley made use of the time entertaining us with an anecdote from his past, about his exploits while he was employed by the Sultan of Brunei. If the truth be told, I secretly wanted to know where Audrey's life went from here. I'm sure the others thought the same, but I felt it would be a little inappropriate to ask. No such worries about inappropriateness for Stanley, however. As soon as Bill returned, he turned his attention back towards Audrey.

"Tell us a little more about your father, my dear." It didn't seem to be inappropriate when Stanley said it, and Audrey was much happier talking about George.

"My father was a wonderful man; he had a way about him."

Audrey's grandfather was something in banking and George had obviously slipped effortlessly into the world of finance. Despite that fact, Audrey still described him as being self-made. The brokerage business in the family name of Calcut was established before Audrey was born. It was quickly apparent that George was a pillar of the financial establishment.

"Why don't you move me further ahead in time my dear, to when you would have been the most beautiful and desirable lady in Oxfordshire," Stanley said, smiling broadly.

Audrey also smiled. The Stanley charm was working. She admitted that she had a long-held ambition to work for her father, but this was not something to be entered into lightly. The world of finance was at that time a male preserve. While it was theoretically possible for her to eventually become a stockbroker, she wouldn't be able to join the Stock Exchange.

This in turn meant that, even if George wanted it, she couldn't become a future partner in the business. The Stock Exchange was run at that time like an exclusive gentlemen's club. Admission was entirely dependent upon connections or family. Like any good club, there was a steep membership fee of several thousand pounds and a yearly subscription and, oh yes, it was gentlemen only. A little later, when Parliament raised the issue of women's exclusion, the members still objected on the grounds that there were no ladies' toilets! Audrey pointed out that it wasn't until 1973 that the first group of ladies was permitted to join the Stock Exchange and so, as far as her father was concerned, a future partnership was not an option for her.

Her brother John had decided to go into medicine. So, if George secretly harboured any ambitions to see his business retained within the family then, despite the obvious problem presented by the Stock Exchange, Audrey would be his only option. There were many things to be considered and Pam the nanny was one of them. Obviously, her job as a nanny no longer existed, but Audrey was adamant that Pam must be retained within the household. Her mother, Isabelle, was agreeable to this arrangement because in all regards Pam was now a companion rather than a nanny. Accommodation for Audrey in London was not going to be a problem; she would stay at her father's London house in Kensington.

At this point in the conversation Stanley hardly needed to ask Audrey any questions. She was much more relaxed, and he had a way of prompting her to continue simply with a facial expression. Audrey was by now smiling and describing her life enthusiastically. It quickly became apparent that, after months of discussion, George had finally decided to take Audrey into the business.

Chapter Three
THE STOCK EXCHANGE

Audrey continued her story with increasing enthusiasm. It was the summer of 1964, she was just nineteen years old and she was going to London to work with her father. It must have been one of the most memorable days of her life. She described it well.

"It was a glorious morning when we arrived at Father's office. The sun was just climbing above the buildings opposite and shining onto the top half of our building. I immediately thought *House of the Rising Sun*. The song by The Animals was a big hit at that time." Audrey admitted with a cheeky smile that it was ages before she realised the true function of the house in the song!

It was clear that here, at last, there were happy memories. She had become, for the moment at least, her usual animated self. She'd opened the door onto a completely new world of work, and a new life. We were all just as keen to walk through that door as Audrey was all that time ago. Stanley was evidently pleased with his work, having somehow cajoled her to this point. Lizzy, however, was not quite clear about the rising sun. She was convinced it must be a pub.

"Did you work as a barmaid, dear?"

We all had a little laugh, and then sat back waiting for Stanley to work his magic once again.

"Now, my dear," Stanley continued with great enthusiasm, "do tell me about your life as a stockbroker."

Audrey answered with equal enthusiasm.

"Well, I certainly didn't start out as a stockbroker!"

She explained that her first jobs consisted of fetching and carrying, filing paperwork and making tea. She was initially concerned that the rest of the staff might not accept her. After all, she was the privileged boss's daughter.

"I think they quickly saw that I was not just a pretty face."

She continued to wax lyrical about the brokerage business, so much so that Stanley couldn't get a word in. Eventually he interrupted her flow.

"Slow down, my dear, you're leaving us all behind. You're describing a world that you intimately understand, but it's one of which we poor mortals are completely ignorant."

"Oh dear, did I get carried away? I'm so sorry. Let me explain."

Of course, one should bear in mind here that, before this, none of us had any idea that Audrey had anything whatever to do with stockbroking. When she started to give us an unscripted presentation, we were all more than a little taken aback.

Audrey spoke fluently and confidently in that refined Home Counties accent of hers, for maybe half an hour or more, detailing every aspect of her father's business and the function of the Stock Exchange. She explained to us that the broker's job was to sell or purchase securities on behalf of the client. The broker essentially acted as agent because, at that time, the Stock Exchange operated with a clear division between the client-purchaser and the stock or the commodity. The Stock Exchange was the marketplace where people came together to buy or to sell, and the people who did the buying and the selling were called stock-jobbers.

The jobber was the market-maker. He would buy and hold stock in his own book and would fix prices depending upon supply and demand. The broker, having received instructions from his client, would then instruct a jobber to buy or sell the stock at the best price. The broker made his money from a commission. The jobber would make his money from the difference between the purchase price and the selling price, known as the spread. The reason for this apparently cumbersome system was in order to keep the client and the trade separate to avoid a conflict of interest.

So far so good. I think we all understood that, but it was the detailed description of how this worked which amazed us. The Stock Exchange, as Audrey had already explained, was run as a gentlemen's club. Bowler hats and furled umbrellas were all a part of the uniform. Just like a long-established club, its way of working was based upon tradition as much as of necessity. There were attendants who wore a uniform reminiscent of a hotel concierge. They were even called waiters, their role being to act as a contact for the jobbers.

Record-keeping was a long paperchain with many links missing. For example, the Exchange was supposed to publish its daily turnover in terms of both trades and value. This was achieved by the jobbers jotting down these details on a scrap of paper and placing it in a box at the end of the day, though many didn't. Even the sale of thousands of pounds worth of stock was no more than a verbal order and a note on a notepad. At 3.30pm when the Exchange closed, the jobbers would go back to their firms and hand over their scraps of paper for the clerical staff to process into contract notes.

It came as no surprise to hear that the Stock Exchange at that time was entirely self-governing, nor that the jobbing system only existed in the UK. Audrey also brought us up to date by explaining that this arcane system ended abruptly in 1986 when the 'Big Bang' overhauled the Stock Market. From that moment, one firm could execute all functions. Bill, who would have understood all this far better than the rest of us, offered an intelligent question.

"If the market-makers, brokers and clients all ended up under the same roof, what happened to the notion of avoiding self-interest?"

Audrey was quick to reply.

"You have a good point, Bill. You might also point a finger at the repeal of the Glass-Steagall Act in the USA in 1999. This removed the separation of investment banking from retail banking. How do you think we ended up with the current financial crisis?"

This was not remotely the dippy Audrey that we knew. We were flabbergasted by what we'd just been told. Why did we know nothing about this? Why had she deliberately kept all this a secret? It was clear that Lizzy understood even less than the rest of us.

"I don't understand it, dear. I think I'll get ready for dinner." With that, she staggered off.

"I'd no idea it was so late! I think I must be getting ready as well," said Audrey, suddenly noticing the time.

This left us gentlemen by ourselves to ruminate upon events. We were all somewhat lost for words.

"I'm simply dumbfounded!" said Harold.

Even Bill, who normally seems to understand everything, was at a loss to explain it. The Audrey that we knew lacked self-confidence, but the woman we just witnessed was the complete opposite. She was self-assured, incredibly knowledgeable and, well, simply magnificent.

Stanley sat quietly, looking rather pleased with himself until Bill asked him if he could explain it. He sat back in his chair with his hands clasped around his ample middle.

"Well, of course, I've only just met you all, but I do wonder. You say Audrey was not forthcoming about her past, but did anyone actually take the time to ask about her life?"

I looked at Bill who looked at Harold, and for a moment we sat in silence.

"The thing is, Stanley," I said, "I think we probably all felt the same. It just seemed to be bad form to ask."

What I really wanted to ask Stanley was why it didn't seem to be bad form when he asked those questions, but obviously it would have been bad form for me to ask him!

Stanley did have a point; we are a bit tied up with our interpretation of polite society here, but I was not sure that he was entirely right. I was still convinced Audrey had deliberately avoided sharing her past with us and I couldn't help but feel what a waste that had been. I had long since found it impossible not to find Audrey attractive and this new self-assured Audrey was even more appealing.

Chapter Four
FREDDY'S
IRRESISTIBLE CHARM

We don't always dine together in the evening. Sometimes we have the men on one table and the ladies on another. Audrey says it gives us the chance to discuss men's things. I'm not sure what men's things are but, if the situation arises, Lizzy tends to panic a bit. She'll say something like, 'Oh dear, quickly Audrey, I think it might be men's things.'

Generally, however, it seems to work out okay. The dining room is quite delightful. This is despite the designers, who have done their best to make it uninteresting with their unexciting mix of the usual harmonised neutral colours. The effect, however, is to draw your attention to the rather fine collection of prints, curtains and furniture. Even the contract carpet is well chosen. The lighting is important in a dining room; things like chandeliers can make or break a room like this. A cheap-and-cheerful plastic monstrosity would be a disaster. Someone here had the good sense to install two genuine Georgian gilt chandeliers, with some matching wall lights. Even the conversion to low energy lighting has been done well. I suspect it must have cost a fortune, but then again, we all know who's paying for it. The final essential is a crisp tablecloth. Remember tablecloths in a restaurant?

On this occasion, I arrived at the table first and was quickly followed by the others. Only Stanley was still to arrive. The only slight problem was that the half-bottle of wine which I had left over from the night before was a rather delightful red that I'd made a point of not sharing with the others. It wasn't a top-flight wine, but a Sarget de Gruaud Larose, a second label wine produced by Chateau Gruaud Larose, one of the top producers of Bordeaux. It's rather good, though not ideally suited as an accompaniment to the halibut which I'd decided upon. I always feel a bit awkward keeping a bottle to myself, but it really is only Bill who has the faintest idea about wine. For the rest, I'm sorry to say it's a bit like feeding strawberries to donkeys!

Stanley arrived moments later and invited himself to our table. The trousers were the same daytime attire, as were the shoes, but the tweed jacket was replaced by an equally thread-bare blazer. The tie had been replaced by his yellow and red MCC one. He actually looked very presentable, as we all did. It was an essential prerequisite that we all dress for dinner. Anything less would be an abomination for Audrey. I have to say in this regard I rather agree with her. I quickly found myself making sure my tie was adjusted perfectly, and as for trying to get away with the odd gravy stain, don't even think about it!

Lizzy had made a special effort with her best evening dress although, with Lizzy, first impressions are always a problem. Perhaps it's the staggering into the restaurant that detracts a little! Audrey is quite tall and slim, she doesn't slouch over like a lot of us, so she seems to look good in whatever she wears. On this occasion, her black chiffon cocktail dress was some-thing of a show-stopper. Her hair is long and I'm never sure if the grey and gold highlights are natural or her hairdresser's additions. She has wonderful bone structure and when she wears her hair tied back, as she had done that evening, she radiates a sophisticated elegance. Her regal presence at the dining table can be quite imposing, so when she gazed around checking that everyone was suitably attired, we all sat upright as if on parade.

"I see you're wearing that same jacket again, Bill," she said, in her best condescending voice.

"Amazing what you can find in the laundry bin," Harold replied, with one of his half-smiles.

Bill as always was impervious to these comments. I'm afraid he always looks as if he has just stepped out of the laundry bin and he can't understand what the problem is.

Harold on the other hand, despite his gruff manner, always looks like the best dressed mannequin in a Savile Row tailor's window.

"You look extremely smart this evening, Harold," Audrey commented.

Harold puffed up his chest, improving his already depressingly perfect posture.

"I try to make a bit of an effort for you, Audrey."

Stanley had only momentarily sat down when he spotted my bottle of wine.

"Ah!" he said. "A bottle of Sarget. Did you know this is the second label of Gruaud Larose?"

He made a lunge for the bottle and promptly commenced filling everyone's glass.

"Is this your bottle, Charles?" he asked, as he drained the last dregs.

My heart sank, but of course I put on my generous face and smiled.

"Do help yourself."

Ten minutes later, there was salt to rub into the wound as Stanley insisted that he should treat us all to another bottle of wine.

"I'm sure the house red is fine," he said.

Harold said this would be fine, Audrey said it was fine, and Bill muttered in agreement the house red would be fine.

"Fine," I replied, while quickly calculating the £45 price difference.

No-one mentioned Audrey's story, and she looked relaxed. We all sat back, having finished our starter course, and Stanley saw his moment.

"Now, where were we, my dear? You'd just entered your father's employment, I believe?"

"That's right, dear, you'd just got a job at the Rising Sun," Lizzy helpfully reminded us.

Audrey kindly explained to Lizzy that this was not quite correct, and quickly moved on.

Within six months, George was sufficiently confident for Audrey to sit in on meetings with clients, and it soon became apparent that she was a considerable asset. When Stanley asked her to explain her contribution, she was surprisingly candid when she answered.

"Father's clients were all men, they all had the same weakness, me! Father said he could always have them eating out of the palm of his hand, but now he didn't need any crumbs."

It was a big surprise to hear that Audrey had this kind of awareness at such a tender age but have it she surely did. The months went by and she consumed every scrap of knowledge that her father could give her. Within two years, Audrey was regularly going to the Stock Exchange with her father, not on the trading floor, of course, but in the public gallery. Within four years, clients were asking for her advice. We were mere onlookers, but even we felt a sense of pride at her achievement. Her hard work and dedication were an inspiration. As she continued her story, it became clear that, by now, her involvement in the business had progressed to a new level.

She suggested to her father how the private client list could be greatly developed. Her idea was that, rather than taking instructions or offering advice, why not offer to take over the client's portfolio and manage it on their behalf? This concept of private wealth management was relatively new in the 1960s but certainly not without precedent. When Audrey suggested it to selected clients, they all embraced the idea. George's commission fee quickly attracted an additional management fee, and this business rapidly expanded. It was the start of a golden age for them.

This was not, however, a golden age for our main courses. We were all so engrossed that most of us neglected our food, and few things look less appetising than a piece of cold and dried-up halibut. The house red did come a close second.

Bill glanced at the halibut.

"If my Sarah had produced a dried-up piece of halibut like that it would have been considered a great success!"

Bill smiled whenever he thought about his beloved wife. We ordered our desserts and we all intuitively looked towards Stanley, anticipating that he would ask Audrey to continue. We were not disappointed.

She moved us forward to the late summer of 1968. Harold Wilson was Prime Minister; the Beatles were singing *Hey Jude* and, somewhat prophetically as it turned out, the Supremes were singing about a *Love Child*. Audrey by now knew all the jobbers with whom her father normally dealt, and I hadn't the slightest doubt that the Stock Exchange had never seen anything quite like Audrey. I assumed it was only going to be a matter of time before one of these types became significant, and so it proved.

One of the jobbing firms George dealt with had a brash up-and-coming young man who'd gained a bit of a reputation on the floor of the Stock Exchange. He was, by all accounts, a bit of a "Jack the Lad". Audrey had met him on several occasions and freely admitted that she had to fend him off with a broomstick. The young man's name was Frederick, but inevitably he was known as Freddy, and we all disliked him immediately! It's strange how we had become a part of

Audrey's life and, like a protective parent, we were looking disdainfully at the child's first boyfriend who could never be good enough.

"If I'd been there, I'd have broken his legs," said Harold. "Bit harsh," I answered. "I'd settle for an arm."

Our retrospective objection to Freddy held no sway of course. Audrey produced a photograph of him, and I suppose we had to grudgingly admit that he did cut a dashing figure. Sorry to say, he was tall, dark and handsome. His hair was terribly well coiffed, all swept back with a liberal coating of Brylcreem. His suit was immaculate, no doubt from Savile Row. It was double-breasted with the wide lapels of the time, plus a white shirt with cutaway collar, and a small neat knot in his tie. We couldn't see his shoes, but we knew they would have been of the very finest quality.

Audrey described the game of cat-and-mouse which persisted for months. I grudgingly had to admire the boy's perseverance. The problem from her point of view was that the Stock Exchange was a small world. In fact, worse than that, it was a gentleman's club and as far as the young single men were concerned, Audrey was the star prize. Everyone knew her, if only by sight, and so there wasn't the slightest possibility of a discreet relationship.

Despite the obvious problems, Freddy's charms eventually proved to be irresistible, and a whirlwind romance inevitably ensued. It would be fair to say that, from Audrey's description, Freddy simply swept her off her feet.

One evening Freddy had a suggestion.

"How about you come down at the weekend to see my parents? We could leave as soon as the Exchange closes on Friday."

"Where do they live?"

"They've just moved from London. I've bought them a house on the south coast."

Audrey was reluctant, but Freddy was insisting, and he won

the day. She stepped into Freddy's red Triumph Spitfire the following Friday afternoon. Feeling apprehensive but excited, she had packed a small overnight bag on the assumption that they were staying with his parents.

"I'd never done anything like that before. There had just been a couple of occasions when I had taken boys home to Father's and we had tea and scones together."

They arrived at Freddy's parents' new house in the early evening and were warmly welcomed.

"This is Audrey, Mum." Freddy proudly announced. "Didn't I say she's wonderful!"

Freddy's parents were typical East End Londoners, a little rough around the edges but the salt of the earth, though not altogether what Audrey was expecting. It was a very small terraced house. She couldn't help but notice that the entire ground floor was about the size of the living room in her father's London house. They enjoyed a pleasant enough evening, with a passable meal of sausages and mash, not something Audrey had ever eaten before. Freddy had brought two bottles of wine with him and Audrey, not feeling quite at ease, was happy to drink several glasses.

During the evening, Freddy's father asked, "Where are you staying tonight, son?"

"I've booked us into the Grand."

"Shame we don't have room for you here, son. The Grand will cost you a pretty penny."

For Audrey that penny had indeed dropped. She'd known nothing about this, and without the inebriating effect of the alcohol dulling her senses, the outcome may well have been different. However, no more than an hour later, she was walking into a sumptuous suite at the Grand Hotel with Freddy.

"I had truly been swept off my feet," Audrey said awkwardly. "It's not that I didn't want to go to bed with Freddy. Of course, I did, but I'd always thought that it would be on my terms."

There was no doubt that Freddy had not behaved like a gentleman. However, the little half-smile on Audrey's face hinted that he might not have been entirely without encouragement. Stanley, ever the gentleman, intervened.

"Say no more, my dear. I think it's time we decant ourselves into the lounge."

I looked at my watch to see that it was ten o'clock. We were the last people in the restaurant. As we left, Alan the barman ran after us.

"Whose account should I put the wine on? I'm afraid I've forgotten to do it."

Stanley gestured to Bill.

"Can you take care of that, Bill?"

I looked at Harold who had a broad grin on his face.

"The old bugger, he's got deep pockets and short arms."

Despite the late hour, there was no question of calling it a night, and we all duly headed for some comfortable chairs.

"Cups of coffee all round?" I asked.

"Good idea Charles, make mine a single malt. How terribly kind of you to offer," said Stanley.

Bill's knees were playing up, so he sat down, and Harold and I went to the bar. When we sit on the bar stools together, I find it impossible not to notice Harold's straight back. I, on the other hand, look more like a melting candle, gradually leaning over. Harold couldn't wait to get me alone.

"What about that little shit Freddy!" he said. "I can't go back and break his legs then, but I could now!"

I was used to seeing Harold enraged about one thing or another but, on this occasion, the veins on his forehead were pulsating more than usual. It was almost as if the scar on his right temple was moving. The fact was that this was *our* Audrey who had been taken advantage of by Freddy.

"Have you ever taken advantage of a woman quite so deceitfully?" Harold asked very seriously.

To which I truthfully replied, "Absolutely not!"

We agreed. Freddy was a little shit. However, I couldn't help but smile a little to myself. Almost the exact same situation that Audrey described in the hotel room had happened to me once, except that the roles were reversed. Perhaps I had been taken advantage of. It was nevertheless the most wonderful experience of my life, and I suspected from her tone of voice that maybe Audrey felt much the same.

We walked back with Stanley's single malt.

"How did I end up buying this? I was talking about coffee!" I said.

Stanley settled us all down again with another of his little anecdotes. On this occasion, he was culling kangaroos in Australia with a high-powered rifle, shooting from a helicopter. He then quickly moved on from this 'everyday occurrence' and once again turned his attention back to Audrey.

"Now then, my dear, are we to assume that this relationship with Freddy developed into something, shall we say, permanent?"

Audrey didn't hesitate with her reply.

"Yes, you could say that. We were married four months later, and my daughter Fiona was born in next to no time."

Once again, her candour and confidence had reduced us all to silence, while she appeared to be unmoved. Stanley realised the timing of the baby's arrival was a stone best left unturned.

"How wonderful, my dear. Once again, your life has completely changed direction. Do tell me where it goes from here."

It was clear from Audrey's description of this period that being a full-time mother wasn't going to be an option. She was determined to get back to her father's business. Freddy sold his London flat and purchased quite a nice house in Chelsea, not far from her father's house in Kensington.

Another part of the plan was obvious as far as Audrey was concerned. Pam the nanny was still a part of the Oxfordshire household but, despite some resistance from her mother, Pam was installed in the new house, together with a housekeeper and a maid.

Audrey was able to get back to work within a couple of months, and again she was very candid about this stage of her life.

"Pam was the key to everything as far as I was concerned. I couldn't have trusted Fiona with anyone else."

Even Lizzy grasped most of the story, although she wasn't clear who Pam was. Lizzy said that it was very late now, and she would call it a day.

She staggered off, muttering to herself.

"Very naughty that Freddy. Wish I'd met him."

Bill looked at me in amazement.

"Did you hear that?"

Audrey also looked very tired and Harold stepped forward.

"Let me walk you to your apartment, Audrey."

I could see that she was taken aback. Harold wasn't known for his empathy, much less his caring. She looked at me because it had latterly become one of my pleasures to escort Audrey to her apartment, but then she smiled and turned to Harold.

"That would be very kind, Harold."

I had lived every moment of Audrey's life with her; I guess we all had. I was so tired that, much as I wanted to discuss it further I, too, decided to call it a day. I wished Stanley a good night and said I would see him the next morning, to which he made his usual reply.

"If I'm spared, dear boy, if I'm spared."

I made my way to my apartment while Audrey and Harold made their way in the other direction. I remember thinking, this wasn't what I had in mind.

On looking back, I think this was the moment when I realised just how much Audrey meant to me.

-o0o-

The following morning the weather was beautiful. I pulled back the curtains to find the sun shining straight into my face. This wasn't seven o'clock; I had overslept! In fact, I was so late that I'd already missed breakfast! All I could think about was Audrey's story and was I missing anything. I quickly washed and shaved and hurried across to the lounge. On the way, I met Harold who'd overslept just the same.

"Couldn't damn well sleep," he said. "All I could think about was Audrey. She's magnificent, isn't she?"

We agreed; she was magnificent. Stanley and the rest of them were in a corner of the library.

"Come on, you two," said Stanley. "I don't know about you, but I'm desperate to know what happens next in Audrey's life."

Like schoolboys late for class, we quickly sat down.

"We both overslept, missed breakfast," Harold said.

Lizzy was really concerned that we had missed breakfast. Before we could dissuade her, she was staggering away toward the kitchen. Stanley entertained us with yet another of his anecdotes. On this occasion, he was advising the Chinese Communist Party about the rural breeding of rabbits for consumption. Lizzy duly returned, with a mug of tea in both hands and her stick over her arm.

Without the stick to balance her, Lizzy tends to stagger to the left and then to the right as if she's negotiating the deck of a storm-tossed ship. Obviously, we all wanted to assist her, but she is always so offended by these offers. As she lurched to the left, I raised myself up from my chair onto my arms, ready to assist. Then she would lurch to the right and Harold would raise himself up, also ready to help. For what seemed like an eternity I raised myself up and down. I would be raising myself up as Harold was lowering down, in time with every change of direction.

Stanley didn't understand how offended Lizzy would be if he were to offer some help. So, filled with good intentions, he struggled up from his chair and walked towards Lizzy who was currently involved with a starboard tack away from him. Harold and I could see it coming a mile away. As Stanley approached, Lizzy changed tack with a violent lurch to port, and what was left of both mugs of tea went straight down his waistcoat.

Lizzy thought the interference was dreadful and gave Stanley a real dressing-down. We all collapsed with laughter, including Stanley. Once again Lizzy had inadvertently raised everyone's spirits, as she so often does. Lizzy really is the archetypal 'little old lady'. Goodness knows how old she is. Despite it all, she seems to have an uncanny gift for combining her apparent frailty with an unexpected robustness; she can crash into the hall table and continue as if nothing has happened. The first moment I met Lizzy, she reminded me of Mrs Wilberforce in the wonderful old film *The Ladykillers*. I could almost see her asking Alec Guinness about the 'loot'.

After such an entertaining start to the day, it seemed like a good time for Audrey to resume her story. So, after draping his tea-soaked jacket and waistcoat over the back of a chair, Stanley made himself comfortable in his chair.

"My dear, you must tell us. What happened next?"

Audrey continued her story, telling us that her father's business was going from strength to strength, built upon the private clients' managed portfolios. Freddy, meanwhile, was flying ever higher, while baby Fiona was a joy to them both. Both Freddy and Audrey were very successful in their own right, but it sounded as if no amount of success was going to be enough for Freddy. He was always on the lookout for a new angle and, while the separation of broker and jobber was long-established, Freddy was keen to push the boundaries. Audrey was highly principled, obviously as a result of her father's upbringing, and she had made it quite clear that Freddy's desire to get closer to her private clients was inappropriate. Freddy, however, was undeterred, and approached Audrey and George with a proposal.

"What if," he said, "rather than you building up a portfolio of stocks and securities for your private clients, why not form your own investment trust that your clients could buy into?"

Lizzy, of course, had no idea what an investment trust was. Audrey smiled and explained it all in very simplistic terms, saying that an investment trust was just the name of a type of collective investment fund. Rather than a client buying shares in fifty different companies, they could instead buy a share in a fund which itself owned shares in fifty different companies. This was altogether more convenient. The value of the fund was the sum of its assets, and the price of a share in the fund was calculated as the value of those assets divided by the number of shares issued, simple.

Investment trusts had been around for a long time. The first one was formed in 1868 by Foreign & Colonial, so they weren't a new thing, but they were still something of a niche market at that time. In fact, Audrey explained that some investment companies used their trusts simply as a holding vehicle. Audrey made all this seem very simple and straight-forward. Lizzy, however, tends to fixate on the words that she understands, and 'holding vehicle' became her centre of attention. She couldn't grasp why an investment company had to hold vehicles.

George was apparently very cautious about collective investments, but Freddy explained there would be tax advantages. For example, the buying and selling of stocks held within the trust didn't incur capital gains tax at 30%. The fund could, therefore, be managed at a much lower cost to the client. It was clear that both George and Audrey had reservations, but Freddy obviously wasn't going to drop the idea; he was evidently very persuasive.

George and Audrey did set up the trust, which was called the Calcut Investment Trust, and then instructed Freddy to buy certain stocks. The initial capital was very considerable; some came from institutional investors or from investment banks. A large part of it came from clients who were keen to get in on the ground floor of what Audrey and George had promised them was a great opportunity.

Stanley stopped her at that point.

"This is absolutely fascinating, my dear. I can't wait to see what happens next, but do you realise it's lunchtime?"

Reluctantly we all agreed and made our way to the restaurant. We all enjoyed a light lunch, discussing the weather and other trivia rather than asking the one question that we all wanted to have answered. Audrey seemed relaxed, so perhaps it was just as well. There was some background music playing which half of us enjoyed, and the other half hated with a vengeance. Most of us haven't heard a pin drop in a decade, but we can still hear the odd word that's spoken, and some of us enjoy the music. The problem is that few of us can hear both at once.

On this occasion, however, it was one of those old favourites reminding us of days past when we could tie our shoelaces without groaning. Someone asked for the sound to be turned up and no-one objected. It was that wonderful classic *American Pie*, and we all sang along. I felt sure that each of us had been transported back to some special time and place. It was indeed a song we all knew well, but who was the singer-songwriter? I almost asked Audrey who the singer was but alarm bells rang at the prospect of no-one knowing. Then disaster struck as Stanley spoke.

"Oh isn't it silly! I just can't think who that is."

My heart sank. Desperately trying to remember singers or song names is one of our most frustrating preoccupations.

We spent the next hour in absolute torment, until finally we agreed it was Scott McKenzie, and the relief was palpable. Feeling exhausted, we made our way back to the lounge with our heads aching. We encountered Charlotte on the way who was puffing a little having just walked the dozen paces from her office. I'm not sure how Harold gets away with it, but he greeted her as he usually does.

"Afternoon, Commandant."

He related our sorry tale, which was just another in a long series of these 'who was singing that' torments.

"Oh, wonderful song," Charlotte said. "How could you forget? It was Don McLean."

Harold summed up our thoughts perfectly. "For God's sake, it was bad enough when we didn't know. Who was the idiot who said Scott McKenzie?"

This was our one moment of salvation. Stanley beamed from ear to ear.

"Surely you must remember, old boy? You were the idiot!"

We sat in the lounge and, apart from Harold, we were all jubilant that our collective memory loss had been eclipsed, if not expunged, by Harold's greater foolishness. Our smugness was short-lived, however. He obviously considered his gamble carefully and, having weighed up the probabilities, he rightly assumed that he had a winning hand to play.

"You might be smug now," he said, "but what was the song that Scott McKenzie made famous?"

Game set and match to Harold. We wasted the entire afternoon submerged in memory loss.

Sensibly on the stroke of five o'clock, Bill spoke up.

"It's past the yardarm."

Stanley responded immediately.

"I'll have a single malt."

Bill and I duly returned with a trayful of drinks, and we all knew it was the appropriate time for Audrey to continue her story.

Stanley savoured his single malt, not knowing on this occasion what it was. He embraced his glass delicately with just three fingers and smiled lovingly at it, rather like a mother might smile at her new-born baby.

"I would say this is a Speyside, a touch of honey and a hint of mint, must be the Aberlour 10-year-old," he said confidently.

"Bugger me," whispered Harold. "The old sod doesn't pay for them, but he certainly knows his whisky."

Stanley was pleased with this demonstration of his expertise and sat back in his chair looking just a touch pompous.

"Now my dear, you were telling us about the Calcut Trust."

Audrey seemed eager enough to continue her story.

"The trust really took over our lives," she said. "All of our private clients wanted it and very quickly it became our principal business."

Within the first two years, the value of the trust had increased by about 30%, totally unprecedented at that time. Audrey put all of this into context by reminding us that this was the period when the miners voted to go on strike. Unemployment had doubled since Ted Heath became Prime Minister (exceeding one million by then) and all the while the IRA was stepping up their terrorist outrages. Investors were generally becoming cautious and, in this environment, the Calcut Trust offered a safe haven for their clients.

Stanley asked Audrey how this success affected them and once again she was very candid in her reply.

"The money simply poured in, and it quickly became a flood."

Freddy, it seems, was still not content. Interest rates of 6% were low by historical standards, so he decided they should increase their mortgage to the maximum by purchasing an even bigger house. This was despite having barely had time to settle into the current one. Audrey could see no reason for moving and tried to dissuade him, but it was to no avail.

Stanley, of course, had to know the detail about the new house, which Audrey described as being palatial. It was what the agents described as stucco-fronted and built in the mid-nineteenth century, located in Knightsbridge, not far from Harrods. It had six bedrooms plus the master suite, four bathrooms, main and secondary reception rooms. There were cast iron balconies, and staff quarters on the fifth floor. Stanley enquired about the exact location of the house.

"Oh yes, I know the road, sold a house there myself. I think I can picture the house you describe."

He then asked her, "You were still so young, my dear. How did your newly elevated social position change your life?"

What a perceptive question! It was obvious that the life which Audrey described before she married Freddy already occupied an elevated social position. Stanley's question about her 'newly elevated position' was subtle. Perhaps her new social position might not actually be elevated at all.

It became clear that Audrey knew full well that all the money in the world wasn't going to elevate Freddy's social status. They mainly socialised with Freddy's friends who were often uncouth and loud.

Conversely, Freddy considered her friends to be a bore because he had so little in common with them. George had been correct about Freddy right from the start. When they purchased the new house, George had made a comment she would never forget.

"When the race is over, the only people who would like it re-run are those who aren't standing in the winner's enclosure," he said.

"We had it all, but Freddy simply didn't realise that he was already standing in the winner's enclosure. He always had to risk it all again on another bet," Audrey said.

Audrey described aspects of their social life together in some detail, or rather how they were not really 'together'. We heard about occasions when she was embarrassed in front of friends, and times when Freddy made a fool of himself.

Some of the stories made me cringe on her behalf, but when Stanley offered his sympathy and understanding, she gave him a wry smile.

"As Freddy would say, you ain't heard nothing yet!"

Chapter Five
THE PARTY

Audrey went on to describe the first big social function they held in the huge reception room of the new house. I could picture with such clarity the scene which Audrey described. The room full of Freddy's jobber friends, laced with a few favoured brokers, their wives, and various social acolytes. The only saving grace from her point of view was that her father was unable to attend, or perhaps didn't want to. The men all wore their Savile Row black dinner jackets, with wing collar shirt and black bow ties. The ladies were in their glamorous evening dresses.

As the guests arrived, it would have been a procession of sophisticated grace and style, the ladies each competing for the unofficial title of Belle of the Ball. Above all, this was a room full of testosterone-emboldened bravado, young men who lived on a diet of stress and adrenaline. And in the middle of it all, was Audrey; young, beautiful and sophisticated. She didn't spell it out in as many words, but we all had a good idea of the impact Audrey would have had upon the boys of the Stock Exchange. By working there, she'd inadvertently entered a competition where she was the star prize. For many of these traders, this was no genteel lottery. These were players who played to win.

Now, if there's one thing that a young testosterone-filled trader hates above all else, it's to be out-traded by a fellow trader. The elegant procession of sophisticates entering the party all had one thing in common, they were all losers. The single men had failed to win the star prize, and the glamorous wives and girlfriends were never going to be the Belle of the Ball while they were standing in the long shadow that Audrey cast over them. We didn't need to be there to feel the tension in the air.

As soon as she had set the scene for this social gathering, I had a sense of foreboding. Just at that moment, a spider ran across the floor. Audrey hates spiders.

"Oh! Get *rid* of it, Charles! *Do* something!"

Bill glanced down at the beast and casually commented, "Large house spider, Tegenaria Gigantea, probably a male, looking at the length of those legs."

Lizzy, meanwhile, was leaving the room at full speed, which normally would have been a situation that could only end in disaster. However, as fate would have it, a collision was averted by the timely arrival of an old boy who was walking past on his way outside for a smoke. Puffer, as he is so appropriately known, is either outside smoking, or on his way to or from a smoke, so we see very little of him.

On this occasion, he just happened to be in the right place at the right time and it was into his arms that Lizzy fell.

"It's been a long time since a lady threw herself at me!" said Puffer, whereupon he commenced a fit of coughing.

In normal circumstances, anyone offering Lizzy assistance would receive a terrible dressing-down. Perhaps it was the tobacco fumes or the copious spray from the coughing, but Lizzy was totally silent as she reached for a handkerchief to dry her face.

Puffer assisted Lizzy back to her seat, and with a final cough and splutter, he relinquished his grip upon her. She fell into the seat as if in a state of shock and just sat there, handkerchief over her face.

We had quite forgotten the spider which was by now long gone. Puffer has just one redeeming feature as far as we are all concerned, he has a wonderful sense of humour.

Looking back as he continued his onward journey towards another cigarette, he said, "What did the fly say to the spider?"

"What did the fly say, Puffer?" I asked.

"You must be joking, you're not going to eat me, you're just pulling my leg."

Trust Puffer to offer us a touch of humour at an opportune moment! It was late now, so we all decided we should have a quick change of clothes and head towards the restaurant. Lizzy stayed put, saying she couldn't face any food.

We changed and were sitting at the dining table in record time, although Audrey still looked as fabulous as if she'd spent the entire afternoon getting ready. I found myself gazing somewhat adoringly at her. No sooner had we placed our orders than Stanley put us out of our misery.

"I'm sorry, my dear, but I don't think we can wait a moment longer to hear about what happened at your party."

Audrey was visibly upset, saying, "The party turned into the most excruciatingly embarrassing moment of my life. I've never talked about it to anyone. It really upsets me even now. It's so difficult to talk about."

Stanley, seeing her discomfort immediately, said, "In that case my dear, let's just leave that memory in the past."

Audrey, however, was obviously determined to expose this particular demon, and insisted that she would continue.

"It was all going well enough," she said, "but as the evening progressed and the champagne flowed, I couldn't avoid hearing various comments. It started with one particularly objectionable character asking Freddy about the Grand Hotel."

The ghastly character asked Freddy if he had found the beds comfortable. Freddy could have dismissed the comment but he didn't and, instead, both men laughed knowingly. Audrey tried to pretend she had no idea what the joke was, but then the ghastly man asked her if she knew the Grand Hotel. Audrey said she didn't recall such a place.

The man then said, "If you don't remember it, that's not saying much for Freddy!"

There was more laughter, and another three men became involved, as this revolting character continued with his hideous innuendo.

The full implications of these comments hit Audrey in an instant. It was obvious Freddy must have boasted about their first night together at the Grand Hotel the other year; perhaps the entire trading floor knew about it.

Her heart was pounding, she felt faint and just wanted to run away in shame, but her legs seemed incapable of carrying her. The situation went from bad to worse. One of the other undesirable characters decided that he too would add to her discomfort.

"Not only comfortable beds. I find the Grand to be very discreet," he said.

The man's wife, standing next to him, said in a loud voice, "What do you mean, discreet?"

He tried to laugh it off, but his wife obviously understood the meaning of his comment only too well from previous experience. She did no less than raise her champagne glass and pour the contents over her husband's head!

Inspired by the woman's actions, Audrey lifted her glass and threw the contents at the ghastly man who'd started the whole sordid affair. Taken aback, with his pride damaged, he was initially angry. Then, as the champagne bubbles ran down his face and into the wing collar of his shirt, the absurdity of his situation turned his anger towards embarrassment.

Feeling empowered, Audrey stood defiantly, enjoying the dreadful man's obvious discomfort.

She looked him straight in the eye.

"You are beneath contempt sir. I can't imagine where the vile aspect of your person would be tolerated, but it's certainly not here in my presence. Get out of my sight!"

She looked at Freddy with an equal degree of loathing. Completely dispossessed of his previous swagger, he gestured at the ghastly man, pointing towards the door.

Audrey now turned her attention towards the three remaining men who had contributed to her embarrassment.

Seeing the demise of their loud-mouthed friend, the eyes of the room were upon them. There was a buzz of anticipation; perhaps they too had met their nemesis, and so it proved.

Audrey glared contemptuously at each of the three in turn.

"I find all three of you equally disagreeable. I suggest you try to imagine what a gentleman would do in your circumstances, and act accordingly."

Lowering their heads in shame, they each apologised and left. Audrey felt a mixture of emotions, triumph, certainly, but as the adrenaline of that intense situation subsided, she also felt isolated and vulnerable. The guests in the room remained silent, which increased her feeling of isolation.

Then the lady who had poured champagne over her husband's head started to clap. One or two more guests started to clap until, a few seconds later, the whole room was applauding and cheering her.

Audrey was as overcome with emotion now as she had been all those years ago, needing a moment to regain her composure. I just wanted to hug her, but instead I clapped my hands just as the people had done that night. We all clapped. I think we were all so proud of her. Harold was more emotional than I could ever recall seeing him.

"She's magnificent," he said, for the umpteenth time.

Upon that matter, we were in complete agreement. We'd eaten the odd morsel from our various courses, but our evening meal had largely been wasted. We seemed to have lost all track of time, totally engrossed in Audrey's story. We even failed to order any wine, a point which hadn't escaped Stanley. Feeling emotionally drained, I suspected Audrey was feeling weary. Stanley, however, had one final question.

"Tell me my dear, how did the Stock Exchange and your wider circle of friends react to these events?"

It quickly became apparent that, rather than being the subject of ridicule, Audrey gained enormous respect, out of all proportion to the incident. It turned out that the ghastly man, particularly, was just endured rather than liked, while Audrey seemed to be in receipt of everyone's admiration.

Unfortunately, the same couldn't be said for Freddy. His lack of gallantry towards her was condemned by all his colleagues.

It had certainly been a long day, so we decided to call it a night earlier than usual.

"Would you walk me back to my apartment, Charles?" Audrey said.

I was delighted to be of service and offered her my hand as she lifted herself from her chair. I'd done this dozens of times before but, on this occasion, I didn't realise that neither Audrey nor I let go of the other's hand.

We left the restaurant and went out into the cool night air which was full of the aroma of freshly cut grass.

We had walked some distance before I realised her hand was still in mine. We had a close relationship, but we didn't usually hold hands quite like this.

When I realised, I wasn't sure what to do. Should I let go her hand, or should I pretend I hadn't noticed?

At that moment of indecision, we arrived at Audrey's apartment and stopped at the door, still holding hands.

Audrey squeezed my hand, leaned forward and kissed me, saying, "Charles, do you realise you're my dearest friend?"

What I should have said was, 'My darling wonderful Audrey, am I really so stupid that you need to ask?'

Sadly, what I said was, "That's kind of you, Audrey."

We effectively shook hands and I bade her goodnight and left.

As I walked to my apartment, I just kept repeating to myself, '*idiot*'! I simply couldn't explain my ridiculous behaviour.

I was really attracted to Audrey; in fact, it was becoming more than that.

Why on earth was I holding her at arm's length?

Chapter Six
STOCK MARKET CRASH

The following morning, we all arrived for breakfast at the same time. Audrey seemed none the worse for my glaring ineptitude, but I still felt like a complete idiot. After breakfast, Bill suggested we should all sit outside in the garden, and so we set off in anticipation of Audrey's continuing story. The grounds are quite extensive and meticulously manicured. There are numerous walks and little private areas between the apartments and the main building. We wanted somewhere quiet and a little private. Eventually we grouped a table and some chairs together on a small paved area. We had a row of lavender to one side and a bed of begonias on the other. It was clear which the bees preferred as they buzzed in profusion among the lavender.

Lizzy was greatly alarmed. "I can't sit here, look at them all."

"Don't be so bloody daft," said Harold. "I will personally kill every bee that takes an interest in you. Just sit quietly."

As it happened, none of the bees took an interest in Lizzy, not with all that lavender about. Nevertheless, she was on tenterhooks all morning.

Stanley wasted no more time. "Now, my dear," he said, in his fatherly and comforting voice, "you left us at that point in your life where the space between you and Freddy had widened, while I suspect the space between you and the Stock Exchange had narrowed. Why don't you bring us forward a little in time?"

What Audrey had thought would be her downfall turned out to be the exact opposite. Considering that she could never enter the Exchange other than via the public gallery, she was almost treated as an honorary member. In fact, it turned out that our Audrey occupies a small place in history. She amazed us all by saying that on the first of February 1973 she was one of the very first group of women elected to join the Stock Exchange.

"One of the last great bastions of misogyny had been torn down, and I'm quite proud of my small part in that!" Audrey said proudly.

This also opened the way for George to make her a partner in the business. Stanley was elated, as we all were. Our Audrey, our magnificent Audrey, had helped to change the course of history!

"I think Audrey can do anything she puts her mind to; she's so remorseful. What a shame about her dodgy knee," Lizzy said.

Harold was brimming with pride. I knew exactly what he was about to say, so I pre-empted him by saying, "She's magnificent, isn't she?"

"She certainly is," he replied.

I thought again about the night before when she kissed me, and I shook her hand. Idiot was the only word that kept coming to mind. Stanley wasted no time getting back to Audrey's story.

"Now, tell me my dear, the Calcut Trust was such an important part of your business. I think you should tell us about its progress."

Audrey said the trust increased in value very well. From 1969 to 1973, when she became a Member of the Stock

Exchange, the fund had increased by 50%. What none of them knew then was that the country was heading for a deep recession and the second largest Stock Market crash of all time. We had the miners' strike, power cuts, a 3-day week and an oil crisis, not to mention inconveniences like joining the EU and the introduction of VAT. The situation was going to be not far from a re-run of the 1929 Depression.

"People today just have no idea!" Audrey said.

Initially the investors stayed put, because the fund didn't lose value but, as the crash unfolded, the steady stream of investors wishing to sell their shares in the fund became a flood, and the value of the trust collapsed virtually overnight. There was complete chaos as their investors invaded the office, demanding their money. Investors know that when the tide falls, it lowers all the boats. The problem was that the trust had fallen in value disproportionately to the rest of the market, and even worse was the fact that they could hardly sell their shares at all. There were no buyers which, therefore, rendered their shares valueless.

Stanley adopted his apprehensive face and grave voice.

"What you describe, my dear, is a terribly serious situation. What had gone wrong?"

George and Audrey immediately examined the fund structure, and from their side, there were no irregularities. However, all was not what it should have been as far as the trades were concerned. It took a long time to unravel the situation. Jobbers were notorious for not keeping records, and so they had to make some assumptions.

Audrey reminded us again how the shares of the trust were valued, which was the value of its assets, known as the net asset value, divided by the number of fixed shares. She explained it very simply by saying that if we imagined a fund with an asset value of £100 and with 100 issued shares, then each share was obviously worth £1. However, if demand was so high that each share was selling for £1.20 then it would be said to be selling at a 20% premium.

The price of both the assets in the fund and the fund price itself were set by Freddy. The premium grew as large as 40%, which accounted for a substantial percentage of the increased share value. This figure appeared in their company accounts for the trust and, while it raised a few eyebrows, Audrey said it was accepted.

What they hadn't known was that the premium was not a consequence of market forces. Freddy had manipulated it. When the Stock Market collapsed, the premium was unsustainable. The fund was simply not worth the share price, which accounted for its dramatic fall.

Fixing the trust share price and, therefore, the premium, was serious, but it all became far worse. There were lots of companies in the trust which Freddy had recommended they should include. George and Audrey had understood that some of these were newly listed companies, but when Audrey insisted that she see the company accounts, they turned out to be shell companies, not really operating businesses at all.

A shell company was often a failed business, but its structure and constitution had been retained because crucially it could provide a ready-made Stock Market listing for a third party. The value to a buyer had nothing to do with what the company might once have been. The real advantage for a non-listed company was that it provided a ready-made route to the Stock Market without the need for a full prospectus, and without complying with full corporate governance. There was nothing illegal about trading shell companies, but she knew Freddy must have been up to something because it gave him the opportunity to trade a listed company within the Calcut Trust which was not actually a real trading company.

Stanley quickly pointed out that, if Freddy had been involved in fraud, she would also be implicated. Audrey had been only too aware of that. She realised that Freddy must have traded the trust in every respect to his own advantage. The newly listed companies were probably fraudulent, the share price premium had been manipulated, and his spread-gain on each transaction was excessive.

Stanley asked the obvious question. "How did he expect to get away with it?"

Audrey answered in a very matter-of-fact way.

"It's the oldest story in financial fraud. If the subject of the fraud is making a lot of money, you believe what you want to believe."

Talk about events changing history! I was dumbfounded. One moment Audrey was one of the first ladies to join the Stock Exchange, and the next moment she's involved with a fraudster! What on earth were the consequences going to be? I could only envisage disaster.

I looked at Harold and was a bit alarmed to see the veins in his forehead pulsating, a very bad sign. Harold is one of those characters whose face tells you a lot about the person. No one part of his nose is quite sure in which direction it should be pointing. His short stubble beard, like his far too ample head of hair, covers up various past encounters. His physiognomy tells you in no uncertain terms that life has thrown a lot at him. I am in no doubt that life came out the worse for the encounter! His anger was palpable and for the first time I really did believe that he would be capable of killing Freddy. Harold really cared for Audrey. Why had I been so slow to realise that? Idiot!

Bill and Stanley both looked worried, as did Lizzy who thought that a shell company meant eggshells. She put two and two together and came up with chicken farms.

"I hope they weren't battery farms," she said.

Audrey wasn't paying proper attention, and she thought Lizzy hadn't heard because of her hearing aid batteries.

"No, Lizzy, nothing to do with your batteries."

Lizzy was pleased. "Oh good. I use Duracell, you know."

Harold was exasperated. "For pity's sake, Lizzy, pay attention! Can't you see Audrey is upset!"

Lizzy was going from strength to strength. "I'm a little hard of hearing Harold, you must be more patient, but I was right you see, it was about batteries, that's why Audrey is upset. I'll give her one of my Duracell's."

Suddenly Harold could bear no more. Audrey was in real distress and we had descended into farce!

"That's the last straw," Harold growled. "I can't cope with any more damn batteries. For goodness sake just allow Audrey to tell her story."

Lizzy was finally content that the battery issue had been resolved satisfactorily, so Audrey could continue. She was distraught, explaining between tears how the clients who had purchased the trust were queuing in the office to sell their shares, but there was no-one to buy them. There were still many details about Freddy's dealings with the trust which hadn't come to light, but they already knew enough to under-stand that they were potentially involved with fraud.

The pressure was so great upon her father to maintain their reputation that he decided to personally buy back some of the shares in the hope of a recovery. He also persuaded Audrey to do the same thing. Between them, they managed to maintain the impression that the Calcut Trust was functioning normally and when some clients realised that George and Audrey were purchasing shares themselves, they stopped selling for a while.

At this time, early 1974, the Stock Market had declined considerably, and it was possible that the end of the crash was in sight. Clinging to this hope, George and Audrey invested everything they had, and much that they didn't have, propping up the trust. Even Freddy, desperate to keep his activities away from the public gaze, provided considerable funds. Had the market turned, they might have got away with it, but what no-one knew at the time was that the crash had much further to run, until December 1974. The result was inevitable and very sudden.

Audrey expressed it well when she said, "It's like bailing out a sinking boat; you stay afloat as long as you keep bailing but, the second you stop bailing, you sink immediately."

Calcut Stockbrokers became insolvent in September 1974, and so George and Audrey were both eventually declared bankrupt. Freddy, however, suffered no such fate. The new house had little or no equity in it and had to be sold, but when the stock market finally bottomed in December 1974, a rapid recovery ensued, and Freddy was back in business.

The prospect that our Audrey had become a bankrupt was incomprehensible to all of us. We could only imagine the shame and disgrace that she and George must have felt as she recalled what we assumed must have been her most ghastly hour. We were all desperate to hear how the bankruptcy affected them, but she obviously needed a rest, and it was Harold who stepped forward to escort Audrey to lunch. We set off towards the main building and the restaurant, when Lizzy suddenly made off at a rate of knots.

"What the hell's going on?" I said.

"It'll be the bees," replied Harold. "You couldn't make it up, could you!"

Lizzy at full speed was obviously tantamount to disaster so I hastily went after her and offered my arm. As I did so, I asked myself why I was escorting Lizzy and not Audrey. Harold lacks most of the social graces, in fact maybe even all of them, and yet here he was, escorting my Audrey. Suddenly I was aware that I was calling Audrey 'my Audrey'. We were late as we sat down for lunch and Puffer was already on his way out for a smoke.

"What we need," I said to Audrey, "is one of Puffer's jokes to cheer us up."

Bill looked in horror. "Don't ask him over, he'll cough all over us."

Just as I was thinking that Bill had a good point, Puffer made a beeline for us and stood with his hands resting on the back of Lizzy's chair.

"We all needed cheering up, Puffer," I said.

As I said it, I knew it was a mistake. Puffer can't say more than a dozen words without inducing a coughing fit. He started to tell us one of his jokes, but he had already gone over his limit. There was a rasping sound, and we all knew what that meant. Sure enough, Puffer erupted into a prolonged coughing fit, all over Lizzy's head and most of the table. We changed our knives, forks and plates and, except for Lizzy, who said she was no longer hungry, we settled down to a nice lunch.

We really should have allowed Audrey to relax a little but, no sooner had we finished our starter course, than Stanley said, "I can't imagine, my dear, how terrible you must have felt. Did you lose everything?"

Audrey seemed completely resigned now to the completion of her story. In fact, I was beginning to realise that, by shining a light into this dark past, she was consequently making her future brighter.

She continued saying, "Yes, we lost absolutely everything. Father lost the business, and his London house. I lost my future in the business. I lost my newly acquired Membership of the Stock Exchange. I lost my house and my husband."

Stanley stopped her at that point.

"Did you divorce Freddy as a consequence of his handling of the trust?"

Audrey was very honest when she answered, saying that she thought they would have divorced anyway. George said afterwards that he always felt Freddy was using her, and in the light of what had happened, he was proved to be right.

As we finished our lunch, I couldn't help but think that at least Audrey could sink no lower. Little did I know that the worst was yet to come. We went back to the lounge, and Stanley wasted no time with his next question.

"You must tell me, my dear, did Freddy's fraudulent activities ever come to light?"

Audrey reminded us of the state of the economy and the

market at that time. There were so many people going bankrupt, and so many questionable transactions coming to light, the failure of the trust might have gone unnoticed.

Unfortunately, one of the private clients was a City lawyer who lost a huge amount of money, and he went through the trust's holdings item by item. He realised that the so-called newly listed companies in fact had no value, and that this deception constituted fraud. He also made the correct assumption that the share price premium had been fixed, and so he went to the police, who instigated a fraud investigation.

Not only were they bankrupt, but they now faced the possibility of going to prison. Both George and Audrey had benefitted from the trust's rise in value in the form of their commissions and their fees. Freddy had benefited from his excessive price spread, but none of this was illegal.

The trust's increase in value was largely due to the unusually high price premium, but it was impossible to prove Freddy had manipulated the trust share price which was supposedly supported by the value of the newly listed companies.

What the police needed to prove was that there had been fraudulent manipulation of the share prices of the so-called newly listed companies. Both Audrey and her father were interrogated like criminals, for hours over many days. The stress must have been unbearable.

"The police naturally assumed that, as husband and wife, Freddy and I must have been accomplices, so I was treated as a criminal. It was awful."

The police, however, were struggling to find anything incriminating. Eventually the case was dropped, due to lack of evidence, and they were never charged.

"Oh, my dear, what a relief for both of you, but what of your reputation?" Stanley said.

"What reputation?"

They had both been declared bankrupt. They lost everything. Lots of City companies became bankrupt during the market crash, but George and Audrey were among the few people investigated by the police. They had lost their reputations irretrievably. Harold was incandescent with rage. I worried that the veins in his forehead would explode. The fact that Freddy had caused our elegant and sophisticated Audrey to be subjected to cross-examination by the police was reprehensible.

No doubt Stanley had the matter in hand, but Harold couldn't wait.

"How did the bastard get away with it?"

Freddy wasn't forthcoming with any answers, but eventually Audrey managed to piece together what had been going on. Freddy had encouraged Audrey and George to set up the Calcut Trust as a vehicle for him to sell what effectively were worthless assets to the private clients without anyone realising. The so-called newly listed companies were not new expanding businesses with exciting prospects at all. They were shell companies which had little or no value. They didn't attract attention because they were bundled together.

Freddy, who was the sole trader in the stock, would greatly inflate the share price of a chosen shell company which he owned, and he would then sell it to the trust. George and Audrey had trusted his recommendations and had authorised his purchases with little or no scrutiny.

Having sold a shell company to the trust at a large personal profit, Freddy would then manipulate the price back down, and eventually sell a legitimate shell company on behalf of the trust to a third party. The shareholding then disappeared from the trust accounts. The net asset value of the trust declined, of course; this had gone into Freddy's pocket. He then manipulated the trust share price so that the loss wasn't evident to the trust shareholders. This was why the trust share price premium became so high.

Stanley was still not quite clear how Freddy got away with it.

"Surely, my dear, the police could trace the proceeds of the sales back to Freddy?"

Freddy was much brighter than any of them suspected. The businesses which he claimed to be valuable newly listed companies were all owned by a holding company registered in Panama. There was no connection to Freddy, but we could all assume that he owned the holding company. The police strongly suspected fraud but, with no evidence, Freddy got away with it.

Audrey was really distressed. "I would freely confess now, that Father and I failed in our fiduciary duty to the trust shareholders. We broke with the code of separation between broker and jobber. We were gullible, having trusted Freddy."

The rest of us had struggled a little to keep pace with her detailed description of events, but Bill obviously had a better grasp of all this detail and offered an interesting observation.

"I've not heard of this scam before, but the use of pooled assets to hide worthless assets is at the heart of this latest financial crisis."

Audrey agreed with Bill, he was quite right. Although the nature of the asset was quite different, what Freddy did was not so different to what had only just happened two years ago in 2008. He had bundled dubious assets together and concealed them in a much larger financial instrument.

"You mark my words," said Audrey. "This current crisis has a long way to run. The problem will come when they have to unwind this so-called quantitative easing."

"Where's Freddy now?" asked Harold menacingly.

I was relieved when Audrey said she had no idea. He hadn't contested any aspect of their divorce and, although he insisted upon his right to visit Fiona, that gradually reduced. He did, however, pay a generous amount of maintenance which had enabled Fiona to have a private education. She suspected it was his way of easing his conscience, but she hadn't seen him for twenty years.

Stanley now had a contented look, I suspected that he was pleased with his part in the telling of Audrey's story, but there was one more tragedy that we didn't expect. He asked Audrey what happened in the immediate aftermath of the bankruptcy. A tearful Audrey quietly explained that during the police investigation, George suffered a life-changing stroke, and was in hospital for several months, severely disabled.

"When I thought we would be convicted of fraud, I thought things couldn't get any worse, but when Father collapsed in the police station, I realised then just how low the human spirit can go."

We sat in absolute silence for what seemed like an eternity. I wanted to take Audrey in my arms, and I suspected that Harold might have been thinking the same thing, but all we managed to do was just sit there. Bill and Stanley both looked forlorn while Lizzy, who'd obviously managed to hear most of the story, was just as tearful as Audrey. We all sympathised with her as well as we could, but nothing anyone could say was going to console her as she relived her darkest hour.

Stanley, who only half an hour ago had been looking rather pleased with himself, had now lost his sparkle. Perhaps he felt some remorse for his part in returning Audrey to that ghastly situation. Maybe, like me, he was pondering whether to ask Audrey to finish her story, and so draw a line under the whole sad affair, or should he perhaps leave it for another day. My thought was that we couldn't come this far without hearing the final episode. Like having a tooth filled at the dentist, it's better to get it over with.

I took matters into my own hands, I put my arm around Audrey saying, "We all admire you so much, we're here for you."

"I've spent my entire life reliving these events, but I've never shared them with anyone. Not even Fiona knows all the details I've told you. Please tell me that none of you think worse of me for the part I played in the scandal, because I'm so ashamed."

Stanley quickly reached out for her hand.

"My dear, we're all shaped by past events, but the past is yesterday. Today you're the product of those events, and I must tell you that we very much like the result. Nothing from the past can change that."

He certainly had the knack of getting to the heart of the matter! Audrey had obviously made up her mind to conclude her story and so, with new composure, she continued.

George had always been a cautious man, and it came to light that one of his cautions was to have the Oxfordshire house registered in Audrey's mother's name, as well as various small accounts.

The result was that, while they had effectively lost everything else, the Oxfordshire house wasn't affected; it was her only lifeline.

George suffered terrible disabilities following his stroke, but he did eventually leave hospital and Audrey drove him home to Belmont in her mother's car. Somehow George's catastrophic fall from grace, combined with his devastating disabilities, seemed in some way to ameliorate Isabelle's lingering hostility caused by his brief affair. Pam the nanny obviously moved back to Belmont with Fiona, who was nearly five years old now, and between them all another phase of life began.

Audrey described a life which was very sad in many respects, due to George's disability. Fiona grew up at Belmont exactly as Audrey had done. She went to the same village school and to the same private boarding school.

There was an obvious omission from Audrey's story which Stanley was not about to overlook, but Audrey answered him before he could finish the question.

"No," she said. "Before you ask, I didn't remarry. Perhaps I would have, if the right man had come along, but he never did."

Stanley didn't pursue it, perhaps he detected a hint of regret in Audrey's voice. Instead he asked whether she'd managed to return to her financial career. She smiled and said that it wasn't easy to get a job in finance when you're a bankrupt. Eventually, by being economical with the truth, she did get a position as a financial analyst, and her past never came to light.

Another tragedy in Audrey's life was the premature death of her brother John. Her father George lived until he was eighty years old and, although he never regained the use of his right side, he did regain much of his speech. Audrey remained devoted to him until his death in 1999. Isabelle's condition was better understood in later years and various medications were eventually a great help. She lived to the commendable age of eighty-eight. Pam married very late in life and both she and her husband now live together in a care home in Yorkshire. Pam and Audrey remain devoted to one another, in touch by telephone on most days.

Despite her tears, Audrey had somehow managed to share her tragic story with us, but it was obvious from her expression that this was not the end of it. Stanley must have sensed it too.

"My dear, you have so courageously shared your story with us. What is it that still troubles you?"

Audrey looked as if the weight of the world was upon her shoulders; tears welling up in her eyes once again, she drew a deep breath.

"Don't you see?" she said. "My father meant everything to me. He put his faith in me when I was only nineteen years old. He saw something in me that I was not aware of, and he devoted himself to my future. He was my mentor in so many ways. Everything I achieved in my professional career, I owe to him."

Audrey struggled to continue, clearly holding back a huge weight of sorrow which only required one more word to allow it to burst free. That word was 'blame'. She forced the words out of her mouth.

"My father trusted me, and I single-handedly destroyed his business, his reputation, and I have no doubt that I caused the stroke which removed whatever vestige of dignity he might have had left. I'm to blame for everything."

The huge weight of guilt and sorrow that she had been holding back suddenly burst free. It was a harrowing moment to see her in such anguish. I rushed forward to comfort her, as did Harold. We all did what we could, but nothing was going to ease her pain.

"If I may say, my dear, I think you overlook the role that Freddy played in this whole affair," Stanley said.

Somehow, she managed to answer him in a very matter-of-fact way. "If I'd never met Freddy, my life would no doubt have taken another turn, as would my father's. The fact is, I made the decision to get involved with him against my father's advice. I was both gullible and stupid. I can't blame anyone else."

Bill looked positively tearful when he said, "Audrey, are you telling us that you've spent the rest of your life weighed down with this burden of guilt?"

"That's exactly what I'm saying, because it's true. It was all my fault."

Stanley did his best to return to his fatherly understanding expression.

"Put aside the issue of guilt, my dear," he said. "The real question you should ask yourself is can you forgive yourself for whatever it is you think you might have done? Before you tell me you're unworthy of forgiveness, let's have a show of hands. Who thinks Audrey is worthy of forgiveness?"

Everyone raised both hands and, for a light-hearted moment, Stanley had managed to relieve just a little of Audrey's tension. I so much wanted to say something significant. As we know such things usually elude me, but on this occasion, I was determined.

"Audrey, surely you realise that we all love you, and now that you've shared your story with us, we all have to shoulder the burden with you. I'm sure I can speak for everyone when I say that we'll shoulder the burden with you for as long as you need, but wouldn't it be better if we could all just cast it aside?"

Stanley was pleased. "Well said, Charles."

Harold was quiet, even by Harold's standards, while Bill said, "Charles is absolutely right, Audrey. You really have shared your burden among us, let's deal with it together."

Audrey couldn't take any more of our well-meant intentions, and burst into a flood of tears once again, whereupon we all stepped forward and formed a group hug. It's a strange thing when human emotion is concentrated like that. It really does appear to generate a power greater than the sum of the individuals.

Audrey sobbed aloud with complete abandon, but now her tears were a mixture of both distress and joy.

"Thank you all," she said. "I don't deserve friends like you, but I'm so pleased to have you."

We all stood with our arms around her. I was in no doubt that the dippy Audrey had left the building.

Chapter Seven
THE PUB

The following day, Fiona arrived. She and Audrey went out for the day to visit some stately home or other. Lizzy was adamant that she needed a quiet day after all the excitement and so this left the rest of us to ponder over Audrey's remarkable story. Bill suggested that a change of environment was needed; perhaps we should pop out to the pub.

"Capital idea," said Stanley. "You can drive, Charles."

We set off, our heads full to the brim with yesterday's events. Audrey's story was revelatory to say the least, and none of us could concentrate upon much else. The traffic was light, and we drove for at least fifteen minutes without a single incident of road rage from other drivers. At roundabouts especially, I'm never quite sure which lane I should be in. Consequently, I'm often entertained by an irate driver waving a clenched fist or a raised middle finger.

Finally, and without incident, we came across a nice pub which wasn't of our acquaintance, but Stanley liked the look of it. It was a charming pub, thatched roof over a bent and leaning timber frame, with a wonderful covering of climbing roses. Inside, it was original old English brickwork with very low timber beams. Sad to say, I always notice boring things like brickwork, and these were good old nine-inch bricks so were pre-eighteenth century. Of much more interest was the selection of real ales. Stanley sat down, saying he would have a pint.

"Do you think he'll ever pay for a drink?" Bill said.

We agreed that the prospect looked unlikely. Negotiating the low oak beams was something of a challenge, but finally we raised our glasses in a toast to Audrey.

"Did anyone have the faintest notion about her past?" asked Stanley.

We all agreed that not one of us had the faintest idea. I said that I'd had a few suspicions from some of her comments, but not this.

"It all goes back to what you were saying, Charles, about events changing the course of history," said Bill. "Just imagine what might have been if she hadn't fallen for Freddy, or her brother had gone into the business."

Harold agreed and added, "If only she hadn't met that little shit Freddy! None of those tragic events would have happened!"

My thoughts turned to George.

"That poor man, it sounds like he was a really good egg. A decent honest bloke who only wanted the best for his daughter. It does make you realise how one or two events can change your life forever. I still can't understand how Audrey could have fallen for the little shit's false charm."

"I've been married twice, and divorced twice," Stanley said. "I think I can say with some experience that affairs of the heart are not rational decisions."

Bill looked extremely thoughtful when he said, "Of course you're right, Stanley. Emotive decisions don't always have the best outcome, but let's not forget that, while a hasty decision may be irrational, it might also be intuitive."

"Trust you to bring philosophy into it, Bill," I said. "Are you saying there are times when our intuitive actions are more rational than a conscious well-considered decision?"

Harold put down his glass of beer, saying, "Intuitive thought is often irrational, which is why we need training to cope with difficult situations so that our response is automatic and not the result of an irrational process."

"I know I made two very bad life-changing decisions because I wasn't being rational," Stanley replied.

Bill smiled, "Perhaps intuition is irrational, but I made the best decision I ever made, despite all common sense telling me otherwise."

I didn't like to ask Bill what decision he was talking about.

"That's really fascinating," I said. "I tend to agree with Stanley. I've made a series of disastrous decisions as far as women are concerned."

Stanley interrupted me. "When you say disastrous, Charles, was that decision only disastrous with the aid of hindsight?"

"Good point Stanley, I suppose to be really objective about it, some of the traps I fell into were simply not visible, but others had a great big warning sign above them."

"My second wife carried one of those signs," Stanley said with a broad smile.

"My wife carried one of those signs as well," said Bill. "It was flashing neon and would have lit up a football pitch!"

What was Bill trying to tell us, I wondered? The one thing we all knew about Bill's wife was that he doted on her and, in all respects, they appeared to have shared a perfect life together. In fact, if I'm perfectly honest I would have to admit that I feel more than a bit envious of Bill's relationship with his wife and children. His life experience in this regard would appear to be the exact opposite of mine. My marriage was a disaster and I hardly ever see my two girls. Bill has become my constant reminder that the opposite face of joy is despair. Harold had contributed an interesting element to this discussion, but he remained quiet as far as affairs of the heart were concerned.

"Quite right about training, Harold, but the manual is a bit thin as far as women are concerned," Stanley said.

"You're right there. I could do with a training manual in that department, never understood the fairer sex."

Keen to move the discussion away from himself, he went on. "I know a couple of Audrey's decisions were ill-advised, but in light of what we've been discussing, can anyone really blame her?"

"Absolutely not," said Stanley. "I've known few women with Audrey's degree of intelligence and determination. If she was duped by the little shit, I think it's fair to say that we all would've been."

"You know what's even more distressing? She's carried that burden of guilt for so long," I said.

Bill replied, "This is obviously why she has never spoken about her past before. In fact, I've hardly ever heard her say anything that even hinted at that enormous intellect of hers. Come to think of it, this is probably why she chose to come to the Village in the first place."

"You're right, I think she must have created 'Dippy' to hide behind," I said.

"What a tragedy, but perhaps now we will see the real Audrey," said Stanley.

"That's a happy prospect," replied Harold. "How about one for the road?"

Stanley looked over towards the landlord. "Another four pints of your finest ale, my good man."

We all hesitated to see if Stanley might be considering paying, but no such luck.

"I'll get it," Harold said, and proceeded to the bar.

On his way back with a tray of four beers, the landlord shouted after him, "You've forgotten your change."

Harold half-turned his head to reply and crashed straight into one of the oak beams. The beer went directly over us, while the beam went directly across Harold's forehead. Once we had established that Harold's injury to his pride was greater than the one to his forehead, we all fell about laughing. Being completely soaked in beer, we thought it best that we head off towards a change of clothes so, having apologised to the landlord, and still laughing out loud, we started our journey back.

We hadn't driven more than a mile or two when the first roundabout appeared and, of course, I do get a little confused at roundabouts. As I exited the roundabout, I just might have inadvertently cut across in front of a Range Rover Sport. It was a black one; I'm not sure they make them in any other colour. This resulted in a good example of road rage, fist shaking alternating with the ubiquitous one-finger sign. I'm entirely used to this and I find it terribly amusing. Bill shares my sense of humour and we laughed even more. Stanley was new to all this, but he soon began to see the funny side of it.

No sooner had we exited the roundabout, than the young man in the Range Rover came racing up alongside us, put his window down and shouted a torrent of abuse about my driving skills, and how I should be banned from the road. The boy made a complete arse of himself. Bill and I were in fits of laughter. I have two standard replies to enraged drivers. I have, 'I know, it's terrible, isn't it?' and 'I can't hear you, can you shout louder?'

On this occasion, I used the first option which worked very well. The boy was apoplectic, and we now had a series of threats to various parts of my anatomy. Bill summed up the situation perfectly, as he so often does.

"That poor chap must be so full of stress, and here we are, relaxed and enjoying our day; there's much to be said for retirement!"

With that, the Range Rover swerved and very nearly clipped the wing of my Audi.

"I think I'd better let the poor sod go past before he kills himself," I said.

A lay-by conveniently appeared, so I pulled in. The Range Rover, having driven on a few yards, stopped abruptly and reversed back to us with smoke billowing from its tyres. The enraged young man jumped out of his car, running enthusiastically toward us.

"Oh dear," I said. "It's only funny when the enraged driver stays in the car."

Harold, who had said very little, nursing his forehead, opened his door and stepped out of the car.

"You'd best leave this to me," he said.

The young man, who was probably in his early forties, looked at Harold who was soaked in beer, with a trickle of blood running down his forehead. His better judgement should have told him that it simply wasn't sporting to punch an already injured man who was twenty years his senior. However, this young man had left his better judgement way back on the carriageway. He advanced toward Harold, swinging a windmill of a right-hand punch, which would probably have missed him anyway.

Harold brushed the swinging arm aside but retained a hold upon the boy's sleeve, while at the same time taking hold of the fellow's lapel with his other hand. In an instant, the young man hit the ground with a thud that made *my* back ache, let alone his! The next thing we knew, Harold was twisting the boy's head off. Bill and I rushed out of the car and grabbed Harold.

"That's enough, Harold!" I said. "Leave a bit for the stretcher bearers!"

None of us had ever seen anything like it. We bundled Harold back into the car and I quickly checked to see that the boy was still alive.

"Who *is* that guy?" he asked.

"Do you know," I replied, "I have no idea."

We set off once again in the car, but we'd only travelled a few miles when I noticed a blue flashing light in my rear-view mirror. It appears that a police car had turned into the lay-by just as we left and encountered the irate young man who told them the story about the four violent drunks.

"How much have I had to drink?" I asked the others.

"Only the one," said Bill. "We're wearing the last round."

We pulled over and a policeman soon arrived at the side of the car. I lowered the window with a distinct sense of foreboding. The smell of beer was overpowering, and the poor chap physically recoiled as the fumes rose up out of the window.

"Been having a drink, have we, sir?" he asked, and turned to his colleague in the car, saying, "You've got to see this!"

The two policemen stood a safe distance from the fumes, looking at Harold's injured forehead.

"Are you gentlemen capable of getting out of the car?" one of them asked sarcastically.

We got out of the car, looking as sprightly as we could manage.

"This is not how it looks, officer," I said.

"It looks like four brawling drunks to me. Which part of that have I got wrong, sir?" he replied.

Stanley took over the situation and explained what had happened. The two policemen didn't believe a word of it and produced a breathalyser.

"Would you like to blow into this, sir, or shall I just wave it around you?"

I duly blew into the contraption and miraculously it was negative. The policeman asked me to do it again, which I did, and again it was negative. This turn of events seemed to be of considerable irritation to both of the policemen who then started to question us about the 'assault'. Stanley stepped forward again and pointed out that they were taking the word of one very dubious character, and that he found their manner both insulting and patronising. They were essentially accusing four law-abiding citizens of giving false evidence.

"Remind me, young man, who is your chief constable?" Stanley asked.

Before he could answer, Stanley was scrolling down the contacts in his phone and said, "Ah yes, Robert Evans. Before

I call Bob, you might just like to consider the implications for your careers."

Both the policemen were somewhat taken aback.

"I don't think that will be necessary, sir," one of them said. "I think it's clear there's been a misunderstanding."

"Not on my behalf, there hasn't," said Stanley. "I'm minded to pursue this matter further."

With that the two policemen offered profuse apologies and scuttled off to their car. Obviously, we were all jubilant.

"Bloody hell," I said to Harold. "He really does know everyone in the entire world!"

"What luck, Stanley, that you should know the Chief Constable," Bill said.

Stanley smiled triumphantly.

"I don't know him. He was on the TV the other day, and I remembered his name!"

"But he's listed in your phone?" said Harold.

"I didn't say he was in my phone, did I?" said Stanley.

Once the penny had dropped, we heaped praise upon him, while he sat in the back of the car, beaming from ear to ear.

We were desperately hoping to arrive back at the Village as clandestinely as possible, but sod's law proved itself to be as infallible as ever. As we entered the Village, who should drive in right behind us but Fiona and Audrey.

"What do I do?" I said.

"Keep your head down," replied Harold.

"Some hope," said Bill. "Perhaps they'll think it's a driverless car".

"Don't let them see me!" said Harold.

With that, Audrey opened my door. "What on earth has happened to your head, Harold?" she asked.

I stepped out of the car, to be immediately greeted with a hug from Fiona.

"How are you, Charles?" she asked. Then she gasped, "Oh my God, what on earth is that smell?"

Audrey put her head into the car to get a better look at Harold's head and was almost overcome by the beer fumes.

"Oh, my goodness! What on earth have you all been up to?"

Stanley, still revelling in his triumph, stepped out of the car with all the swagger of a four-star general about to address the troops.

"That, my dear, is the sweet smell of success!" He rolled up the bottom third of his tie, squeezed out a handful of beer, and set off towards his apartment.

"How do you put up with this lot?" Fiona joked to her mother.

"Oh, they simply rub off on you!"

Chapter Eight
THE FALKLANDS

Presentable again, we all arrived for an aperitif at about six o'clock. The only clue to our adventure was Harold's forehead, which by now was quite impressive. We related the story about the oak beam, the spilled beer and the road rage incident, not to mention our encounter with the law. None of us mentioned Harold's dispatching of the young man, as we all knew that was going to be a long story. Audrey was on great form; she thought our adventure was hilarious and was just calming down when she looked again at Harold. There was a silent moment before we all started laughing again.

A little later, I was quietly chatting to Bill as we dined, and we agreed that Harold's dispatching of the young man raised a lot more questions than it answered.

"There's a hell of a lot more to Harold than we know," said Bill.

I agreed, saying, "I think he must have had a military career. He's such a confident dashing figure. I can't believe that he has so little to say about himself."

Bill looked very thoughtful until finally he said, "Think about Audrey. We thought she had little to say, and now look at her."

He was right, and I started to say, "I wonder if….."

Bill interrupted me, "That's what I'm wondering. Let's wait and see if there's a pattern here."

After dinner, we sat in the lounge again, relaxing in the comfortable chairs. I made a dash for the chesterfield, knowing that meant I could rub shoulders with Audrey. We enjoyed a cup of coffee each, while Stanley contentedly sipped a glass of Dalwhinnie 15-year-old, courtesy of Bill on this occasion. I felt sure that today's events would provoke a question or two for Harold, and sure enough, Stanley's opening gambit quickly followed.

"Do I detect just a hint of a North West accent in your voice Harold? Were you from the Manchester area originally?"

Clever Stanley! Ask a question and make it clear that you already know the answer, then there's nothing for Harold to lose by answering. Harold tried not to get involved, but he did confirm Stanley's assumption.

"Terraced house in Manchester. Nothing of any interest for you, Stanley."

"Everyone's of interest to me, Harold, especially people who lose their Mancunian accent." replied Stanley. "It tells me they left the area of their birth at an early age."

Harold agreed, "No harm admitting it. I was out of there at the age of sixteen."

Stanley was ready to pounce.

"Sounds like you were running away, dear boy. What caused you to run away?"

"The usual things," Harold replied. "Dysfunctional household, really nothing out of the ordinary, nothing interesting."

Perhaps Harold realised or perhaps not, but that single sentence opened a tiny crack into his past, and Stanley made it his own.

"Now then, old boy, you must tell me. What did your father do during the war?"

Now why did Stanley ask such an innocuous question? I assumed it was just to keep Harold talking, but then I realised that if the household dysfunction had anything to do with the father, then Stanley was already ahead. I think maybe Harold realised this only too well, and he wasn't keen to allow Stanley into his very private world. He tried to prevaricate for a while until Audrey intervened.

"Harold," she said, "I think you're missing the point of Stanley's questions. Your answers aren't for our benefit, they're for yours. I've spent a large part of my life consumed by guilt. I couldn't allow anyone to have even a hint of my past. You all know how difficult it was for me to talk about it, but now I have, I can't tell you what a relief it is. I only realised how heavy my burden was when I put it down."

Harold seemed to be taken aback by Audrey's unexpected intervention, but finally said, "I know you're right. It's not that I have any great guilt or shame to hide, it's simply that the ghosts of the past are less troubling when they stay in the past."

Audrey leaned across, holding Harold's hand as she spoke. "Let your ghosts out, Harold. If you let them fade in the light of day, they won't trouble you again."

"You could convince me of anything, Audrey, but I'm afraid you'll find my life a disappointment."

Stanley was invigorated by Audrey's intervention, and wasted no time in reiterating his question about Harold's father.

Harold said his father had served with great distinction during the war in the 6th Airborne Division. He was one of the first to land at Normandy on D-Day, where he was awarded the DCM. This was clearly a matter of great pride for Harold, but he hinted that all was not well when his father returned from the war.

"So often the case," said Stanley. "Was it what we now call post-traumatic stress?"

"I suppose that's exactly what it was but, at the time, there was no recognition of it."

With a little more encouragement from Stanley, it gradually

came to light that Harold's father was in every respect a war hero many times over, awarded his DCM for leading a successful attack on a German gun emplacement during the Normandy landings. His squad suffered terrible losses. In fact, he was the only survivor. Despite his own injuries, he carried a badly wounded comrade several miles back behind the Allied Lines only to find out he was already dead. Harold explained that his father was never able to forgive himself. Apparently, despite his heroism, he felt he was to blame for the deaths of his comrades.

"How did it affect him?" Stanley asked.

"In a word," said Harold, "drink."

"How sad, for a gallant man to have overcome such odds, only to succumb to drink. How did this affect your childhood?"

Harold didn't reply at first, but eventually said, "When he was sober, my father ruled the house with a rod of iron. When he was drunk, he hit us with it."

Audrey leaned forward to touch Harold's arm.

"I can't imagine how terrible it must have been for you. I'm so sorry."

I'm not sure how much sympathy Harold had ever received in his life, but he looked really touched.

"Another drink?" asked Bill.

"Good idea," said Stanley. "I'll have a single malt."

Bill and I went to the bar.

"Stanley's got him, you know," said Bill.

"I think you may be right, Bill. I can't say that I'm surprised about the army connection. He does have that air of authority."

Bill agreed. "It's just like Stanley did with Audrey; you remember that pattern we talked about? Talking of Audrey, have you noticed the change in her? It really is as if a great weight has been lifted. She looks wonderful. By the way, when are you and Audrey going to become an item?"

"Oh dear, is it that obvious?"

"Of course, it's obvious, but if you don't do something about it, I think Harold could take over. Audrey isn't the kind of lady to wait for anyone."

I knew Bill was right, but maybe a bit of competition might be the motivation I needed. Just as our drinks arrived, Bill and I heard an unmistakable rasping sound behind us. We looked at each other in complete horror. There was no need for words, we both knew what this meant; immediate evasive action was required. Bill isn't too quick on his feet, so I grabbed the tray and we beat a hasty retreat. A second later, Puffer, who'd been standing behind us, erupted into a coughing fit all over the bar.

There's always a selfish satisfaction when a disaster that could so easily have been ours is instead bestowed upon some other poor sod. One of those unfortunates at the bar was wiping his face with a napkin and said to us, "You had a lucky escape!"

Puffer, who is always oblivious to the effects of his coughing, latched onto the comment and instantly recalled a joke about an escapologist.

Bill and I arrived back with the drinks, laughing our heads off.

"What's tickling you two?" asked Audrey.

We related Puffer's joke and we all agreed that it was one of his better ones. Stanley, however, was keen to pursue Harold's story while he had the chance, so he continued.

"Do tell me, dear boy, is that why you left home so young?"

Harold agreed, saying he couldn't wait to get away. Reading between the lines, I sensed a deep conflict in his mind about his father, but he didn't intend to be forthcoming. Stanley didn't dwell on the subject and asked where he went and what he did when he'd left home. Harold said he only ever wanted to do one thing as a young man. He always wanted to join the army like his father, and he apparently had his father's support to do that.

He wanted to join the Parachute Regiment, so eventually he was stationed at Catterick in North Yorkshire to complete pre-Parachute selection. From there, he later joined the 2nd Battalion Parachute Regiment at Colchester.

"That was it." he said. "When I eventually put on the red beret, I knew this was going to be my future."

He had various overseas postings, and it sounded like Harold really excelled in the Regiment. A few years afterwards, Harold applied to join the SAS, and described to us the selection process based around the Brecon Beacons. It's one of the toughest selection processes in the world. It seemed almost impossible to me that anyone could pass the test which Harold described, and indeed very few do. Harold, however, was one of the few in more ways than one. He again excelled and was accepted by the SAS. Eventually he served through the ranks to become captain, second-in-command of a squadron.

Stanley was very keen to explore his SAS career, but Harold made it quite clear that much of his covert activities needed to stay exactly that, covert. The SAS role in the 1982 Falklands campaign was, however, well-known and he was reluctantly prepared to describe his role in that campaign. It came as no surprise to find that Harold had served with the SAS. Although he had never spoken about it before, everything about Harold spoke of a military career. I was left wondering why we always had to wait for Stanley to join the dots together.

Harold started to tell us about his involvement in the Falklands campaign, though it was immediately obvious that he had no great enthusiasm for the task ahead.

On the 14th of May, the SAS carried out a highly successful raid at Pebble Island where they destroyed several enemy aircraft.

On the 21st of May, they carried out a diversionary attack at Darwin and Goose Green, the idea being to draw attention away from the main landings taking place at San Carlos. Despite their low numbers, it was later found out that the Argentines believed they were being attacked by a whole battalion.

Harold's next role, nearly a week later, on the 26th, was to provide reconnaissance for his old battalion, 2nd Para, as they fought to capture Darwin and Goose Green. SAS operations are always meticulously planned but this operation had little time for their usual preparations. Following the landing at San Carlos, the UK forces had secured the landing site and dug in, but there were no ground operations. The landings were being consolidated in preparation for the march towards the capital, Stanley. Back home, the politicians were concerned that the landing force might appear to be stalled, and they were under more and more threat from the Argentine air force.

Goose Green and Darwin weren't of strategic importance as far as recapturing the island was concerned, and the original plan was to bypass Darwin, but the powers-that-be decided an attack upon Goose Green and Darwin would break the log-jam and give the invasion some momentum. The order was only given on the 25th of May.

"My orders were to take a recon team to a position near Darwin Ridge, where we were to assess the Argentine forces and to direct the artillery fire, in particular night-time fire from HMS Arrow, which was to provide naval gunfire support for the ground assault."

In theory, Harold's squad would arrive at their position undetected and hang around for a couple of days providing intel and target coordinates. Then when the Paras came along, they would slip away without firing a shot. There's always a Plan B, however, and they had as always to be prepared for any eventuality. Harold didn't anticipate any circumstances where they would extend the mission much beyond the planned two days but, to be safe, they allowed for four days of food and water rations. The nights were cold, so sleeping bags were essential. There were radios and batteries, of course, together with all the standard survival kit, night vision kit, navigation equipment, spade, field dressings, antibiotics, rehydrate drink packs, etc.

They carried morphine around their necks. In that way, everyone knows where it is in an emergency. Due to the nature of the mission, they probably wouldn't need much of the kit that an SAS patrol would often carry, such things as Claymores, Elsie mines, plastic explosive or detonators. The need for a disposable anti-tank weapon was debatable but, in the event, not one of these items was available anyway.

Harold recalled all the details as if it was yesterday, and when Stanley asked him what Plan B was, he answered immediately. Plan B was what they would do if they were compromised and, because that was a high risk, they had to take every precaution. Their only option in the event of being compromised was massive firepower to support a tactical retreat, and so the priority was weapons and ammunition.

None of this equipment or terminology was familiar to us, but for Harold this was all everyday jargon. The standard weapons of choice for the SAS in those circumstances were the M16 Armalite with the 203 40mm grenade launcher, and the Minimi light machine gun. The plan was for two of them to carry an Armalite, and two would each carry a Minimi, together with as much ammunition as they could reasonably carry. Harold also wanted as many of the 40mm bombs for the 203 as possible.

In many respects, the operation was a last-minute decision and, as such, the usual meticulous SAS planning was simply not possible. The patrol might face unknown unknowns, and the usual SAS procedure is to work through every possible scenario, each with a corresponding response so that, in the event of an alternative plan being required, the response is automatic. Harold was concerned that there was insufficient time to put this kind of planning into place. Following the diversionary attack a week ago, they had to assume that the enemy had made improvements to their positions, but the latest intelligence about the Argentine positions wasn't clear which, of course, was why he and his men were being sent to Darwin Ridge in the first place.

The other complication was the terrain in the immediate area, which was rolling, treeless ground with grassy outcrops, sporadic gorse and peat bogs. 'High ground' was a relative term, but the Argentines were occupying what little high ground there was. An ideal surveillance position would normally be at a safe distance and from higher ground, but this wasn't an option at Darwin. The patrol would have to get as close as possible.

Getting as close as possible without being detected is one of the classic procedures for which the SAS trains, and the prospect of silently crawling several miles in the mud didn't worry him at all.

They set off as soon as it was dark. There was a crescent moon but plenty of cloud cover, giving them occasional visibility as well as offering the enemy the same advantage. The first few miles were a routine 'tab', what he called a march, but the last mile or so was a crawl. It was obviously essential that they remained concealed both visually and audibly, but in such a featureless terrain with a Bergen backpack, it does require special skills.

All the terrain was wet if not actually bog so, in some areas, it was possible to slither over the wet surface. Gorse areas were to be avoided because you get caught up in it, and it can create noise, so they had to cut around those areas, always trying to keep grassy hillocks between them and the Argentines. Every movement had to be slow and deliberate. Any rapid movement could draw attention, and the slightest noise, such as the clunk of two pieces of kit knocking together, could be fatal. Even heavy breathing must be avoided. The advance was much slower than they had expected due to the terrain. It was six hours into the darkness before they were approaching their target.

Stanley asked an obvious question.

"How did you know where to set up your surveillance in such a dark and featureless terrain?"

Harold explained that they had night-vision goggles and a scope, so they could see, but in that kind of landscape all you see is even more featureless landscape, so what you rely on is the enemy revealing themselves by movement or noise, or even by glowing cigarettes. If the enemy was as concealed as they themselves were, they might even stumble upon them, with disastrous consequences.

As it turned out, they were lucky that the Argentines weren't as disciplined as they should have been. They were able to spot several trenches and gun emplacements simply because the troops moved or made a noise. The only worry was about the troops who were properly disciplined and who would remain concealed. On two occasions as they approached Darwin Ridge, they found themselves in a dangerous position and had to backtrack.

On the third approach, towards the end of the ridge, they found a slight depression surrounded by grassy hillocks. Looking to their right, it was about five hundred metres from the positions which they had boxed around earlier. With clear higher ground to their left, this wasn't the best of vantage points, but Harold decided it was the best they might find before daybreak.

The possible noise of scraping out a deeper depression was too risky, so they hunkered down beneath camo nets and waited to see the sun rise. They didn't have long to wait; it was already getting light. Looking around, moving very slowly and deliberately, they could see the positions to their right were quite extensive. The troops were moving about, seeming relaxed. Five hundred metres was a safe distance. They found themselves thinking it had all gone very well, all they had to do was to sit tight until it was dark again.

At that moment, they heard Argentine voices. It was very

faint and was coming with the wind direction, but it was a lot closer than five hundred metres. None of them spoke as they each scanned what ground they could see, but there was no sign of an enemy position. Either they were on the other side of the ridge, or there was a trench invisible from their perspective. Content that they weren't compromised, they would remain concealed. It wasn't ideal, but neither was it a big problem, so long as they just kept their heads down.

Bill asked an interesting question.

"What goes through your mind when you have plenty of time on your hands like that?"

Harold smiled one of his condescending smiles and replied.

"If you drift off into your own mind, you aren't alert, and we must always be alert."

Time is filled with normal procedure. One at a time, firearms are taken apart, then cleaned and oiled. Ammunition magazines are checked to make sure they are exactly where they should be. Hand gun, grenades, fighting knife, everything is checked. If there is time, there are cold rations but, above all, they rehearse between them what each one should do in every possible scenario should they become compromised. Only when every eventuality has been covered do they then set about their principal job of providing intel. Jim Owen was the navigator so, having marked the map with all the Argentine positions that he could see, including some assumptions about the ones he couldn't see, he radioed back their intel, including the coordinates for the naval bombardment. Any remaining time was for sleep with one of them on watch, changing every two hours.

"There's never any time for introspection," Harold said.

Bill looked as if he wished he hadn't asked the question. It demonstrated a profound ignorance about the workings of the SAS. The trouble was that we were all equally ignorant about these things. Stanley adopted his all-knowing expression as if to say, '*of course I knew that*'.

Lizzy was very concerned about the cold and damp.

"Did you get a hot cup of tea?" she asked.

Harold was unusually polite, assuring Lizzy that they were fine without a cup of tea for a day or two, but this wasn't good enough for Lizzy.

"I suppose you could've gone back for a nice hot bath if it got too cold."

Once again, Harold was uncharacteristically polite. I was hoping Lizzy wouldn't pursue the matter further, feeling sure that with two polite responses, he was already over the limit!

"Do we assume then that you remained undetected until dusk?" asked Stanley.

Harold explained that once they were in such a position, only extremely bad luck was going to compromise them. Normally the SAS welcome the dark, as it usually works to their advantage, but of course that didn't apply to this coming night. At ten o'clock, all hell was going to break loose.

HMS Arrow in San Carlos Bay was going to start an extensive naval bombardment on the coordinates which Jim had given them. His job was to continue guiding those shells onto new coordinates, and to provide intel to 2nd Para who would be advancing towards them. Harold knew that, at precisely ten o'clock, the bombardment would begin, so they checked watches.

He said to the lads, "Here we go, heads down."

The first coordinates were half a mile along the ridge and HMS Arrow should first find their range, then their fire would be guided as necessary. The bombardment didn't go according to plan. The first they should have seen was the flash of the shells landing half a mile away, followed by the sound of the explosions, but instead they heard the whistle of incoming shells. There was no time to do anything other than to press themselves into the ground.

The first shells landed about fifty metres below their position, the second group fell almost directly upon them. Jim and

Harold were a little further from the blast than the other two lads, who didn't have a chance. Shells continued to fall around them. Jim kept calm and was immediately on the radio, giving their call sign to HMS Arrow.

"Come in Arrow, come in Arrow".

Harold looked at the radio, which was completely silent. Jim turned it over, only to see a hole in the back about the size of a fist.

They had a second radio which was with the other two lads, so they didn't even need to check it out; just a glance told them there was no hope. More shells dropped until one landed very close and Harold thought he'd had it. They were both blown clear out of their position.

"I've no idea how long we lay there, but, as I became conscious, the shells were still raining in."

Stanley was really concerned.

"What on earth did you do?"

"I couldn't hear anything; my ears had gone, and you assume the worst."

He was totally disorientated and groped to feel his limbs, expecting to find his body smashed and broken, but everything was there. The next thing he remembered was Jim dragging him into a shell crater. He could see Jim's lips move and guessed what he was probably saying.

"Are you okay, Harry? Harry, are you okay?"

Harold said, "These are the moments when your training really kicks in. You want to panic, you really want to get away from the danger, but your training says: regroup, assess the situation, collect weapons and equipment."

They were both confused and disorientated but, as he said, the training did its job. As the shells continued falling, they picked up what kit they could and stumbled away from the position, fully laden. The shells were falling mainly below their position. Shrapnel flew around their heads, earth and debris rained down from the sky, and the air was full of toxic smoke.

There was no point moving toward the concentration of fire, so they moved in the opposite direction. What they didn't realise in the smoke and confusion was that they were moving towards the Argentine positions.

They cleared the smoke and managed to put about a hundred metres between them and the barrage. This wasn't far enough, but they couldn't risk walking any further in plain sight of the enemy. As soon as the smoke cleared, it was back to crawling. They had only covered a few more metres when Harold could see movement in front of them, perhaps seventy-five metres away. He signalled to Jim and they stopped in their tracks. Surely, they'd been seen? Their silhouettes would have stood out against the shell blasts. They waited and sure enough the Argentines had indeed seen them, and opened up with machine gun fire. They could both see from the tracer shells that the Argentines didn't know their exact position. Their proximity to the enemy had placed them in a perilous situation; it was sink-or-swim.

The Argentines were conscripts, and certainly not as well-trained as they themselves were. Harold said their best option was to employ their SAS training. When the odds are very much against you, it's imperative that the enemy doesn't know that. If it had been known there were only two of them, they would have been quickly overrun. Jim had one of the Minimis with as much ammunition as he could carry, Harold had his Armalite with the 203-grenade launcher. They had a lot of firepower.

Their plan was to advance toward the enemy. One of them would lay down enormous fire power while the other would advance forward. Then he would fire the same while the other advanced. In this way they created the impression of a much larger advancing force. Their hope was that the Argentine conscripts would retreat to their main defensive position, enabling them to exit in the other direction, but the reality was quite different.

Harold was sure that, in the dark, the Argentines did think they were a larger force, but they were very brave men and some of them still stood their ground. This was the worst possible scenario. They had risked all with an advancing frontal assault which amounted to an enormous bluff, but the enemy had called their bluff. It was clear their options had run out. They couldn't retreat, and their ammunition wouldn't last forever.

Harold admitted he thought they had surely reached the end of the line, but it wasn't as if they had any options. All they could do was to continue the assault, however futile that appeared to be.

The Argentines had prepared positions including a series of trenches and, although the two of them had driven the main force back to their main defensive position, one group had taken cover in an outlying trench. If Harold and Jim could seize this trench position, it would provide them with cover. They concentrated all their considerable firepower upon that position, but the intensity of the action was such that they were starting to run low on ammunition. Harold signalled to Jim that he was low, and Jim indicated that he had just one magazine left for the Minimi. Harold had fired all his thirty grenades with the 203. Their only remaining armament was one hand grenade each and handguns.

They were by now only fifty yards from the leading Argentine position, so they quickly formulated a plan. Jim tossed Harold his one remaining grenade; he would provide covering fire with the Minimi while Harold advanced upon the trench. Jim suppressed the Argentine fire power to a great extent, but this still meant that Harold had to half run and half crawl, fully exposed, toward their trench. In the dark, he needed to get close enough to be sure the two grenades would both drop into the trench. He could just make out that the trench was V-shaped with the arms being about thirty feet long. He tossed one grenade a few yards from one end. Then he crawled a few more yards and tossed the other one into the other end. As the grenades went off, Jim ran from his position to jump into the trench at one end, and Harold did the same at the other end.

What they found in the trench was horrific. Bodies lay everywhere. He was sure that most of the victims were already dead before the grenades went off, but each one had to be checked for any signs of life. His matter-of-fact way of describing these events was a little disturbing to those of us who have killed nothing larger than a spider. However, I could understand that heroism like his was only possible with a large degree of detachment.

Audrey, probably sensibly, suggested another cup of coffee.

"Very sensible suggestion, Audrey," said Stanley. "I'll have a single malt, and I think the gravity of Harold's situation means that Laphroaig 10-year old would be the appropriate choice."

Bill and I stood at the bar discussing the evening's events.

"Did you have any inkling that Harold was capable of this kind of thing?" I said.

"Not really, but I can't say I'm surprised."

"I know what you mean, and this certainly explains our friend in the lay-by the other day."

We could see Puffer coming in from another smoke, so we quickly went back to our seats, just in case!

Stanley sipped his Laphroaig with great satisfaction.

"A haggis of a whisky," he said, and proposed a toast to Harold.

"To the courage of our armed forces, and to you Harold. Your country is proud of you."

"Hear, hear!" we all said in unison.

"That's very kind of you, Stanley," said Harold, "but I was only doing the job I was trained for."

"What on earth happened next, after you occupied that trench?" asked Stanley.

Although they had control of the trench, the enemy had more positions close by. The only hope was that the Argentines might not realise their trench had been overrun. All the two could do was to keep their heads down, which worked until dawn when the Argentines sent a squad down to check. Harold and Jim collected all the Argentine weapons and ammunition, only to find that their ammunition was also low. Nonetheless, they opened fire with what they had, catching the advancing squad out in the open.

All the time this was going on, the main force of 2nd Para was moving closer to their position. They themselves were at the base of Darwin Ridge, and 2nd Para were not far away at Coronation Ridge. He and Jim only had to hold out long enough for the Paras to overrun their position.

Having successfully repelled the reconnaissance squad, the Argentines assumed that Harold and Jim were the leading edge of the main invasion force. The enemy opened fire from the other side of the ridge with artillery and mortars. Once again, shells fell all around them as they crouched in the trench. Miraculously they weren't directly hit, although Jim was hit by shrapnel in the neck. It was a nasty wound, and he was bleeding profusely. Harold did all he could to stem the flow of blood, but he knew he only had a short time to get Jim to the medics.

He could see 2nd Para advancing further along the ridge, but the resistance was formidable. Time and again they were repelled. 2nd Para's response to the artillery and mortars was to keep the enemy pinned down with their own mortar fire. In that single engagement, the Para's mortar crews fired a thousand rounds.

"We were now in a position where we could be killed by either side," Harold said. "Shells were falling and there was gunfire everywhere. I had to assume that the Paras knew about us, following the fire-fight, but they wouldn't know exactly where we were. Jim was bleeding to death; it looked like the end of the road."

Bill had to excuse himself for one of his bathroom visits, and although the rest of us were riveted to our seats, frankly, I think we welcomed the break. Obviously, Harold had escaped but how did he manage it and what had happened to Jim? It was very late, but nobody suggested calling it a day. Stanley reached for his glass of whisky, forgetting that it was empty. He looked at his empty glass with much the same disbelief that you might look at your car after you'd just dented it. He inhaled the remaining distinctive peaty aroma of the Laphroaig, but it was no substitute for the golden liquid. He looked around mournfully in the hope that someone might say, 'would you like another whisky?' but no-one did! We were only interested to hear how Harold had escaped!

I remember thinking at that moment how calm Harold was. In fact, Stanley was more emotional about his empty glass than Harold was about reliving his past. Then I thought about the contrast between Harold and Audrey. He gave us the impression that he had little or no emotional capital invested in these past events, whereas Audrey had been the complete opposite. They say opposites attract, but could it really be possible that Audrey and Harold could make a perfect couple?

Bill returned saying, "Sorry about that."

Harold admitted that the situation was hopeless. If he'd been by himself, he thought his best plan would have been to stay put in the trench, perhaps surrounding himself with whatever was available, including the bodies. If a shell fell directly into the trench, it was probably the last goodbye, but he would at least have been safe from the gunfire. However, with Jim bleeding to death, he felt he had no option but to take the only other course of action available. Jim wasn't a big fellow, so Harold put him over his shoulder and climbed up out of the trench and into the maelstrom of shells and gunfire above. He set off, heading towards the advancing troops of 2nd Para.

From the very first faltering step, time appeared to stand still. He could see and hear the mortar shells and bullets all around him but none of it seemed real. He could hear the zip of bullets passing close to his head, and the zing of bullets ricocheting off the ground, and all the time the acrid smell of cordite.

Harold gained maybe twenty-five yards before being hit by a piece of shrapnel. He just felt it as a dull thump which felled him to the ground. Struggling up, he was hit again. Jim fell from his shoulder; he was hit as well. Back on his feet, he again slung Jim over his shoulder as if he was no heavier than an old blood-stained raincoat. Another twenty-five yards and another thump, this time to his arm. He could no longer support Jim, he had to stop and change shoulders, and then another stumble.

2nd Para were perhaps another two hundred yards away. It seemed impossibly far, but he continued. Then a mortar shell landed directly in front of him, sending the pair of them crashing once more to the ground. The shock wave from the explosion hit Harold's chest like a sledgehammer and completely winded him. Dragging Jim forward, the two tumbled into the shallow smoking crater left by the shell. His eyes were full of debris and stinging with the smoke. With only one objective in mind and struggling to see, he once again hauled Jim onto his shoulder and stepped up again into the hell above.

The troops of 2nd Para could hardly believe what they were witnessing. There was a great cheer from the lads willing Harold on. They were probably calculating how close he might get before he fell for the last time. Harold's ears were ringing, he could hear nothing; then little short of a miracle happened.

In among the deafening noise, his brain somehow registered the sound of the lads cheering in the distance. It was as if new energy infused his legs. Barely able to see, hear or stand, Harold somehow propelled himself again towards the sound of salvation. Another twenty yards and a bullet went clean through his side which sent him spinning to the ground. The cheering stopped abruptly. Struggling up, first onto one knee, the cheering started again. When Harold regained his weary legs, the cheers became a wall of sound.

With Jim once again over his shoulder, Harold struggled towards the sound. It seemed there was no immovable object that this irresistible force of nature would not overcome. The lads of 2nd Para were equally inspired, and a large contingent broke cover and rushed forward with covering fire. With every stride, the space between the irresistible force and the advancing Paras shrank. Against all odds, the Paras advanced straight past Harold and continued towards the enemy.

The deadlock in the battle was broken, and Jim and Harold were being carried behind the lines. That jolt back into reality hit Harold far harder than any of his four wounds. Suddenly his body was consumed with pain and he could hardly move. Jim was unconscious, his leg shattered below the knee. He had lost pints of blood. Looking at Jim, the medic thought there was little hope.

He turned to Harold and said, "Let's deal with you first," making ready a shot of morphine.

Harold forced himself back into consciousness, looking at the medic with all the anger that he could muster.

"Why do you think I've just carried that man through hell to get here. That's Corporal Jim Owen; he's the reason we're here. You tend to him first."

The medic did his best for Jim, but it looked like a hopeless task; there were several wounds all bleeding badly, as well as his original neck wound and his leg. Miraculously, none of Harold's wounds were critical but, like Jim, the blood loss was taking its toll. Harold was drifting in and out of consciousness, and only vaguely remembered the medics getting him back to San Carlos, to be shipped out to the SS Uganda hospital ship.

His first clear memory was waking up on the ship, looking into the beautiful eyes of a nurse. Harold described the contrast between the hell of Darwin Ridge and this girl's beautiful eyes as 'utterly indescribable'. She represented for him everything in life that was worth cherishing. Where he had just come from represented everything in life that was barbaric and grotesque.

"I just wanted to hold her," he said. "I just wanted the things she represented to be as close to me as possible, and for that other life to be excluded. I attempted to reach out to hold her, but neither of my arms responded to my command, so I said, 'Please hold me,' and to my surprise she did exactly that."

For a moment, Harold never felt so happy in his entire life. Moments later, a matronly figure appeared and barked at the young nurse.

"What on earth are you doing? Get away from that patient."

The nurse wasn't flustered in the slightest. Kissing Harold on the cheek, she said, "I thought I'd lost you. Welcome back."

"I'm pleased to be here, thank you."

This was a side of Harold's character that none of us had expected. It was such a touching scene that Audrey was in tears. Lizzy, who had been very quiet throughout, was clutching her handkerchief, and I had to turn away for a second to wipe my eye.

"What of Jim, your Corporal? I suppose he didn't make it?" Stanley said.

Harold smiled a huge irrepressible smile. "They put a gallon of blood into him, removed a couple of pounds of shrapnel, gave him a wooden leg, and sent him on his way."

Harold's story had left me emotionally drained. It was late, and this was surely an appropriate time for us to call it a day.

"I need a courageous man to escort me to my apartment," Audrey said.

It was quite clear who she had in mind. There was only the one courageous man around here, and it certainly wasn't me. Harold and Audrey left together, and I was reminded of the time when I was a young schoolboy at the end of term dance. The girl that I was secretly in love with asked the boy next to me to dance. I was left standing there like the proverbial lemon that I surely must be.

Chapter Nine
NORTHERN IRELAND

The following morning we'd made tentative arrangements to go out for a picnic together but, as we were all gathering for breakfast, so were the clouds; gathering, that is. Also, Lizzy said she had to see the Doc about her legs so, all in all, we decided to abandon the picnic. After breakfast, Harold could continue his story instead. He seemed less than delighted at the prospect.

"Come on now, Harold, you know you need to do this," Audrey said. He reluctantly agreed.

We had a very pleasant breakfast before heading off towards the library. This is a charming room, oak bookshelves and panelling. The chairs are the same as the ones in the bar, except that they are upholstered in a not altogether unpleasant fabric.

"I love the smell of the books in here," said Bill.

"I agree," I replied. "Shame about this contract carpet."

"We need to wait for Lizzy," said Stanley. "What's the problem with her legs?"

"She knows someone who had a deep vein thrombosis in their leg, so of course she's now convinced that she has one as well!" I replied.

"What happened to the gallstones?" asked Audrey.

"Indigestion," I said.

Stanley once again kept us entertained with one of his anecdotes while we waited for Lizzy. On this occasion he recalled a fishing trip to a remote part of the River Usk in Wales, where he managed to fall into the river. Soaked to the skin on a hot summer day in a very remote location, Stanley decided to take his clothes off in order to dry them. At this point, he described his utter disbelief as a large contingent of the local Women's Institute suddenly appeared in front of him!

We were still laughing at Stanley's embarrassment when Lizzy appeared staggering through the door, looking very pleased with herself.

"I told you, didn't I? The Doc says it's the veins in my legs that are the problem. They're too close together."

Harold intervened, "What the hell are you talking about, 'too close together'?"

Lizzy proudly told us exactly what the doctor had said, and she was in no doubt that he said her veins were very close together. I suddenly realised what he must have told her.

"I think you mean varicose veins," I said.

"That's it," she said. "My veins are very close."

We all fell about with laughter, Stanley clutching the buttons of his waistcoat which were straining against the buttonholes.

"If I laugh any more," he said, "I'll end up with a tailoring problem!"

Lizzy, who could never see the funny side of one of her verbal confusions, gave Stanley a good dressing-down.

"I don't think my close veins should be a source of amusement. It's very rude."

Stanley apologised. "You're quite right, Lizzy. I do apologise. I wouldn't find it humorous if it were *my* veins."

That only started us off again! When we'd all finally calmed down, Stanley slipped effortlessly back into his inquisitorial role. Settling back into his armchair, fingers entwined in front of him, he took a deep breath, seemingly lifting his chest up with his hands.

"Now then, dear boy, we can see that you recovered from your horrendous ordeal, so what happened next?"

Harold smiled a faint smile. "I had a couple of months of R&R back in the UK, but really I'd been incredibly lucky. All my wounds had avoided vital organs or arteries, so it wasn't long before I had another posting, which was to Northern Ireland. Ireland was a typical SAS counter-insurgency job, but it was all a bit 'close to home'. It wasn't a posting any of us enjoyed."

Stanley leaned forward just a little as if to whisper a state secret.

"Were you involved with the so-called shoot-to-kill policy?"

Harold didn't blink an eye, simply answering, "Of course, that was a part of our mission, but surveillance and intelligence were the more difficult part. The whole point of urban counter-terrorism is dealing with an unseen enemy. Once you'd identified the enemy, eliminating the bad guys was the easy part."

This description of events seemed a bit simplistic to me. While I was pondering a significant question to ask, Bill said, "Is that not the real problem, sorting out the bad guys from the message-carriers?"

Harold agreed this was exactly what makes urban terrorism so difficult to deal with, and why ultimately all our efforts were unsuccessful. The reason that the IRA campaign eventually failed was partly because they finally realised that in order to achieve a political change, they needed to bring the people of Northern Ireland with them. They needed to win hearts and minds, and if you want to find the one thing which doesn't endear you to the people, then killing and maiming them will do it every time.

Audrey looked concerned for Harold, and asked him, "Did you ever come into harm's way over there?"

Harold paused for some moments before answering, and finally said, "Physically no, but emotionally yes."

He didn't want to elaborate upon this comment, but Stanley wasn't about to let it drop.

"When I think about what you went through in the Falklands, I'm left wondering what on earth could have happened to you in Northern Ireland that could have left you emotionally scarred?"

Harold bowed his head slightly in a gesture which might equally have been one of regret or of shame, and his answer soon made it clear that it was both. He told us that when you infiltrate a community you need to look credible, and above all never give anyone a reason to challenge that credibility. To achieve this, you always remain on the edge of the community, maintaining a shallow profile. In other words, you need to look like a blade of grass in a field.

On one occasion, they were in the middle of a surveillance operation at night in circumstances where there was the possibility of an action, when suddenly a young woman blundered right into it. She might have been IRA for all Harold knew, but she was a lovely young woman and was in harm's way. He should have abandoned the operation. Having been a long time setting it up, Harold had a sudden impulse, a rush of blood to the head, call it what you will. He broke cover, walked over and took hold of the woman by the arm, practically lifting her off the ground. He told her she needed to get out of there right now, and to let him help her. She might well have shouted or fought back, but instead she was compliant.

As soon as it was safe, Harold said, "Be on your way now, and don't look back."

She did as he said and left. A few seconds later, there were several gunshots, and it was immediately obvious that the surveillance had indeed turned into an action. The rest of the squad appeared, so they could now melt away into the night. Later that same week, Harold bumped into her again quite by accident, and she recognised and approached him.

"Hello," she said, "I want to thank you for the other night."

Harold said he had no idea what she was talking about, but she had no doubt about it.

"At least let me buy you a cup of coffee," she said.

He should have walked away. She could have been IRA. Even if she wasn't IRA, you never, ever, fraternise with the locals. Never compromise your cover. But she was lovely, charming and irresistible so he foolishly agreed to the cup of coffee. Very quickly Harold was quite sure that she wasn't IRA or political in any way. In fact, she was one of those rare things in Northern Ireland, a genuine neutral. She'd spent quite a while in England before returning to Ireland to be with her mother after the loss of her father.

Harold said, "I think I fell in love with her before my coffee cup was empty."

This was an altogether different situation as far as we were all concerned. We'd never heard Harold mention a woman other than his brief encounter with the nurse. His falling in love was a difficult concept to visualise, a bit like me saying I was going to win the London Marathon. Did Harold really have the capacity to be emotionally involved with someone? Well, apparently so. The tone of his voice, however, wasn't that of someone recalling a loving encounter. All his experience and training had been telling him to walk away but, try as he might, he simply couldn't. It was obviously a bad idea, but he'd found himself suggesting that they meet again.

Harold didn't tell her his role in the army; he didn't throw caution to the winds. But he did explain that, as a member of the armed forces, he was a prime target for the IRA, and by association she would be as well. He told her, if they were going to meet, it would have to be secretly, and she really needed to be aware of what was a very real risk.

"Perhaps I was trying to suggest that she should have the strength to do what I was unable to do, to walk away," he said. "I think I was hoping she would say no, that it was too difficult. But she didn't, and so it began."

Harold employed all the skills he had, making sure he wasn't followed, and that he didn't create any recognisable patterns. They met regularly for several months, behaving like furtive lovers having a clandestine affair. His only promise was that, when his tour was over, they would go back to England together.

Stanley looked worried, and we were all apprehensive as we could tell from Harold's tone that this lovely story wasn't going to have a happy ending.

"Perhaps you'd better tell us what happened," said Stanley, fearing the worst.

Harold was resigned to it and said that he was late for one of their clandestine meetings. When he finally arrived, she wasn't there. He pulled every string he could think of. He even had his boys looking for her. Then about two weeks later, following a tip-off, they found her body on waste land outside Derry. She obviously had little to tell them, but the bastards had given her a hard time before shooting her in the head. Harold refrained from giving us the details. Informants later told Harold that the IRA thought she was working for the army. Had he not been late that eventful day, the IRA had intended to kill them both.

"I was completely broken," Harold said. "Her name was Rachel and she offered me a glimpse of a different kind of life where the touch of soft skin or the warmth of a spoken word was more important than looking over my shoulder. It was one of the very few moments when I allowed myself to think about the possibility of another kind of life, and it was the violence of that present life which put an end to it."

These events must have been totally devastating for Harold. When I thought about the man we knew, and then thought of him in that situation, it was too awful for words.

Audrey put her arm around him and said how sorry she was. I did what we gentlemen do best, I placed a hand on his shoulder and said nothing. The others sat looking equally glum. Stanley gave him a reassuring pat on the knee and asked what he did next.

Harold said that his career in the SAS was over as far as Northern Ireland was concerned. He was a known face and, reading between the lines, I suspected that the killing of the young woman was perhaps the last emotional straw for him. His mind had been made up and he got out of the SAS on medical grounds, post-traumatic stress. It wasn't the kind of triumphant send-off this courageous soldier deserved.

Chapter Ten
CHINESE RESTAURANT

Harold's story had taken us on an emotional roller-coaster ride. We were exhausted; there was much for us to mull over, and we were all subdued. Lunchtime was approaching but there was no enthusiasm for anything. It had been a strange kind of morning. We'd half-planned to go out for a picnic and because that hadn't happened, we all felt a bit disjointed. These had been such painful memories for Harold to recall that I felt we should all be rallying round him to lift his spirits, but instead we were moping around. I suddenly had an idea. Most of my ideas prove to be bad ones but I thought no-one else had any suggestions so perhaps I should run it past them.

"What about going out for lunch?" I said.

Audrey's face lit up. "Wonderful idea, Charles, but it's lunchtime already. Where can we go at this short notice?"

Bill thinks about food far more than the rest of us and he naturally had the solution, saying, "There's a local place where I would bet that we can still get a table for six and be sitting down in less than fifteen minutes from now."

I was puzzled. "You're not talking about a take-away, are you?"

"No," said Bill. "The local Chinese restaurant."

A minute ago, this would have seemed like a silly idea, but now it seemed to be a masterstroke.

Audrey suddenly panicked. "I can't be ready to go out in five minutes! That's preposterous!"

Harold stepped forward to take charge of the situation and said in a very authoritative voice, "Audrey, you always look beautiful, and so do you Lizzy, and as for us gentlemen, no amount of time will make any difference. We'll simply go right now, exactly as we are. We'll need two cars. I'll take mine. Charles, will you take your Audi? Right, let's go."

Harold has such an air of authority about him that nobody questioned his orders. We got up and did exactly as we'd been told. Of course, Bill was right. We were indeed sitting down in the restaurant within fifteen minutes, and all looking terribly pleased with ourselves. Sensible as ever, Bill reminded us that we hadn't told the restaurant back at the Village that we had gone out for lunch.

"Who has a phone?" I asked.

It seemed that in the rush to leave quickly, none of us had taken one. Except, that is, for Audrey who had the new phone Fiona recently insisted she should have.

"Okay," said Audrey, "leave it to me".

She left the table, insisting that the signal was bad, and stood by the window, fumbling with the contraption. After watching her for a few minutes, I went over.

"What's the problem?" I asked.

"Can't find the number."

"Is it stored in your contacts?"

"I'm sure it is."

More time passed, and more things were pressed, with no obvious success.

"Would you like me to do it?"

Audrey was pleased to pass me the phone. I looked at the thing which was completely different to mine. Nothing was the same. I poked at the screen, looking extremely authoritative. It soon dawned on me that I didn't have the faintest idea how to access the contact details. Then I had a good idea. I said to Bill that I didn't have my glasses and I couldn't see the damn thing, could he do it? He had a go but ended up taking a photograph of his ear.

It was no good asking Stanley or Lizzy, what about Harold? He picked up the device and placed it to his ear and said, "Come in Village, this is Alpha Foxtrot Six, do you read me?"

We laughed more in despair than anything else. With that, a young Chinese girl came over to the table. She was the daughter of the owner and must have been all of eight years old.

"May I help you with your phone?" she said, terribly politely.

"Thank heavens," replied Lizzy. "None of these idiots knows how to use it."

Suitably deflated, we accepted the help and within seconds the child had achieved what we couldn't. This wasn't a good start, and then just to confirm that we'd made a bad impression, the waitress came over to us and promptly destroyed our remaining self-esteem by asking if we needed help to read the menu. I was just in the process of putting together an esteem-restoring response when Lizzy spoke up.

"Oh, how kind of you, dear. I'm sure I wouldn't understand it by myself."

I looked at the others and said, "Fickle thing, credibility. Just as you think you have it, just as quickly it can disappear!"

Lizzy beckoned to the waitress who was, in fact, very kind to her and went through the menu. The waitress asked if she would like an appetiser.

"Spare Ribs, perhaps?" she suggested.

"Only if there *are* any spare ones," said Lizzy.

The waitress glossed over that and said, "What about Kao Poon, madam?".

"No, that's alright, dear," said Lizzy. "I'd like to try the chopsticks."

"May I suggest the Dim Sum, madam?" the waitress said.

"Okay, I'll have some dim."

"What would you like for your main course, madam, we have some very good beef, Au Yuck."

"If that's what you think of it," said Lizzy, "I'd best avoid it!"

The waitress had the patience of a saint and she followed with another suggestion.

"What about Korean Beef, madam?"

"Certainly not! I'm not having beef from Korea!"

We sat in self-disciplined silence while this was going on. There was a little coughing and nose blowing. The most distracting thing was that some of the shoulders were starting to move up and down, combined with some puffing up of the cheeks, it was becoming difficult to hold it together. The young waitress had long since regretted her offer of help but persisted heroically.

"May I suggest Satay Chicken, madam."

Lizzy looked up in horror. "It's Tuesday! I'm not having Saturday's chicken!"

That was it, we could contain ourselves no more. There was an eruption of laughter. Some unfortunate people were sitting on a table nearby, and one of them was so enraged about our disturbing their lunch that he came over and gave us a piece of his mind. Actually, it was quite a large piece of his mind, though I doubt that he had very much to start with.

While it was all very entertaining, we did need to get on with ordering our lunch, so I was wondering what our best strategy might be. We could get Lizzy to explain to him the problems that she'd had with the waitress; that might take the sting out of his vitriol. Alternatively, we could unleash Harold, but I decided that would be cruel.

"I think this is a job for you, Stanley," I said.

He obviously relished the opportunity and wasted no time.

"I do apologise, old boy, on behalf of my rowdy friends,

but what's so much more interesting is that slight Yorkshire, or is it Lancashire accent, that you have? Now, tell me old boy, if I said Shipley, would I be far out?"

With that, Stanley put his arm around this strangely compliant man and led him back to his table, no doubt telling him about the very house he lived in!

When he came back, we all asked in unison, "How did you know he came from Shipley?"

Stanley smiled and whispered, "I overheard them talking earlier."

It was clear to me that Stanley missed nothing and had an uncanny ability to retain any scrap of information that might prove useful. We ended up with a good lunch and remained on our best behaviour despite consuming a little too much cheap wine. Listening to Harold's story earlier had been exhausting, and we clearly needed to unwind. Even Lizzy had a couple of glasses, which is most unusual. We all agreed that, despite one or two little incidents, our lunch had been a great success. A change of atmosphere was exactly what we had needed. Harold said he really appreciated everyone's kind thoughts and that he would pay the bill. Stanley's eyes lit up at the prospect.

Lizzy said she would just pop off to the loo and wouldn't be a minute. She staggered off in the general direction of the toilets, but suddenly there was a lurch to starboard. She then applied a corrective manoeuvre to port, acting as if she was on a steep downhill slope. Lizzy might well have regained her composure had it not been for a table of diners directly in her way.

It was a relatively minor collision by Lizzy's standards. One of the diners was slightly inconvenienced by the initial encounter, but the damage to his glasses was purely cosmetic. I was sure the arm could be replaced. The real inconvenience was caused by Lizzy inadvertently grabbing the tablecloth as she descended to the floor. We quickly pointed out to the diners how much worse all of this could have been had they still been enjoying their main courses. The spilled coffee was a minor distraction by comparison. Admittedly three of them did have coffee running down their clothing, but we managed to distract them from that problem by helping Lizzy to her feet. She's very adept at playing the badly shaken up dear old lady. She does, of course, get a lot of practice!

The deficiency in our strategy was that, rather than appearing to be a dear old lady, the diners had it in their minds that she was a drunken old lady. There's an enormous credibility gap between a dear old lady with balance issues, and an inebriate with balance issues. We knew Lizzy was the former and seldom the latter, but I could see that we had no snow beneath our skis.

Our demise was greatly exacerbated when the diner we'd aggravated earlier decided to give us the benefit of his expansive intellect. Despite a creditable performance from Stanley, the situation wasn't redeemable. We insisted upon paying for all damages, dry cleaning and the man's wretched glasses, but this wasn't enough to pacify them. We even offered them a meal in the restaurant at our expense, but they said they would be too embarrassed to return.

Finally, Audrey insisted that they should all be our guests one evening at our Village Restaurant. My heart sank. There were three generations of them. Probably because the Village was seen locally as a bastion of wealthy privilege, they agreed, or perhaps out of curiosity. The restaurant owner kindly called us a cab, insisting that we were unfit to drive, and perhaps we might like to dine elsewhere in future.

We arrived back a little crestfallen but, being determined to put this unfortunate incident behind us, we decided an early arrival for afternoon tea was probably the best idea. We sat down and commented upon the weather. I think we were all a bit embarrassed about our encounter.

Audrey was the first to mention it. "I've never been banned from an establishment in my life! How dreadfully embarrassing. You should all be ashamed!"

Harold agreed, so did I, and Bill apologised for his part in the fiasco.

"It was awful, but didn't Stanley do a great job with that grumbling idiot," he said.

"I agree." Harold said. "Great job Stanley, and what about that manoeuvre of Lizzy's. The best one I've seen in ages!"

We all started to laugh. "The best part was that chap sitting there with his glasses hanging down his nose," I said.

Suddenly we were in fits of laughter. Audrey was trying not to laugh, insisting that we had behaved badly. Finally, she said. "I suppose that poor man did look rather ridiculous with his broken glasses and coffee stains!"

With that, Audrey laughed as well. The only person with a straight face was Lizzy.

"I suppose it was one of my more embarrassing incidents." she said. "Never mind, I expect I'll have forgotten it by tomorrow."

We all enjoyed our afternoon tea in high spirits. We'd managed to turn our disaster into a triumph, and all agreed we didn't want to go back to that restaurant anyway.

Chapter Eleven
UGANDA

Everybody had a freshen-up and returned for aperitifs an hour or so later, feeling well pleased with ourselves. Audrey looked fabulous in her cream evening dress. I was just about to say how wonderful she looked when Stanley stole my thunder.

"Audrey, my dear," he said. "May I say how absolutely sublime you look this evening."

Sod it, another opportunity lost! Harold then appeared, wearing his usual double-breasted blazer and a very smart two-tone shirt with white cutaway collar and blue pinstripe body. Tonight, however, was very different. For the first time, he wore a tie bearing the SAS emblem, and in addition he wore an SAS lapel badge. This was clearly a significant moment for Harold, and one of which Stanley was only too aware

Stanley offered his hand to Harold. "If you can't wear that badge with pride, I don't know anyone else who could. I'm proud to shake your hand."

I was proud of Harold as well, but I could never have expressed my thoughts as well as Stanley did, and in a strange way I found I was becoming proud of Stanley as well. In so many respects, he was still a mystery. He had simply appeared among us and started changing our lives. I'd never met anyone like Stanley. He was a force of nature, this much was clear. But was he a malevolent force, or the kindest and best-intentioned person I had ever met?

My thoughts turned to drink, and I was thinking, following on from this afternoon's indulgence, a soft drink would be appropriate. I suggested this to Stanley, who told me not to be ridiculous. In the end, I even found myself asking him if he would like a glass of whisky! What a ridiculous question!

As I went to the bar, I was left wondering how Stanley did it. Was there a human equivalent of a horse whisperer? I arrived back with a tray of soft drinks and Stanley's whisky, to find that Stanley had Harold sitting down opposite his inquisitorial chair. He had already straightened his tie and was by now adjusting those buttons on his waistcoat which were bearing the greatest stress. It was obviously time for Harold to continue his story.

Stanley sat there exuding an air of contentment as he contemplated his glass of 15-year-old Dalwhinnie. It appeared to take some effort to draw his attention away from the golden fluid, as if it was interrupting a conversation.

Eventually he said, "Now, tell me, dear boy. How on earth did you adjust to a life out of the armed forces after your experiences in the Falklands and Northern Ireland?"

Harold told us that an awful lot of SAS people go straight into a PMC but he had been determined not to go onto the circuit. His determination had lasted for about a month, but then he got a call from an old mate with an invitation to join him as a partner in a new PMC he was setting up. Apparently about a month is the usual time it takes for ex-Special Services to realise that there is no other job for them in civvy street. Someone just had to ask what I thought was an obvious question, or was I the only person who had no idea what a PMC was?

In the end I asked him, "What on earth is a PMC?"

Harold gave me one of his half-smiles and said, "I suppose

this is the reason we don't fit into society. People don't even know what it is we do."

He then went on to explain that a PMC is a private military contractor. They have all the skills of the Special Services and up to a point are available for anyone to hire. He was quite right, I certainly had no idea about these things, and I don't think any of the others did either. Even Stanley, for once, didn't profess an intimate knowledge. Harold obviously knew this would be an opaque subject to us and so, in the same matter-of-fact way that, say, a builder might explain the workings of his industry, he explained the workings of what he called the 'circuit'.

There have probably been fighting men available for hire for as long as there have been fighting men, but the sector in its current commercial incarnation is a relatively new enterprise. It all started essentially as an offshoot of the SAS. The founder of the SAS was David Stirling and in 1965, together with a chap called John Woodhouse, they founded the first PMC. It was all terribly above-board. They even had an office in Sloane Street, and later in Mayfair.

The sector soon grew into a diversified field of specialists who can undertake just about any mission that the SAS might take on. They also do all manner of other work such as personal protection and training. It was the scale of these operations which surprised me. Apparently, there isn't a place on earth, perhaps with the exception of Antarctica, where a PMC hasn't operated. In the US, for example, Harold said that during his time, PMC's accounted for 49% of the intelligence community spending. The sector is huge. It was a fascinating insight into an area that none of us had ever thought about.

Stanley asked about the kind of work in which Harold's company specialised.

"We'd consider just about anything, but we do have a good reputation in the area of personal protection and hostage negotiation. In other words, we would protect someone, but if they became a hostage, we would also negotiate their release," replied Harold.

"Have you ever had a client taken hostage?" Stanley asked.

Harold squinted his eyes in obvious disapproval. "No, I was joking, we never lost a protected client. Hostages are generally people who don't understand the risk."

Bill asked who he had protected, and Harold said that it was all manner of people. Lots of business executives operating in foreign countries, politicians, even the leaders of some dodgy countries, but he'd never lost one of them.

"Did you ever come close to losing one?" asked Stanley.

Harold thought about his reply for a moment and said they certainly had some attempts made against them, but the key to success is meticulous planning. If they knew an abduction or assassination attempt was likely to involve a lot of firepower, they would always be sure to have far greater firepower. If they had definite intel about an attempt, they would change location or intercede beforehand. The most difficult threat to overcome was the skilled lone assassin, especially the long-range sniper or even the suicide bomber.

"What about hostage negotiation? That must be difficult?" Audrey asked.

Harold agreed, saying they had expert negotiators, but it very much depended on the people with whom they were dealing. There are situations, especially where groups act outside of state control, when negotiation is extremely difficult and isn't always successful. Stanley detected a nuance in Harold's voice.

"Tell me, old boy," he said, "are you thinking of one case in particular?"

Harold breathed a deep sigh and admitted that there was one event which still haunted him above all others. It was one of the earlier jobs, when he was still involved with some of the field work. They'd been called in to negotiate on behalf of a mining company manager whose wife and children had been kidnapped in Uganda.

The first problem was that this guy was not one of the top brass. He didn't have the $250,000 that the kidnappers were demanding. Perhaps the company might pay, but it made the negotiations difficult. The company were paying for Harold's involvement and they wanted to limit their liability.

The second problem was that the kidnappers were a lawless bunch, under the control of the local warlord; these were extremely unpleasant people. This was 1985, and the country was still in disarray following the overthrow of Idi Amin. The government was led by Milton Obote but there was considerable unrest. It was effectively a civil war against the government, led by Yoweri Museveni and the National Resistance Army, the NRA. It was unclear exactly who the kidnappers were. They might have been affiliated to the NRA or they might just be an opportunist bunch. In either event, it's always an ideal situation to operate in a country where they can avoid upsetting the government. The old saying always applies; the enemy of my enemy is my friend.

They negotiated for a couple of days, trying to persuade the company to pay the ransom on the manager's behalf and then, just as they were coming around to the idea, the warlord said it had taken too long, and the ransom had consequently gone up; it was now $400,000. Harold advised that this group had a track record of killing hostages unless the ransom was paid immediately. They had no regard for the lives of their hostages and simply moved on to another victim. His advice was to initiate a rescue attempt as soon as possible. What the client didn't know was that, as a routine part of the negotiation, Harold would always investigate the hostage-taker, and, in this case, it wasn't difficult to answer the two key questions: who they were, and where they were.

In truth, he wasn't sure exactly who they were, and what they called themselves was immaterial. All that he needed to know was that they were a totally undisciplined group, relying upon strength of numbers. They were holed up in a camp in the bush; Harold had a surveillance team watching them.

The mining company, and even the unfortunate manager, finally agreed that a rescue attempt was the best hope for his wife and two children. Harold was asked what he thought the chances of success were and, in those circumstances, he had to be completely honest, so he said that a rescue attempt would have no more than a 50% chance of success, plus a hefty invoice from them. They accepted the offer.

Stanley looked puzzled. "If the hostage-takers were becoming impatient, how did you set up a rescue attempt quickly enough?"

Harold said that from the moment they took on a negotiation, there was always a Plan B in place which, in this case, was a rescue attempt. It was just a case of getting the personnel and the equipment on the ground. They planned for this kind of response meticulously; all the men were ex-Special Forces. They knew exactly who they needed and what equipment was necessary for any kind of job. Their personnel were always on standby so within twenty-four hours of the word being given, they were ready to go. One of the surveillance team came in to brief them, having managed to get an aerial photograph of the camp.

It seemed to be the textbook operation they'd practised a dozen times before. In these circumstances, overpowering the opposition was not the problem. They would go in with a surprise attack under the cover of darkness. Provided they could get into position without being compromised, the opposition would have no chance. The big problem as always would be getting the hostages out in one piece because the captors would kill them, given the chance.

The surveillance team counted thirty-four men in the camp, and a further ten who'd left as a group the day before to go who knew where, so they had to assume at least forty-four men and children. He said 'children' because they were now sure that these people were NRA; they all wore camouflage military uniform and the group was notorious for indoctrinating children to their armed cause. Unfortunately, when faced with a uniformed person aiming an AK47 at you, the distinction is not relevant. They were heavily armed with AK47s and several RPGs.

The hostages were being held in a wooden building in the centre of the compound, surrounded by outbuildings. The compound was obviously a long-standing settlement of some kind that they had taken over, adding several new buildings. The central building, like all the rest, was of timber construction, but very solidly built with a corrugated metal sheet roof and heavy door.

The kidnappers operated with four sentries on watch at any one time, but surveillance indicated that they were poorly disciplined, not always changing watch on time, and often falling asleep. Harold's plan was to get within five miles of the camp on transport, and then quickly 'tab' the last five miles. Once in position, their surveillance team would confirm that the situation was unaltered. The four on watch would be quietly eliminated, and then Harold would lead a team into the camp unnoticed, break into the building where the hostages were held, and make their escape under the cover of overwhelming firepower.

He made it seem very matter-of-fact, rather like planning a day at the allotment, but Stanley was obviously being very attentive because he asked Harold a rather pertinent question.

"Why did you elect to lead this rescue attempt yourself? As the man in charge, wasn't your place back at your HQ?"

Harold replied, "I suppose you're right Stanley. Until this operation I'd been leading from the front but, in fact, this was the last time I would lead an operation of this scale."

Audrey looked very concerned and said, "Why did you have to keep putting yourself in harm's way, Harold? You're a worry."

He smiled, evading the question.

"Let's not worry about that now, Audrey. I want to know what happened," said Bill.

Harold had fourteen men in place, plus the three-man surveillance team, which they considered to be overwhelming odds in their favour. They had all their usual armaments, plus three NATO issue .308 Winchester sniper rifles with night vision scopes. They even had two L16 81mm mortars, should it be necessary to cover an emergency withdrawal. They had the firepower of a small army. They didn't expect to use it all but would never enter a conflict without that degree of superiority.

They loaded up the transport and were on their way by early afternoon. It was going to take about three hours to get to the drop-off point, during which time Harold went over the operational plans. At last light, as planned, they arrived at the drop-off, and immediately commenced the 'tab' through the bush. The route took them through some difficult night-time terrain, having deliberately chosen this difficult route to ensure they wouldn't bump into any hostiles moving in or out of the camp. It also meant they approached the camp from the most advantageous position. Surveillance radioed in to report the return of the ten hostiles who'd left the camp. This was good news from their perspective as they much preferred knowing where those ten were. The Plan B which they had prepared, covering the possibility of the ten returning during the assault, could now be discarded.

Everything was going according to plan. Despite their heavy loads, they made excellent time and found the camp exactly as they had expected, with at least one of the hostiles on watch asleep. Surveillance reported that the watch had changed about an hour ago, so their absence wouldn't be missed. The position of one of the watches was preventing their preferred approach to the camp, so the main force held well back while four of their specialists silently set off into the night to eliminate them. Harold said that approaching and eliminating a person in total silence is extremely difficult. It's not like shooting an anonymous figure five hundred metres away; it takes a large degree of dispassionate ruthlessness. All their personnel were capable of doing it, but only a few would admit to being good at it. It was those few who set off into the darkness.

This was one of the critical moments of the operation. If the alarm had been raised now, they wouldn't be able to execute their preferred plan. There was an alternative plan, of course, but the outlook for the hostages would be bleak. They waited in silence, intently listening for whatever sound might fill the night air. They had sight of one of the sentries from their position, and while they couldn't see their man approaching him, they knew he was there. There was a specific time when all the men should strike, but this can only ever be an optimal scenario. In practice, each man must take his chance as circumstances dictate.

Harold could see the nearest sentry clearly through his night-vision scope and at the exact stroke of 1.15am, his man appeared out of nowhere. He wrenched the man's head back and cut his windpipe with one very powerful motion of his fighting knife, followed by another. The hostile immediately went limp and was eased silently to the ground. Knowing he would be within view, his man gave Harold a thumbs-up sign. There were no other sounds from the bush other than the soft drone of insects.

The second phase of the operation went straight into action, each man silently deploying into his allotted position. The snipers had the best vantage points around the camp and would remain in those positions throughout the operation. The rest of them took up concealed positions just metres from the outlying buildings, from where they could clearly see the central building, which had no additional guard protection. From Harold's perspective this seemed incredibly lax, but very fortuitous.

The plan had assumed that the elimination of an additional compound guard would be very high risk, but this new situation raised the possibility of the operation remaining covert for some very useful additional minutes. Harold signalled to the men to go into action. He led the hostage release team; the others broke up into three groups to cover the hostiles' sleeping quarters. The release team carried a tool kit to achieve the rescue. They had bolt croppers, crowbars, hammers, etc, and, because they didn't know how secure the building was, they also carried some plastic explosive.

Within moments, they were in position. They would attempt to release the hostages as silently as possible, and mayhem need only break out as and when they were discovered. The heavy wooden door of the building had two exterior hasp and staple padlocks. Harold could hardly believe it; these locks could be broken off in seconds. He signalled a thumbs-up to the squad and placed the bolt croppers over the locks. There was a loud crack as the locks were cut, but nothing dramatic, and no-one stirred. The hinges made an audible creak as he eased the door open and shone a torch through the opening.

He whispered, "We're here to rescue you, stay calm."

There was no reply and, when he entered the building, he saw there were no hostages. Instead, it was stacked from floor to ceiling with munitions of various kinds.

Harold looked at the others and they said almost in unison, "Oh shit." Intel was clear that the hostages were there, but they wouldn't keep hostages together with these munitions. What was going on? Intel had reported clearly seeing the hostages being moved about the camp, so this was obviously a case of mistaken identity as far as this building was concerned.

In one moment, this had become a totally different scenario but, as always, it was one that Harold had considered. With the hostages under their control, and hostiles asleep, they could have effectively destroyed the camp with no risk to themselves. However, not knowing where the hostages were meant they could be in any of those buildings. The only option in these circumstances was to draw the hostiles out into the open and to avoid any firing into the buildings.

This gave the hostiles an enormous advantage, and Harold had already concluded that, in this event, he would have to consider abandoning the operation. The risk of losing several of his men while trying to save three hostages from an impossible position wasn't an equation which made a lot of sense, so with a finger drawn across his throat he signalled an end to the operation.

At that precise moment a single shot rang out. They all recognised it immediately as the .308 sniper rifle. One of the hostiles must have stepped out into the night. In the space of seconds, the plan had changed three times; now they were back to drawing the hostiles out into the open. The men knew exactly where they should be for this eventuality, and the squad automatically deployed.

The sleeping hostiles were slow to react, which was exactly what Plan A had intended to exploit. After what seemed like an eternity, heavily armed men rushed out of two of the buildings. The snipers dropped them one after another, while the squad remained concealed. Immediately there was heavy covering fire from AK47's coming out of the windows, and Harold decided to engage them in those two particular buildings. At the same time, hostiles appeared from other buildings, firing wildly. Harold was looking for a building that didn't contain hostiles, in the hope that maybe the hostages were there but, in the confusion, it was impossible to be sure.

Their positions were known now, and Harold said they came under heavy direct fire as the hostiles began to coordinate themselves. The added confusion provided by the darkness was their single biggest advantage. The squad had night-vision goggles while the hostiles were literally in the dark. The hostiles were heavily armed but, in the panic and confusion, their fire wasn't effective. While this contact appeared to be highly dangerous, the squad was in fact firmly in control, until a rocket-propelled grenade appeared from nowhere and exploded close to one of their positions.

They had a man down when another rocket crashed into their position. The snipers had the best vantage point and they reported that one of the launchers was down, but they couldn't see the other. They also reported that a child had climbed out of a window from one of the buildings on the far side of the compound. At last, Harold knew where the hostages were. While not knowing this vital information, they had contained their fire as much as possible, but this new observation came just in time.

The squad hosed down the other buildings with the Minimis and grenades fired from the 203s, while Harold ran from cover around to the other side of the compound in the hope of finding the child. He could see the boy running in panic and shouted to him to lie down. As he shouted, he made himself known to a group of hostiles behind one of the buildings. He had to forget the boy and take cover. Harold fired a grenade from the 203 followed by a burst of automatic fire, then changed his position. He shouted again to the boy to lie down but, in his panic, the boy started to run towards him. One of the hostiles cut him down, and the boy was dead before he hit the ground. Harold described that ghastly moment.

"In that one moment, all the noise and confusion of conflict disappeared. All I could hear was a terrifying scream coming from the hut opposite. The anguish of that mother's scream cut through me like a knife. I'd never before heard such pain expressed by a human being. None of my training and experience equipped me to deal with that God-awful sound."

We could all see immediately how this painful memory affected Harold. I think this was perhaps the first time that he had revealed a vulnerability. Being in the open, he ran towards the hostiles, firing a continuous burst until his magazine was empty. He then went on to admit that he had behaved completely irrationally. He should never have emptied his magazine like that, nor should he have exposed his position to them.

This was a terrible situation, and he felt detached from reality. He dropped the empty mag and was feeling in his belt for another one when a hostile stepped out in front of him. He knew the hostile would fire his AK47 before he could replace his magazine. Harold described it as a strangely surreal moment; he felt calm and resigned to the inevitable. It could only have been two seconds, but it was ample time for him to be aware of his last surroundings and the face of the man who was about to kill him. He wasn't even attempting to load the magazine, completely resigned to his fate.

The hostile suddenly dropped to the ground. It was another second or two before Harold realised that one of the snipers had saved his life. It was several more seconds before the full horror of this awful situation became his reality again. The distraught mother's scream filled the air. Harold replaced the magazine, and opened fire. The remaining hostiles turned tail and he dropped several of them as they ran. He could see that the other members of the squad had broken cover, advancing on the remaining hostiles, not allowing them the opportunity to regroup. This removed attention from him, so he approached the hut.

Harold shouted for them to get away from the door and he fired a couple of shots at the padlock. The woman was completely oblivious to any danger, running screaming out of the hut toward the boy who was lying crumpled on the ground. Harold grabbed the other child, a young girl about four years old. She was small enough to put under his left arm, leaving his right hand free to fire the Armalite. He admitted he wasn't thinking clearly. He thought the woman would leave the boy and make her escape with him but of course that was never going to happen. When he realised that, he dropped his weapon, picked up the dead boy with his other hand and slung him under his other arm.

The poor woman was hysterical, in no position to think rationally, but Harold reasoned that if he made a run for it, she would automatically follow, which she did. Five of the squad broke away from the main group to give him covering fire, and a few moments later the compound fell silent. The only sound was the unbearable grief that this poor woman was suffering. Half the squad pursued the remaining hostiles as they fled into the bush, and the remainder regrouped at their exit point. There was sporadic gunfire in the distance as the hostiles were intercepted, but soon that fell silent as well.

They all regrouped to assess their position. They only had one badly wounded and three walking wounded; all things considered, this was a fortunate outcome for them. They counted 52 dead or badly wounded hostiles. It seemed their intel about the numbers wasn't quite right. They still had a small charge of plastic explosive intended to blow any rein-forced doors, so they rigged that up with a quick timer in the munitions hut, and quickly departed the scene. Five minutes later, the compound erupted in an enormous explosion as they made their way to the meeting point with the transport.

They arrived back at their temporary HQ where there was a medical team standing by to tend the wounded. The good news was that the badly wounded man wasn't critically injured; he was later flown back to the UK where, in time, he made a full recovery. The same couldn't be said for the mining company manager and his wife; whose grief at the loss of their son hung over them like a toxic cloud. The mission was by any measure an outstanding textbook success. Against overwhelming odds, the team had suffered no fatal casualties, having liberated two of the three hostages in circumstances where the death of all three was the most likely outcome, and yet it somehow didn't feel like a success.

The following day the manager and his wife asked to see Harold. He was apprehensive about the meeting, but reluc-tantly agreed. They all sat down in the manager's office, and the couple were much calmer than he'd anticipated. Their grief was just as raw, but they were trying to remain in control. The poor woman had witnessed at first hand the shooting of her child, but she especially wanted to understand every moment which preceded it. Harold explained to her how the operation was planned and executed, and how, following the mistaken intel about the munitions building, they'd had to make the best of a difficult situation.

What she had especially wanted to understand were those last few seconds, those few seconds that Harold admitted he didn't want to recall. Not only did he not want to recall those events at the time, it was clear to us that he didn't want to recall them for us either.

Stanley must have sensed that this was a significant moment for Harold, and intervened saying, "I'm sure you opened your heart to that poor woman because you knew her life would have been incomplete without it. I think the same applies here today for you. Perhaps you need to share this with us for much the same reason."

Harold reluctantly agreed, as he could see how important it had been for the poor woman, and so he recalled the events. He shouted to the boy to lie down but instead, as soon as the boy saw Harold, he started to run towards him. The boy's eyes were fixed to his. The lad had opened his mouth as if to shout, with his right hand outstretched toward Harold.

"That was the moment when I realised that I had no option now but tell the poor woman exactly what happened."

What followed was a startling revelation. Harold told the woman that he stepped forward to put himself between the boy and the gunmen and, as he raised his left arm to reach out to the boy, there was a continuous burst of gunfire from a position behind him. The boy was hit multiple times in the head and chest. One second the boy's eyes were staring into his, and the next he was a broken body, lying at Harold's feet. The poor woman broke down. She'd heard enough.

Once again, Harold was reluctant to continue, so Stanley asked, "What did the woman say after you told her that?"

Harold said the manager ended the meeting by thanking him for saving his wife and daughter. As they were leaving, the woman put her arms around him, and what she said still haunts Harold today.

"I saw what you did," she said. "You didn't just risk your life for my son. You were prepared to exchange your life for his. You're the last human being my son saw in this life, and his final vision couldn't have been of a finer person. I can never thank you enough for what you tried to do."

Harold told us that he'd seen death many times, but he had always somehow managed to remain detached.

"As a soldier you can't allow the reality of death to enter your mind. The boy's death was different. I couldn't look into that boy's eyes and then afterwards exclude the reality of his existence. I've been haunted by the lad ever since. I knew that moment that my active career was over."

-o0o-

Harold was visibly upset. These recollections were difficult enough for us to envisage, let alone for Harold. We decided that, although none of us was hungry, we would go through to the restaurant for dinner. This had been an emotionally charged afternoon. We all needed a break, and there are few things more relaxing than enjoying good food with good company. Gradually our mood lightened and even Harold relaxed a little, but I think we were all quietly thinking that his story had one or two loose ends which still needed to be told. I could see from Stanley's expression he was only too aware of those loose ends, but perhaps the time wasn't quite right.

Just as our meal was coming to an end and perfectly on cue, Puffer left his dining table to go for a smoke. What we needed was one of Puffer's jokes, but what we didn't need was him coughing over us, so time was of the essence. I caught his attention as we prepared to leave and asked if he had a joke for us. Puffer thought about it for a moment, and quickly came up with a one-liner. He then rested his hands against the back of one of the diners' chairs on another table. We didn't stay to watch the outcome, but left laughing.

As we sat down in the lounge again, our spirits were high. I could see Stanley was preparing himself to explore the loose ends which Harold had left dangling.

"The wonderful comment that the woman made; it must have helped you get through such an appalling situation," Stanley said.

Harold agreed, "I'll never forget. It made such a deep impression on me."

Stanley wanted to delve still deeper into the situation and enquired, "Were you fully aware that, by stepping out in front of the boy, you were likely to be shot?"

"Not really," Harold replied, "I didn't reason it through, but I suppose, when I look back on it, I must have prioritised the boy. It was just an instinctive reaction. The inexplicable thing was that the hostile intentionally shot the boy, rather than me."

Harold simply couldn't understand the callous way the hostile had acted. It had certainly affected him then, as it did now. His desire to be on the front line had gone.

"I've planned and organised numerous missions for the company since, but I was never tempted back into action."

I could see from his expression that Stanley was following a train of thought. He always had an inscrutable look about him whenever he thought there was yet another door to open. Harold's military career was a revelation. I needed time to take it all in, but I just knew that Stanley was way ahead of me. As soon as he started to settle into his armchair, I sensed another line of probing enquiry was about to begin.

Stanley started off by saying that courageous people most often risk their lives to save others when they've calculated that the odds of success are in their favour.

He said it was quite another kind of courage when the odds are so much against success that you're prepared to offer your life in exchange for another's. There was simply no greater courage and he would so like to understand the things which had influenced Harold, therefore making him the man he is. He made the point that Harold's father was obviously an important influence during his formative years, and that there was such a similarity between his own incredible exploits and those of his father's in Normandy.

"Do you think your father's exploits influenced your decision to attempt to save Jim in the Falklands or the boy in Uganda?"

That was exactly what I was thinking, but of course I didn't like to ask. Harold thought about it for a long time, finally admitting that Stanley was very perceptive, and he agreed. He needed to lay this thing to rest. It had taken years to understand his relationship with his father. It only started to become clear to him when the army insisted that he saw a counsellor after Northern Ireland.

His father was an extraordinary man, whose bravery was legendary among his men. He appeared to have no regard for his own life. As a kid, Harold would hear all the stories about his father and his army friends, and he had attended some of the presentations. He'd seen all the medals and read all the citations. His father was his hero in every respect, but there was another side to him. He demanded so much of Harold.

This further revelation was obviously difficult for Harold, but he had clearly made up his mind to expose this personal demon, so he continued. The counsellor helped him understand that there were two aspects to the relationship he had with his father. On the one hand, Harold's hero worship was such that he bestowed his father with an aura of infallibility. On the other hand, the standards and demands placed upon Harold were quite unrealistic, if not unattainable.

It took him a long time to realise those two positions were

not compatible with one another. He agreed with Stanley when he made the comparison between Darwin Ridge and Normandy.

Harold admitted that when they were in the trench surrounded by a hail of gunfire, it wasn't just courage which made him decide to carry Jim to safety. He realised he had a fear of disappointing his father. He'd been sure that Jim wouldn't make it. He was equally sure that, if he ventured out into the maelstrom, he wouldn't make it either, so it was more than reckless or foolhardy; it was nonsensical. The fact that they both made it was nothing more than incredibly good fortune. He was even given a gong for it. With hindsight, he said that he shouldn't have accepted the award.

"On that same day, a Victoria Cross was posthumously awarded to an incredibly courageous paratrooper who was cut down while advancing toward the enemy. I was awarded a gong for running away from the enemy," he said.

Stanley appeared to be very pleased with himself. He'd managed to access the darkest corners of Harold's mind and I thought he would be content, but he obviously felt there was yet another stone to overturn.

"Tell us a little more about your father."

Poor Harold was visibly emotional, something we had never seen before. He said his father was taken seriously ill just before the Uganda job came up. He hesitated about taking on the job, but his father was adamant that he should. His father died the day before the attack on the compound, so it was clear to us that he would have been uppermost in Harold's mind.

"Tell me, old boy, was there finally a moment when you felt you no longer had anything to prove to your father?"

"He was there with me when I tried to save the boy, but it all happened so fast," he said. "Later, when my magazine was empty, and with an AK47 pointing at me, he was there again. He was the reason I just accepted my fate. I could almost hear him saying, 'You've done well, son, you can come with me now.' When the hostile fell to the ground, my immediate thought was that my father had gone with *him* and I'd been given a second chance. It was my cathartic moment. I knew immediately my active career was over."

This whole experience had been overwhelming for all of us; we sat in a strange silence. Harold was obviously suppressing an enormous amount of emotion. I was in little doubt that he had spent a large part of his life doing exactly that.

Stanley was also doing his best to stay on top of his emotions; his silence was evidence of that. Perhaps my reassuring but silent hand on the shoulder routine would help. One thing was quite clear, I always knew Harold was a man of some stature, but I had no idea of the magnitude of that stature. With that, Audrey stepped forward wiping tears from her eyes.

"You men are ridiculous," she said to Harold. "You've held all that emotion inside for all these years, and what good has it done you? You've got to shed a tear for your father, for Rachel, and for the boy. Allow yourself to grieve."

Harold looked at Audrey; his eyes were welling up and he seemed quite unable to speak.

Audrey put her arms around him in a tight embrace and simply said, "Now's the moment, Harold, let it go."

It was a moment of complete capitulation. Prior to that, it was incomprehensible that we would all take part in an emotional outpouring centred upon Harold. But now we all spontaneously stepped forward in another group hug, just as we had done for Audrey.

I had the distinct feeling that the Harold who seemed to be devoid of emotion had just left the building.

Chapter Twelve
THE PICNIC

The following morning, we all met for breakfast at the arranged time, each having watched the weather forecast on the television in our apartments. Bill was the first to comment, saying how unfortunate that it was going to rain. Harold disagreed, saying he was quite clear it would be a fine day. Audrey thought she remembered the forecaster saying there was a possibility of some showers, while Lizzy admitted she really wasn't quite sure if it was going to be dry today and wet tomorrow, or was it wet today and dry tomorrow?

Stanley wanted to give us one of his long anecdotes about the unpredictability of the weather in the Himalayas, while Harold looked a little annoyed at all the confusion.

He turned towards me saying, "Surely you saw the same forecast that I saw, Charles?"

I was a little embarrassed to admit it, but I'd once again overslept and hadn't seen the forecast at all. The reason for all this consternation was that we'd been delaying our picnic plans for some time now and, the more the fateful day was postponed, the more imperative it seemed to become. Weather aside, this was a good day for us to get away from the Village. Harold's revelations the day before had left us all quite drained and in need of some diversion. We made our way into the breakfast restaurant, each of us trying to make a good case for the picnic despite our various reservations. As we sat down, Charlotte came over to speak to us, and we all asked in unison if she had seen a weather forecast.

"Sorry, no," she replied, "but I can go online and find out for you."

"Where did she say she was going?" asked Lizzy.

"Online," I replied.

I instantly regretted saying it and quickly did my best to divert her attention elsewhere. Fortunately, Charlotte came back shortly afterwards, confirming my worst fears.

"Showers," she said.

For Bill this meant a good chance of rain, for Harold it meant a good chance of a dry day, and for the rest of us it meant showers. We debated the subject throughout breakfast until Harold, who was clearly exasperated with our indecision, finally suggested a decisive alternative.

"For God's sake, let's just go and chance it," he said.

I was delighted to have my mind made up for me. The debate now turned towards food. What exactly did we need and where should we get it from? Once again, trying to find a consensus was like searching for a smile at a Wagner concert. Bill said it couldn't be a picnic without a pork pie. Audrey said a bottle of champagne was an essential. Harold admitted to a passion for cold new potatoes, while Lizzy couldn't go without boiled eggs. I managed to avoid such an onerous decision by saying that everyone had already mentioned my favourites. I thought it sensible that I leave such decisions to the experts. Bill is our culinary expert, and Harold is our logistics expert. What else could I add?

In next to no time, decisions had been made. Audrey had a wonderful wicker picnic hamper and we borrowed all the necessary plates and utensils from the kitchen, not to mention a range of culinary delights which caught Bill's eye. The next decision was where to find the other essential items? Audrey lamented that Fortnum & Mason wasn't local to the Village, while Bill waxed lyrical about the pork pies at the local butcher. Harold concentrated minds and devised a quick route between the butcher and the nearest supermarket.

"That's it, procurement of rations organised," he said triumphantly. "I suggest we meet up in twenty minutes. We'll need two cars. I'll take mine and we can put all the food in the back of your estate, Charles."

I could hardly believe the change in Harold. Not only had he taken charge of the situation and organised us; he did it all with great enthusiasm and a smile. Neither trait had ever been much in evidence before. Also conspicuous by its absence, was Audrey's previous persona. In a strange way, I missed the vulnerable, defensive Audrey. When Harold suggested that we all meet in twenty minutes, I instinctively anticipated that she would be horrified at such a proposal. I could almost hear her saying, 'Don't be absurd, Harold. A lady doesn't get ready for a social engagement in twenty minutes.'

In fact, her reply was, "I'll need to get a move on then."

I strolled back over to Reception, duly equipped for a day in the countryside, fully anticipating that I'd be the first there. Imagine my surprise upon finding everyone waiting for me!

"Come along, Charles, we can't wait all day," said Audrey.

As we proceeded together towards the car park, it was Stanley who slightly dented our unbridled enthusiasm by asking where we were going? His question was greeted with total silence.

"I hadn't thought of that," Harold said.

We all looked at each other knowingly, expecting someone to have a place in mind, but nobody did. One moment we were about to drive out in organised splendour, the next we had descended into farce. Harold was carrying the hamper which by now was full of crockery and very heavy, and the rest of us were impressively laden with clothing and various necessary items. Stanley said we looked like a procession of pack mules setting out on an expedition to find an ancient civilisation lost in the rainforest. I offered the comment that rather than being lost in a rainforest, this was more a case of being lost in the car park!

We all agreed that our current circumstances fell somewhere between being unsustainable and ridiculous. This was clearly a moment requiring some more decisive leadership, and Harold naturally stepped into the role.

"This is what we'll do," he said. "We'll drive in the general direction of Southwold and, somewhere along the way in this green and pleasant land, there will be an idyllic picnic location."

Audrey intervened. "Don't forget a lavatory, and preferably no more than ten minutes away."

Finally, we were on our way. Audrey and Lizzy went with Harold, while Bill and Stanley followed on with me. The stops at the butcher and the supermarket went like clockwork, with no disagreement or confusion. Suddenly we were functioning as an organised team. The sun was shining, and spirits were high. From our perspective in the follow-up car, this was now a guided tour and we could relax. Stanley was entertaining us with another of his anecdotes. On this occasion, it was his exploits with an order of nuns.

Harold suddenly swerved abruptly off the road, through an open gate and into a field. Naturally I followed, causing our load of provisions to scatter across the back of the car. Harold stuck his head out of the window, smiled broadly.

"What did I tell you, what better location could there be? We passed that pub just a mile away. They'll have toilets, and if we drive down this hill a bit, we'll be out of sight of the road."

I had to admit this field did appear to be ideal. It was just a bit of rough pasture, so I could see no reason why we should upset the farmer. Provided we could find a patch free of cow pats, we were home and dry. Such a patch was quickly found, and we set about organising ourselves. A couple of old thick blankets on the ground, a set of not quite matching folding seats, a collapsible table which we hoped would not collapse of its own accord, not to mention the magnificent hamper.

The main priority was the champagne glasses, followed by the pop of a cork. Stanley poured the champagne with just a little too much enthusiasm, causing one or two glasses to overflow, but it was of no consequence.

We each leaned forward to reach for a glass with the same apparent urgency. These were not life jackets, and this was a green field, not the Titanic, but we nevertheless clasped our respective glasses as if each was a potential life saver. Audrey downed her glass with obvious delight.

"Now we finally have our picnic!" she said.

We all raised our glasses in agreement. I think we were all just a little surprised at the sheer quantity of food which we'd procured. There was ham, roast chicken, smoked salmon, boiled eggs, cold new potatoes, a tin of caviar and the biggest pork pie I'd ever seen, not to mention all manner of salads and dressings. It was little short of a banquet, and we all quickly entered into the spirit of the occasion.

The combination of champagne, good food and equally good company combined with lovely surroundings is an intoxicating mix. I quietly reflected that I couldn't remember the last time I'd felt so at ease with a group of people.

It wasn't terribly long before Bill said, "Excuse me for a moment. I'm just going to take a little stroll along the hedgerow."

Audrey commented that we gentlemen didn't appreciate how lucky we were regarding hedgerows. Inevitably our humour descended for a moment, whereupon Lizzy shocked us all by saying that if it was good enough for Bill, then it would be good enough for her and, as soon as Bill returned, she duly staggered off toward the hedgerow. We looked at each other incredulously, and there was some more ill-advised humour. Audrey was appalled; the mere hint of vulgarity in her presence is like breaking wind during an audience with the Queen.

Some time elapsed before we heard a distressed call for help coming from Lizzy. Harold jumped to his feet and rushed off to help, and moments later we could hear that he was on the receiving end of a fearful telling-off. He came rushing back, clearly very embarrassed.

"This is a job for you, Audrey. Lizzy is stuck in an embarrassing position. She needs help to get up."

Audrey hurried off and Harold assured us that Lizzy would be fine. There was a moment of silence as we all wrestled with an image of Lizzy stuck in the hedgerow in what you might call a compromised position. Eventually, I could see a smile appearing on Stanley's face and it was no good. Humour was inevitably about to supplant gallantry, and we each collapsed in laughter.

Audrey duly returned with Lizzy and said nothing. While we gentlemen did our best to suppress our laughter, Audrey did her best to be cross with us, but it was an impossible task.

Stanley poured both the ladies another glass of champagne, and Lizzy said an unnoticed bramble was the cause of her demise, whereupon Audrey burst into laughter, followed by the rest of us.

The afternoon progressed in beautiful sunshine. I'd be hard-pressed to think of a moment when I was happier. I sat there on my little fold-up seat looking at my friends and valuing everyone. A more diverse bunch you'd be unlikely to find, but we did at least share some of the same eccentricities.

Take Audrey, for example. Here we were in the middle of a field full of cow pats and she was wearing a beautifully tailored cream linen jacket and slacks, combined with a pink lace camisole and a pearl necklace, beneath a wide-brimmed, classic Breton straw hat in sunshine yellow. This ensemble was finished off with equally impractical gold open-toe sandals with a relatively modest two-inch heel.

I looked across at Lizzy and couldn't suppress a smile. She'd confounded us all by turning out in an outfit that none of us had seen before or would ever have guessed that she possessed. It consisted of navy-blue Bermuda shorts and a navy and white striped short-sleeve jacket. She had a white blouse, as well as a hat not dissimilar to Audrey's. The take-home memory was the shoes. Blue and pink striped deck shoes on a very senior lady who tends to stagger is quite an image.

Not surprisingly, the gentlemen had no hope of competing, but it's interesting that, without consultation, we all looked about the same. Jacket and tie, and shiny shoes, we all looked incredibly smart. Maybe Bill's outfit looked as if it was straight from the laundry bin, but was smart, nevertheless.

The fact that we were all dressed so elegantly simply in order to sit in the middle of a field full of cow pats was, for us, the whole point. Moreover, your average onlooker wouldn't even begin to comprehend this display of sartorial absurdity only served to give us greater satisfaction. The danger, of course, was that some new-fangled millennial type might see us and think we were a danger to ourselves and others!

Stanley leaned back as far as his fold-up seat would allow. The threads on his waistcoat buttons were stretched like violin strings, but his satisfaction with the day was self-evident.

Harold looked at ease with himself, which was quite something to behold, but Bill looked a little thoughtful.

Chapter Thirteen
BILL'S DARK SECRET

I noticed Bill's pensiveness, and had no doubt that Stanley was on the case, so thought it best not to mention it. Not so Stanley, of course, who did what only Stanley can do. He relinquished his relaxed posture in a way that told me it was a great sacrifice. He then struggled up to pour everyone another glass of champagne. The whole process seemed to be ritualised, with the champagne being the central deity. As each glass was filled with reverence, Stanley only lacked priestly vestments. Through this process he held everyone's attention for what seemed like an eternity, and all of this without even saying a word! How Stanley can command the attention of a gathering simply by being there is a mystery to me, but I knew we should wait in silence and that something significant was going to be said.

"Oh, my dear friends," he finally said. "Has anyone ever enjoyed a day more sublime than this?"

As we were all agreeing, Stanley turned towards Bill and said, "What is it you need to get off your chest, old boy?"

We all knew and recognised the routine by now, including Bill. It's just that I didn't expect it at that moment! I could see Bill was a little taken aback, as he tried to brush it aside. How futile was that!

Once again, Stanley had total command of the gathering. He sat down again, adjusting his buttons and exhaling in an exaggerated way that signified his deep contentment. I could imagine at that moment Stanley producing his baton and tapping the rostrum to gain the orchestra's attention, before directing all and sundry in their various parts.

I suspected Bill did indeed want to get something off his chest and that he might even have volunteered to confide in us in his own time. However, once Stanley had raised the baton and the rest of us had pulled our seats around, there was only one way forward.

"Quite right, Stanley," said Bill. "There is something I need to get off my chest. I'm afraid I'm not really what I appear to be. There's a period in my past that I have concealed for my entire adult life. At first, I had to conceal it for the sake of my career. Now, I'm just too ashamed to admit it. It's been a terrible burden, and you've all shown me that it doesn't have to be like that."

Maybe, with the aid of hindsight, I might have suspected that there was a lot more to Audrey than she was letting on. I did certainly feel there was a lot more we didn't know about Harold, but I simply couldn't imagine Bill being anyone other than Bill. What he had just said was astonishing! I just sat in silence and let things unfold.

"I've never claimed anything," Bill said. "It's just that people have assumed things and I've chosen not to correct you for fear of being asked to explain. I'm not a professor. I do have a degree in physics as well as a PhD, but not a professorship."

"That's hardly something to be ashamed of Bill, I shouldn't worry about it," I said.

Bill looked very uncomfortable. "I wish that's all it was."

This revelation was greeted with silence. I felt Bill's discomfort and groped for some comforting words, but I didn't find any, of course. I waited for Stanley, who unlike me, knew exactly the right thing to say.

"You forget, old boy, that we're on this journey together. We already know there must be far more to this than meets the eye, so let's just start at the beginning. So, dear boy, tell us a little about your family background."

We'd heard this initial line of enquiry so often by now, and Bill was obviously ready for it. He explained that he was a Londoner, born south of the river in an area which was then considered undesirable, but which now is considered a highly fashionable area.

"How times change," said Bill. "If I owned a house there now, I'd be a millionaire!"

He continued describing an average working-class kid's upbringing in a working-class area where you weren't expected to go to university and an O-level in metalwork was considered as the norm. His comment about the O-level in metalwork really struck a chord with me. This was as far as Bill's education went. He left school at sixteen and it went downhill from there.

Bill said, "I'm profoundly embarrassed to admit it now, but I was a very wayward young man. I suppose a lot of it was the crowd I mixed with, plus the fact that my mother was a single parent who didn't have a great deal of time for me. I can recognise that angry young man's problem today, but of course I didn't see it then. I blamed my mother for everything, probably with some justification. My solution was to take it out on the rest of society."

"Where did it all start to go wrong?" asked Stanley.

"Looking back now, I think what I craved was attention, and a sense of belonging," said Bill. "That's what the gang culture offers you, an identity."

Bill had clearly resigned himself to the telling of his story, so we all sat back to listen. He left school and got a job with the local council in the Parks Department, a gardener really. His slide down the slippery slope of drugs and petty crime followed the usual pattern. First it was cannabis, then some petty crime to pay for it. Then LSD and more petty crime, on an ever-escalating scale. He struggled to hold his job down until eventually he was found once too often in the equipment shed, convinced he was Elvis Presley. Bill had little or no motivation in his life apart from the drugs and his place in the gang. Then he told us that this was when he met Sadie.

"Everything about Sadie was a protest. Whatever convention dictated, she would be the opposite. She dressed outrageously. In that pre-punk era she was, in her own way, ahead of her time. Her hair was cut rather like a Mohican style with a 'rat tail' at the back. It might be coloured red one week, and green the next, or mixtures of colours. She had a dragon tattooed on her left arm. This was supposed to be the new sexually liberated era, but there was no amount of liberalisation enough for Sadie. There was still ample scope for her to shock."

Stanley must have realised that the outrageous Sadie was of some significance.

"Did this young lady have no redeeming features?"

"In the eyes of a young pothead who couldn't see past the next joint, she was the Queen of Sheba," Bill said.

Sadie would have been an attractive young woman in conventional circumstances, but in the gang culture she was known as 'Sexy Sadie', For her, rebellion was best pursued from a position of power, and her power was her sexuality. She would be Queen to whoever was King at the time, but the true power was always hers.

It goes without saying that Bill, despite his background, was highly intelligent. I wasn't surprised to hear that among his low-life contemporaries Bill stood head and shoulders above the rest in terms of intellect. It was a case of being a one-eyed man in the land of the blind. Bill just lacked motivation. It was Sadie who became his motivation. She was sexy, which made her attractive. She had power over the gang which was intoxicating. She was unattainable, which made her alluring. Bill made up his mind that she had to be his.

This was the first time in Bill's young life that he was motivated to do anything; he had an ambition, albeit misguided. He quickly reasoned that trying to appeal to Sadie while in the persona of Elvis Presley was not a great idea. For this one reason alone, he gave up his hitherto growing habit of LSD. He made the decision, and that was it; he never touched it again. He also reasoned that Sadie would have no interest in a lowly foot soldier, so he had to move up through the gang ranks and topple the leader. Bill then set about explaining to us the workings of gang hierarchy.

"If you have read or have seen programmes on TV about primates like chimpanzees, you will know that the alpha male is the only one who gets the girls. He must always be ready to fend off the other males who want the top job. The alpha male does this by a constant display of strength, while any rivals posture and strut from a safe distance. Every so often, a contender makes a challenge, and the loser is either dead or banished."

This was typical of Bill, explaining something clearly and graphically with evidence or analogy. I had never thought to compare gang culture in this way, but it all made sense.

"The irony of my situation was that we were supposed to be non-conformists." Bill said. "We thought we had rebelled against society, against our ancestry. In fact, all we did was to conform to our primate ancestry. We did exactly what evolution told us to do. The only one of us who really did rebel was Sadie. She didn't conform to her female role at all."

The young Bill made the decision to move through the ranks of the minions. The usual currency of power and rank was violence, but Bill had something much more powerful, his intelligence. He would organise their petty crime activities while not actually taking part. When he decided that they would be better off selling weed, rather than just buying it, he organised for others to be in possession of the actual weed, while he was in possession of the money. It was all at a petty level, but suited Bill's purpose.

It didn't take long for Bill to rise through the ranks, and it didn't take long for Sadie to notice the young contender. She carefully nurtured the relationship from a distance, just in case. Bill's analogy with primate culture was still ringing in my ear; a clash between the young contender and the alpha male seemed inevitable. Bill said he knew it as well.

Stanley showed no outward sign of being shocked by the revelations.

"Where were you living at the time?"

Bill shared a flat with three other young men. One of them was a fellow gang member and the other two Bill described as being equally dysfunctional. He didn't need to paint a picture of this environment. My mind painted its own graphic scene which was about as disagreeable as a picnic in a cow shed. Bill admitted that, with hindsight, the squalor of this shared flat probably marked the pinnacle of his underachievement as a young man.

Success and attainment are of course relative terms, and in Bill's world he was quickly becoming recognised as successful. None of this escaped Sadie's attention. She needed to ensure that Bill would remain a loyal subject should his rise to power continue. She knew how to secure Bill's fealty, and Bill perhaps understandably wanted to believe that her warmth was genuine. If there's one thing that will make a young man behave irrationally, then it's a young lady's smile. Bill acted true to type, and asked Sadie to join him in his flat one evening.

"I can't imagine what I was thinking," he said. "There was me asking the Queen of Sheba to attend me at my London residence, where I would be surrounded by my courtiers. The reality of course was a smelly dilapidated flat above a greengrocer, and my courtiers were three low-life deplorables."

Sadie was unimpressed and, when one of the deplorables made advances towards her, she punched him! Bill said it was a moment of realisation for him. Suddenly he saw his life for what it was. Worst of all, he thought his chances with Sadie were over. Having punched the deplorable, she announced her departure and stormed out. She very nearly fell down the unlit staircase and vented her temper on the pile of vegetable boxes in the stairwell. Bill ran after her, more in hope than anger. She continued until a taxi conveniently came along, which she hailed. By the time she was inside the cab, Bill arrived alongside apologising profusely.

Sadie was furious, winding the window down and glaring at Bill. "Fuck off you moron."

Audrey was horrified, "Did she really say that?"

Bill nodded, "That was nothing! Sadie could make an East End barrow-boy blush."

It appeared that the 'deplorable' was even more the subject of her disapproval than Bill. As Bill watched the cab drive away, it suddenly stopped, and Sadie shouted back towards him.

"Get in the cab, idiot."

They drove for thirty minutes or more. Bill didn't even notice where. They turned into a very smart leafy lane where Sadie directed the cabby into the drive of a very impressive detached house. They parked next to a Mercedes-Benz 600 which impressed Bill immensely. Sadie paid the cabby, and as the cab left, Bill stood in wonderment.

Sadie stared at him and pulled him by his lapels towards her.

"This is my folks' place, but if you tell anyone about this, I'll fucking kill you."

Bill wasn't about to argue. They went into what was for him the kind of home he had only ever seen in a magazine; he had difficulty preventing his mouth from gaping open. When her parents appeared, it became immediately clear that Sadie was not a frequent visitor. There were tensions. When they clapped eyes on Bill, those tensions only increased. They took one condescending look at Bill, a look that said it all. Nevertheless, outwardly they were nothing if not polite. They shook hands and exchanged pleasantries. Her father asked Bill what he did for a living and Bill floundered for a moment.

Sadie interrupted, "Bill's in the import business, he distributes plants."

Bill played along, hating every second of the conversation, feeling like something the cat had dragged in. The friction between Sadie and her parents gradually increased until it broke out into open hostility. Bill sat there hoping a great chasm would appear in the floor so that he could step into it.

Seeing Bill's discomfort, Sadie said to her parents, "Don't worry, we'll be gone in the morning; you won't need to meet any more of my friends. Come on Bill, let's go to my room."

She pulled Bill by the hand and marched him upstairs to her bedroom. He had no idea what was going on and wasn't about to argue with Sadie when she was in full flow. Sadie directed Bill towards the en-suite bathroom.

"Do whatever you need to do, I just need to chill out for a moment."

Bill washed and freshened up as if this was all quite normal. He still didn't understand what was going on. This all felt very strange, being in her parents' house. This might have been the new sexually liberated age, but not this liberated. He was very ill at ease and, when he returned, she was sitting on the bed and appeared calmer.

"For God's sake you've still got all your fucking clothes on, you idiot. Get yourself to bed, I'll be back," she said.

As Bill suddenly realised the situation he was in, his heart jumped in anticipation. He was about to go to bed with the Queen of Sheba. After what seemed like an eternity, Sadie finally emerged from the bathroom wearing nothing at all. Bill had only ever seen her dressed in her rebellious dress code. There was nothing rebellious-looking about her now.

She pulled the sheets back and slipped in beside Bill.

"Bit cleaner than that shit hole of yours. If you mention one word of this to anyone, I'm serious, I'll fucking kill you, do you understand?"

With that she made love to Bill and left him in no doubt why she was known as Sexy Sadie. The following morning Bill awoke and, for a moment, he assumed he must have been dreaming. When he turned to see Sadie lying there, he had to pinch himself. His immediate instinct was to take her in his arms again, but Sadie was having none of it.

"None of this happened, okay? I shouldn't have come here," she said. "You know it was just to upset them. Let's get out of here."

The weeks that followed were surreal for Bill. For him, this was the biggest thing that had ever happened to him. For Sadie, it appeared to be of no consequence. Bill couldn't bear it. He wanted her so much he was prepared to do anything. He knew what he needed to do. The posturing contender had to challenge the alpha male.

Stanley, who had been sitting quietly throughout Bill's story, finally said, "I sense this represents a turning point in your life Bill, was that the case?"

It was indeed a turning point. Bill had no intention of violently ousting the gang leader; this was not Bill's way. He hoped he could push him aside by more subtle means. Tony, however, didn't understand subtlety, he only understood violence. The subsequent conflict was inevitable, especially when Tony began to suspect Sadie of giving her favours to Bill.

It all came to a head one night, walking back after a confrontational night at the pub. Tony was drunk, even more drunk than usual. The contender made clear his challenge, and the alpha male automatically resorted to violence to defend his territory, and his right to mate with the females.

Bill didn't understand fighting, but he had to defend himself as best he could. Tony was so drunk, he was uncoordinated and confused, which was probably just as well for Bill.

The event that changed Bill's life happened in an instant. Tony lunged at him, Bill sidestepped him and brushed him aside. Tony fell headlong into a lamp-post. Tony was in a coma for three weeks before he died.

Suddenly, we all had a hint of where this story might be going and, sensing that a pause might be in order, Harold said, "What about some more pork pie, Bill?"

To which Bill replied, "Good idea."

Stanley, obviously pleased with his progress, struggled up and rummaged deep into the hamper for some more champagne.

"Do we actually *have* any more?" I asked.

Stanley looked at me in amazement. "*More? Of course* there's more!"

We all smiled as the cork popped, and we offered up our glasses. We knew by now how Stanley worked his magic, and that, once started, Bill would soon enough continue his story. For the moment, however, there was yet more champagne and food to consume. I suddenly noticed the sky appeared strangely dark towards the west.

"That's a strange light effect," I said.

"Do you suppose it's coming our way?" Audrey asked.

Bill stuck his finger in the air and said, "Well, the wind is coming from that direction so if it's a weather front, then yes, it probably is."

After so much food and wine it becomes difficult to take the threat of a bit of rain seriously and we kind of ignored it until we all became aware that it was getting dark, very dark indeed.

Harold woke up to the emergency.

"It's going to rain."

Despite the obvious distractions, reality did indeed suddenly strike home as the first rain drops fell upon us.

"Quickly," said Harold. "All the stuff into the cars."

Our spirits were so high that the whole episode was viewed as just so much fun, and we bundled everything into the back of the cars, quickly followed by ourselves.

We sat there in the cars as what appeared to be night-time descended upon us. The heavens opened in a downpour which could only be described as Biblical. It fell so hard onto the cars that we couldn't even talk above the thunderous roar, and so it continued for the best part of an hour. However, like the parting of the Red Sea, we knew normality would eventually be restored and so it was, as a patch of blue appeared in the western sky.

"That was fun!" said Lizzy.

Audrey added, "I agree. What an exciting end to a wonderful day! Let's head for home."

We all agreed it had been a most wonderful day as Harold started his car. We watched from my car as he reversed around and headed back up the grassy slope towards the road; except that he didn't head up the grassy slope! Nothing happened, except for a shower of mud flying up from the wheels.

"Oh dear," I said, "That's a rear wheel drive BMW for you."

I engaged first gear and, slowly avoiding any wheel-spin, I too attempted the incline, but nothing happened! We were stuck!

"Okay," called Harold. "We can't go up, so we'll go down instead. If we follow this hedgerow along, there will obviously be an entrance into the field below and with luck a track leading to a farmhouse."

I looked at Bill, Bill looked at Stanley. Was this a good idea, I thought? Harold, however, was nothing if not decisive and, without further ado, he was heading off along the hedgerow, so naturally we followed.

"I'm a bit concerned," said Bill. "We're heading downhill which is exactly what all that rainwater's doing."

Nevertheless, we continued, and sure enough there was indeed a gate, but it stood in the middle of a small pond. Harold seemed impervious to such inconveniences and he did no less than jump out of his car, wading straight through the pond toward the gate. He pulled it fully open until it met the adjoining fence, whereupon he seemed to jump into the air as if in celebration; this man was indomitable!

He waded back to his car, covered in mud but seemingly undaunted. I couldn't imagine what Audrey in his car must have thought of all this! Bravely he aimed the BMW towards the gate and advanced with caution, and to our surprise Harold didn't sink without trace, instead he ploughed through it. Relieved, I successfully followed, and stopped on the other side.

"We'd better close the gate, there are cattle in this field," I said.

They agreed I should be the one to close the gate. I stepped into the water, heading toward the gate. I reached out to grab it and found myself about a metre higher in the air than when I had started. Harold hadn't jumped into the air in celebration! The fence was electrified! Feeling decidedly cross, I grumpily pushed the gate closed and stomped back to the car, feeling rather ridiculous.

Harold continued along the muddy track with us following, but it was as if I'd left my seat belt unfastened. There was an alarm ringing in my head. This whole situation had a feeling of impending doom about it. As we continued forever slightly downhill, so the amount of standing water increased, until Harold faced an area of continuous water. Tantalisingly, we could see dry ground rising beyond it.

Harold, in true Harold swashbuckling style, went for it, making good progress for a while until the BMW suddenly slumped into a hollow and stopped. A waft of steam rose up from the engine and it seemed apparent that his gamble had failed.

"I suggest we don't try that little manoeuvre," said Bill.

I quickly reassured him that I had no such intention. There was nothing we could do but look on from our slightly less precarious position.

"Can you imagine what Audrey is saying right now?" I said.

"I think I can!" said Stanley.

Despite our situation, we laughed aloud. I was already

covered in mud, so I thought I'd better wade over to them. Perhaps a part of me couldn't resist witnessing Audrey admonishing Harold! Sure enough, Harold was metaphorically in hot water, on the receiving end of the worst telling-off I've ever heard.

"Quite right," I said to Audrey.

Then I did something without thinking. I opened the passenger door which, being slightly below water level, allowed the water to rush in. This caused a bit of a commotion, but I managed to blame it on Harold! Now the door was open, and their feet were wet, I suggested that the ladies should leave Harold in the pond and make their way back to my car. Audrey was incandescent with rage. I doubt that she'd ever been this close to mud in her entire life. While I offered Lizzy a helping hand, Audrey stormed off in something of a strop, which wasn't a good idea. Sadly, she didn't see the underwater obstruction that up-ended her, and she fell headlong into the water, white linen jacket, slacks and all.

Was this the most hilarious thing I had ever seen, or was it terribly serious? For a moment I wasn't quite sure, but then Audrey left me in no doubt whatever; this was terribly serious. She righted herself and made her way to my car where she immediately sat inside, mud and all. I followed with Lizzy, and a crestfallen Harold brought up the rear.

It was fair to say that, of all of us, Lizzy had fared the best. Her knee-length Bermuda shorts could have been made for mud wading, but Audrey was another matter. If I thought for one moment that I might have got away with taking a photograph of her dilemma, I just know it would have been an image to treasure for life, but the repercussions terrified me, so I instantly dismissed the idea.

Harold offered no further suggestions, but Bill summed up our predicament.

"We have two options; either we walk on in the hope of finding the farmer, or we walk back to the road," he said.

We all agreed, it was backward or forward. Harold attempted to speak but Audrey intervened.

"Don't say a word, Harold."

We had a show of hands and set off on foot, forward. The only slight inconvenience was that we now had to wade back through the pond. Little did we know that fortunately the farmhouse was just over the rise, and it provided a welcome sight. Just as we approached, a man on a quad bike came rushing toward us, shouting at the top of his voice.

"Are you the idiots who've been camping in my field and let my cattle out?" he said.

Just as I was thinking our predicament had sunk to its lowest level, it had suddenly descended further. I tried to explain but this man didn't have a shred of sympathy for us, and I suppose we did look a little like a bunch of vagrants. He said as much, which enraged Audrey.

"My good man! How *dare* you make such disparaging remarks. You don't have the faintest idea about the kind of people you are addressing!"

Looking at Audrey, I had to admit to myself that any similarity with a vagrant would have been a great improvement. She'd obviously lost sight of the fact that her credibility lay somewhere under the water in a distant field! None of this helped our position in the slightest, and the man rushed off on his quad bike, presumably to round up his cattle. This left us standing there, all soaking wet, with dusk rapidly approaching. The fact that we really needed this man's help hadn't escaped us. Stanley pointed out an open shed, so we went over and stood next to an old tractor. We were feeling cold and bedraggled and by now the funny side of events had disappeared. A little later, the farmer reappeared and continued his tirade against us.

"What are you up to now?" he said. "Planning to steal my tractor?"

I felt so forlorn, I had nothing to say, but step forward Stanley.

"Tell me, old boy," he commenced. "Isn't this lovely old machine a Fordson Major? I recognised it immediately, and I can see you're working on it. Nothing serious, I hope?"

The farmer was a little taken aback.

"Well, yes," he said. "I think I might have bent a pushrod."

Stanley adopted his all-knowing look and started to draw a deep breath. I recognised the signs immediately. He was up to something!

He said to the farmer, "Have you had trouble starting it, and was that when you think you might have bent the pushrod?"

"That's right," came the reply.

Stanley put his hand to his chin with a quizzical look on his face.

"Was your battery getting a bit low, and did you try to compensate for that by starting it with the decompression lever raised up?"

"Yes, that's exactly what I did."

I recognised the hint of a smile appearing on Stanley's face. It started in the corner of his mouth but quickly radiated across his face.

"That's the problem," Stanley said with great authority. "The decompression lever on the Major is only intended for hand turning the engine while you set up the pump timing."

Stanley wasn't content with that. He pursued the man again asking how old the tractor was. The farmer wasn't quite sure, but thought it was probably early 1950s.

"Well, of course," said Stanley, "they didn't make the Major at Dagenham until 1952, and then it only had a production run of twelve years, before it was replaced by the Power Major. I would agree, this old beauty does look like one of the early ones. Now, tell me old boy, where did you buy her from?"

The farmer said he'd bought it from an auction. Well, of course, Stanley knew the auction house, was indeed the best of friends with the auctioneer, and so it went on! With that,

Stanley and the farmer huddled together by the tractor with Stanley one step ahead of him all the way. It ended up with the farmer, who by now was our new best friend Brian, insisting that we come into his house to warm up while he and his son went out in the dark to tow our cars back. Naturally, Stanley's feet barely touched the ground! The Major tractor was indeed yet another of his 'major triumphs'!

We arrived back at the Village very late and very bedraggled, with our cars in need of some serious attention, but the triumph was that we'd made it. From Audrey's point of view, the only thing that mattered was that no-one saw her arrive!

Chapter Fourteen
SADIE'S STORY

The following morning, I woke to see another gloriously sunny day dawning. I thought again about Harold's story the other day. I was in awe of the man; he made me feel quite inadequate. I knew they were expecting my story one day soon, but what did I possibly have to tell them that would compare to Harold's life, or Audrey's for that matter? I did suddenly realise the one thing we had in common. We had each come here to the Village in order to escape our past.

I sat in bed for a while and obviously the events of yesterday came back to mind. There were moments during the picnic when I would be hard-pressed to recall a happier day. How sad that it had all descended into one of our fiascos. Then there was the unforgettable image of Audrey covered in mud from head to toe, and I confess that I found myself sitting there in bed laughing! No real harm had been done, but that was surely the funniest thing I'd ever seen! Then, of course, I felt guilty because, despite the hilarity, I knew Audrey was mortified, and she certainly didn't see the funny side of it. So, the question was: how to deal with the situation this morning? I decided that my best tactic was to be absolutely mortified too, have every sympathy with Audrey, and then to blame it all on Harold. It was a good plan!

I arrived for breakfast just before Harold, who entered looking very sheepish. We all said very little as we sat down to breakfast, but where was Audrey? We waited for some time before she finally appeared wearing a cream embroidered blouse and cream pleated skirt, with high heels and the same pearls as yesterday. She looked incredible, ridiculously over-dressed for breakfast but incredible, nevertheless.

"Lovely day," I said, "and may I say how wonderful you look this morning?"

Audrey didn't respond. Breakfast continued with frivolous conversation about the weather and the scrambled egg. I had the distinct feeling that we were all walking on eggshells.

Eventually, Bill plucked up courage.

"Your knowledge about the tractor really saved the day yesterday, Stanley."

Stanley was justifiably pleased with himself.

"Oh, just one of those little areas of expertise, you know," he said with uncharacteristic modesty.

"What about that pork pie?" Bill said. "Didn't I tell you they were the best pork pies in the world?"

"You know, Bill, I think you're right; it's certainly the finest pork pie I've ever eaten," I replied.

"I must agree, but not just the pie. That was the finest picnic I've ever enjoyed!" Stanley said.

Harold didn't say a word, probably wisely, but then Lizzy piped up.

"I was lucky that I was wearing my shorts, wasn't I, and I was lucky I didn't fall over like Audrey, because it's usually me that falls over, isn't it?"

We sat in silence, but there was more to come.

Lizzy continued with, "I'm always falling over, and I find the best way to deal with it is to look as silly as possible, because then everyone takes pity on you and someone will always help you up. I think you did a wonderful job Audrey! You looked really silly."

The silence was deafening, and for the moment Audrey was expressionless, but it was one of those situations where I could only see one outcome. If I didn't laugh soon, something would explode!

We all waited with bated breath, looking for a signal from Audrey allowing us all to laugh. It wouldn't take much; a half grin or a grimace would do it. She, however, did her best to remain stony-faced. Perhaps it was our red faces and puffed up cheeks but eventually, after what felt like an eternity, she reluctantly raised the corner of her mouth in a gesture that rightly or wrongly we all wanted to interpret as a half-smile.

It was like releasing the cork from a badly shaken bottle of champagne. We all burst into laughter, including Audrey, and we just couldn't stop for an age. Eventually, and smiling broadly, Audrey looked at Harold.

"I don't know what you're laughing at! It was all your fault!"

Harold offered no defence, probably content that there was a hint of forgiveness in the air. We made our way into the lounge, laughing all the way. No-one mentioned it, but we intuitively sat in an arrangement so that Bill could continue his story. For his part, Bill was totally compliant; Stanley had us trained like puppy dogs. We went through the ritual of Stanley adjusting his buttons, the settling into the chair combined with the deep drawing-in of breath. We knew the moment was coming.

"Now old boy, what you described before we were interrupted, was it all as serious as it sounded?"

Bill also drew a very deep breath.

"It was the defining moment of my life," he said. "In the space a couple of seconds, nothing would ever be the same."

Tony's death was interpreted by the police as a gangland killing, a straightforward feud over drug money. Bill was charged with murder! We were all shocked into total silence. It was Audrey who finally said something.

"Oh, my goodness! What on earth happened?"

Bill went on trial for murder where he faced life in prison. He testified that it was an accident; he was articulate despite his lack of education. Sadie testified, confirming Bill's interpretation of events. In his summation, Bill's defence barrister painted a glossy picture of an intelligent but misguided young man who found himself in the wrong place at the wrong time.

Things felt hopeful until the prosecution presented their summation. This was another, quite different, interpretation of events. Bill was portrayed as a young man with no redeeming features. A small-time drug dealer, a gang member and someone who had received two police cautions for shoplifting. A man who wanted to kill the gang leader in order to control the drug money. The jury retired to consider their verdict having been directed by the judge. After two days of deliberation, they returned.

"On the first charge of first-degree murder, how do you find the defendant? Guilty, or not guilty?"

"Not guilty," said the foreman.

"On the second charge of manslaughter, how do you find the defendant? Guilty, or not guilty?"

"Guilty," came the reply.

Bill was sent to prison for eight years.

"I can't believe it, Bill. You went to prison for eight years?" I said.

"Now you know why I'm so ashamed, and why I have always hidden that part of my life," said Bill.

Stanley must have been as shocked as the rest of us, but he didn't show it, simply saying, "I suspect there's more to this Bill. How does a man, sent to prison for eight years, end up with a PhD?"

Bill explained that there was an education programme being run in the prison by an inspirational man who quickly developed a rapport with him. What Bill didn't know at the time was that this man was involved with the creation of the Open University. The OU was founded by the Labour government of Harold Wilson in 1965. It was the then Minister of State for Education, Jennie Lee, who was instrumental in creating the institution. It was still a fledgling organisation at this time, but Bill would unwittingly benefit by it.

With nothing else to occupy his mind, Bill threw himself into GCSE O-levels. His tutor was as gratified as he was amazed. Education for prisoners was not necessarily well received. Bill progressed to A-level standard with unprecedented speed, and this was when an Open University course was mentioned. This, too, was unprecedented; the fledgling OU was not designed for prisoners. Television presentation was just about to be launched, appearing in 1971, not that it would have been an option for Bill. In its absence, educational material was entirely paper, which was available for him. Bill does not know to this day if his course was properly sanctioned by the OU or not, but he ended up with a BA Honours degree. The one thing he is certain of is that his tutor changed his life.

Stanley smiled very contentedly at these revelations.

"What of Sadie, did you see her again?"

"Oh yes, she came to visit me in prison."

Sadie visited quite early on. During her first visit she was her usual hostile self, and Bill assumed he wouldn't see her again, but she came back. On her second visit, a few weeks later, her outlandish hair was gone, replaced by a beautiful and conventional hair style, and it was her natural colour. On her fifth visit she arrived soberly dressed. The term was relative for Sadie; she was now the height of early seventies fashion, but sober by her standards.

She leaned across the table that stood between her and Bill.

"What I said that morning at my folks' place, about only doing it to upset them. It wasn't true."

"What was true then?" asked Bill

"I just wanted you, but I didn't want to admit it."

"But you hurt me saying that, and you probably hurt your parents as well."

"I'm working on that," she said.

Sadie continued visiting regularly throughout Bill's prison term, and he watched her change over the ensuing years. She was inspired by Bill's determination to educate himself, even enrolling for night classes to further her own education. She had a proper job now, working for an estate agent. She had become like an unfolding novel. At each new visit, she had a new revelation, some new act of conformity. Bill found himself existing in two separate states; he was either studying or he was staring into the eyes of Sadie. He was so preoccupied that the prison environment seemed not to exist.

Sadie's final and biggest hurdle was a reconciliation with her parents. Bill knew this, and so when she finally admitted that this was what she wanted, Bill asked her what was stopping her.

"You, you idiot," she said.

"Why me?"

"Because they know you're a fucking prisoner. If they can't accept you, I can't accept them."

"You're a beautiful woman, Sadie. Why can't you sound like one?"

She stopped in her tracks.

"I'm sorry, Bill."

Sadie never swore again, except for just one very notable exception. It was like she had dismissed her last act of rebellion, which made a deep impression on Bill.

Towards the end of his term, which was reduced to six years with remission, he found himself finally thinking beyond prison and making plans for his future. On one visit, he and Sadie talked about nothing else.

"What I would really like is a career in physics, but to get a top position in a university or maybe private industry I need a master's degree and possibly a PhD," said Bill. "Trouble is, after being here, who will accept me and how can I afford to go on studying?"

"I've got a good job now, and I've got my own place. I got you into this mess, Bill. This is my chance to get you out of it. I'll support you."

"You would do that for me?"

"*Of course* I would."

"But why Sadie, why would you do that for me?"

"You know why."

"But I need you to tell me why."

"Because I fucking love you, okay? There, I've said it. Sorry, I mean I love you, I mean … I really do love you, Bill. I want to spend my life with you. I want us to have babies. I want it all."

Audrey was taken aback, "Oh my goodness! What did you say?"

Bill smiled. "What do you think I said? 'Marry me', and she said 'Yes'!"

Audrey was suddenly in tears because finally the penny had dropped.

"Oh, my goodness! Your beloved wife of so many years! 'Sadie' was Sarah's nickname!"

For whatever reason, none of us had associated the rebellious 'Sadie' with being Bill's beloved wife 'Sarah'. We knew he never missed a chance to tell us how wonderful his wife was, and how lucky he was to have spent his life with her. Now suddenly everything made perfect sense to us. Then there were Bill's children, John and Victoria. The story was complete! He lowered his head and took his handkerchief out of his pocket.

"I miss her so much."

We finally settled down again and I remember thinking to myself that, once again, the old expression about not telling a book by its cover had never been truer. I'd always been quietly envious of the relationship Bill had with his wife and children. He so often would make a small comment about how happy they were, and now it all made even more sense.

I think, if truth were told, he has become my constant

reminder of the life I was denied. I suggested perhaps a cup of tea was in order and Lizzy thought that was a good idea, so she staggered off towards the kitchen to organise it. She was barely out of sight when there was a crash.

Harold said, "Lizzy's walked into the hall table again."

"Sounds like it," I said.

Eventually Lizzy came back, carrying a tray.

"Can I pass you your cup of tea, Charles?"

I panicked for a moment and quickly got to my feet in order to avert disaster.

Stanley, however, still had one or two questions for Bill so, when we had all settled down with our tea, he turned his attention back toward Bill.

"Tell me, old boy, how did your career develop?"

"I did get my master's degree, and my PhD, and it was entirely thanks to Sarah. Her job at the local estate agent kept us afloat. I eventually got a job in what is now a part of BAE Systems. My PhD was in fluid dynamics and so, for a while at least, part of my work was being a rocket scientist!"

Stanley looked pleased to hear that, and then he asked, "Did you ever manage to reconcile with Sarah's parents?"

Bill explained how it had taken a long time but eventually, when the parents realised how happy they were together, they came around to the idea, ending up being very close.

Stanley had a final question to ask.

"Did Sarah ever manage to take her education further?"

"No, the kids came along, and she felt she was too old to do it by then, but she did quite well without a degree anyway. She ended up owning a large chain of estate agents. That's the business our Vicky now owns."

There were smiles all round, Bill's story had been uplifting in every respect. The stigma of his offence had obviously been a heavy burden for him to carry all these years, but now that it was gone, we all shared the joy of his new-found freedom.

I had the distinct feeling that the Bill who was weighed down with his dark secret had left the building.

Chapter Fifteen
PANDORA'S BOX

The next few days went by quickly. We had numerous highlights, more of Puffer's jokes, and songs that we couldn't identify. There were a lot those, and we had some excellent malapropisms from Lizzy, and all the while Stanley failed to buy a round! Harold was forgiven for his part in the picnic fiasco; in fact, I couldn't help but notice how close he and Audrey were becoming.

I discussed it on one occasion with Bill who said, "We all thought you and Audrey would make a fine couple, but I begin to think your chance is fast disappearing."

I knew Bill was right, and said as much, but when he asked me why I was letting my chance slip by, I had great difficulty explaining. Bill's experience of relationships was one of happiness, whereas my experience of happiness was fleeting. I understood despair much better. We clearly looked at the same situation from different perspectives, but he was right about Audrey. She was very special to me, and yet I was about to let her go, and for no good reason.

"Perhaps what you need is to sit in the chair opposite Stanley and confide in your friends," Bill said.

No-one had mentioned it, but I knew full well that, following their recent revelations, the others had the expectation that

I would be the next to fall victim to Stanley's interrogation. The prospect frankly terrified me. The following evening, we sat in the lounge having just enjoyed a rather excellent dinner.

"Shall I get us all a cup of coffee?" asked Harold.

Stanley said he'd have a single malt. So far so normal. I did, however, have the most uncomfortable feeling that my time in the chair was approaching.

In desperation, trying to divert attention away from myself, I tried to gain Lizzy's attention.

"Didn't you say that you were a nurse, Lizzy?" I asked her.

She looked distressed. "Oh dear, is someone ill?" she answered.

"No, I said were you a nurse, not that we need a nurse."

Lizzy was relieved and said, "Oh silly me, but you really do need to speak up, Charles."

I was already shouting as loud as I could tolerate, but was determined to continue, so I asked her again.

"Yes, I was a nurse all my working life until I retired, after my last husband died."

I tried again, and said, "You say your 'last husband', Lizzy; I thought you only had the one."

"Oh, did I say only one? Oh no, I had several, I think it was four, let me think. Yes, it was four."

"Are you saying, Lizzy, that you have had *four* husbands? You were married four times?" I asked.

"Oh yes, it was four times, and married in church on each occasion."

I had been hoping to divert attention away from myself, but I hadn't anticipated this degree of success!

Everyone, including Stanley, pulled their chairs around Lizzy. Stanley started puffing up his cheeks and adjusting his buttons. I was off the hook!

Stanley now had command of the gathering and we waited for his opening question which quickly followed.

"Tell me, Lizzy, when did you marry your first husband?"

Lizzy thought for a while and said, "I'm not very good with dates, but I was quite young."

Obviously not content with that response, Stanley approached the matter from a different direction.

"Now then, my dear, tell me about your first husband."

Lizzy thought about it as if straining to recall the name of husband number one, but eventually she replied.

"That's right, it was Tom."

Stanley was visibly pleased with this response. It may have been no more than a name but, for Stanley, this was like unravelling a tangled fishing line and he had managed to tease out one end.

"Tom was a servant to Mr. Mac. I really can't remember his proper name, but I remember Tom often just referred to him as Mac."

Stanley obviously needed more than this, so he asked if Lizzy could remember where or when this was.

Lizzy had no idea when, but she said that Tom was a servant and worked in Whitehall. Stanley tried again to make some sense of it.

"When you say servant Lizzy, was he in service as a man servant or perhaps a butler?" Stanley asked.

"That's right. He was in service; he called it the Civil Service."

"And when you say he worked for a Mr Mac in Whitehall, do you by any chance mean Mr Macmillan?" asked Stanley.

"That's right," said Lizzy. "I remember it now, Mr. Macmillan."

How incredibly insightful Stanley had been; Lizzy's husband worked for the Prime Minister! Stanley sipped urgently from his glass of Ardbeg 10-year-old.

"So, my dear, where did you meet Tom?" he finally said.

Lizzy recalled that she was working as a nurse in a nursing home, where she was taking care of Tom's mother, and how Tom had decided that it would be better for his mother if Lizzy would be prepared to take care of her at his home.

"Oh, I see, so you were living in Tom's house, nursing his mother and you ended up marrying him?"

Lizzy smiled at him. "Yes, it was just before his mother died that we got married."

"How long were you married to Tom?" asked Stanley.

Lizzy had no problem recalling that it was for a year.

"Oh, my dear! That's awful; what happened?" Stanley asked.

Lizzy answered without hesitation, "He died, you know, it was a heart attack."

We were all mortified, poor Lizzy!

"What on earth did you do Lizzy, losing your husband when you were so young?" enquired Stanley.

Lizzy said that she simply went back to work at the nursing home, and that a few years later she met Edward.

"Now, exactly how did you meet Edward?"

Lizzy said she was nursing Edward's mother and persuaded Edward that his mother would be much happier at home, and that she could take care of her. The look on Stanley's face was difficult to describe; we were all spellbound.

Stanley continued, saying, "So, if I understand you correctly, you lived in Edward's house taking care of his mother and then, rather like Tom, you ended up marrying him?"

Lizzy again smiled sweetly.

"That's right, it was just before his mother died."

This was the first time I'd seen Stanley looking as if he was rudderless. Where to go next? But after another long sip of the Ardbeg 10-year-old, Stanley decided to continue with the same line of enquiry.

"Now, tell me Lizzy, what did Edward do for a living?"

Lizzy struggled to remember, but then it came back to her.

"Edward worked for the bank."

Stanley quickly followed that with, "Now do tell me, Lizzy, did Edward work in a High Street bank?"

"Oh no, there were no banks on the High Street; he worked in one of those old buildings in London."

Stanley went straight to the more important question.

"How long were you married to Edward, Lizzy?"

Once again, the duration of the marriage was not something that Lizzy struggled to remember.

"We were married for a year."

"And how did you lose him?"

Once again Lizzy's memory was clear on this issue.

"Oh no, I didn't lose him, he died. It was a heart attack."

I looked at Audrey; Audrey looked at Harold, who in turn looked at Stanley and Bill. There were so many questions, but none of us said a word. Stanley drained the last drop of the Ardbeg and peered into the empty glass in complete disbelief. He then looked towards me with a mournful expression which clearly indicated that he would rather like another single malt. Like the well-trained puppy dog that I had become, I found myself quite involuntarily asking if he would like another one?

"Oh, my dear boy. How unexpected, but if you insist."

I glanced at Harold, and he empathised with me, raising his eyes to the ceiling. I returned with a glass of Mortlach 16-year-old and Stanley's expression was like a child at their first visit with Santa Claus. One sip of the golden fluid, and Stanley was ready for his next question.

"Now tell me, Lizzy, after you lost Edward, what did you do next?"

Lizzy said she went back to work at the nursing home.

"Where were you living, Lizzy, while you worked at the nursing home?"

"I still had my little house where I always used to live." she said.

"Where was that?"

"Not far from the nursing home in London."

Stanley persisted patiently, "Whereabouts in London, Lizzy, can you remember?"

"Oh yes, it was in Marylebone, in Montagu Square."

"And when did you first come to live in Marylebone?" Stanley asked.

"This was where I lived with my first husband, and it was so close to the nursing home, I decided to stay there."

It was obvious from Stanley's reaction that he knew all about this address, but after a moment to regroup he decided not to pursue it.

A quick sip of the Mortlach and he went on.

"You say you had four husbands, Lizzy, so you obviously married again. Tell us about that."

Lizzy said that following the death of Edward, sometime later she met Oliver. Stanley asked where they met, and Lizzy once again said at the nursing home. When asked about the details, Lizzy confirmed yet again that she was nursing Oliver's mother at the home, and then went to nurse her at Oliver's house, where she later married him.

We waited for what seemed like an eternity for the answer to the next obvious question, what had happened to Oliver.

"Oh, he died, you know; we were only married a year when he had a heart attack."

You could have knocked us all down with a feather! We waited in silence for Stanley to pursue it. Finally, he asked Lizzy what Oliver had done for a living.

"Oliver didn't really do very much at all. His father was Mr. Underwood, you know."

"Who was Mr. Underwood?" Stanley asked.

Lizzy looked puzzled, "You must know Mr. Underwood, all those wonderful shops!"

Stanley thought for a moment and said, "Are we talking about Underwood's, the Department Stores?"

"That's right, lovely shops, you know."

We all sat in silence while Lizzy continued to smile sweetly. Stanley glanced towards me and the others as if, for the first time in his life, he was lost for words. He reached for the Mortlach, wafting the glass beneath his nose, but I was quite sure that he was just using the time to consider his next approach.

"Now tell me, my dear, when you lost Oliver, what did you do next?"

Lizzy said that she did just as before, she went back to live in her Marylebone house, and went back to work in the nursing home.

Stanley wasted no time approaching his next question.

"So, Lizzy, how did you meet your fourth husband?"

We all anticipated her answer but there was a sharp intake of breath when Lizzy replied.

"I was nursing his mother at the nursing home, and Arthur invited me to nurse her at his house."

Quite suddenly the atmosphere had changed: my group of friends were seldom far from some light-hearted humour, but not so now! I knew exactly what Stanley's next question was going to be.

He sipped the Mortlach with a sense of urgency while fidgeting with the glass.

"Tell me, Lizzy, how long were you married to Arthur?"

Lizzy once again didn't have to struggle to remember, and simply said, "It was just a year when he had a heart attack."

Stanley quickly followed up with, "And what did Arthur do for a living?"

Lizzy was particularly vague. She said he had something to do with metal boxes. Stanley naturally picked and probed at every detail with his usual insight until finally he asked what was in the boxes.

"All kinds of things, everything came in the boxes."

Stanley came to the realisation before any of us did, the boxes were shipping containers, and his next question was to ask what was painted on the side of the containers.

Lizzy thought for some time, trying in vain to recall the name. "I do remember they had a red line around them."

Once this had become clear, Stanley asked what Arthur's surname was, to which Lizzy replied Riddle.

This meant nothing to me and apparently not to Stanley either, so this looked like another dead end, but cometh the hour and cometh the woman.

Audrey immediately said, "Red Line Shipping."

Audrey, as we now knew, had worked as a financial analyst and it was her business to know about these things. She quickly explained.

"Arthur Riddle was Red Line Shipping. When he started the business, he decided not to call it 'Riddle Shipping'. The connotations were obvious, so he used 'Red Line', which was as near to Riddle as he could think of."

We were momentarily carried away by Audrey's triumph. Harold inevitably said, "She's magnificent, isn't she?"

I had to agree, but moments later Stanley brought us all back down to earth.

"And so, tell me Lizzy, after Arthur died, did you go back to the nursing home again?"

Lizzy sat smiling sweetly. "Oh no, I thought I would retire."

Stanley followed up, asking what retirement meant for Lizzy, and her reply left us all aghast. She told us that she'd had lots of holidays and had travelled a lot. She'd spent most winters in her house in Bermuda, providing that she wasn't staying in her house in the Italian Alps, where she liked to ski. When asked if she was lonely without a husband, she said she wasn't alone, because she had lots of friends and she always travelled with her maid and her driver. The silence in the room was thunderous as we each sat with our individual thoughts.

I couldn't get past the image of Lizzy skiing; even the words 'Lizzy' and 'skiing' were incongruous together. There were so many questions we all wanted to ask, but Lizzy had found the whole process very tiring, and it was well past our usual time to retire for the night, so she excused herself and staggered off to her apartment.

We were all drained and desperately tired, but there wasn't the slightest possibility that anyone was going to bed. Audrey was the first to say something as soon as Lizzy was out of sight.

"Four wealthy husbands, all died after one year, and all died of a heart attack. Is anyone else thinking what I'm thinking?" she asked.

"I think we're all ahead of you, Audrey," said Stanley.

"It stretches credibility to think that it could all be a coincidence," said Bill. "But think about it for a moment; you know what we're effectively accusing Lizzy of doing!"

Stanley said, "I think the best thing we can do is to say no more about it for now. We should all sleep on it and see what we think in the morning."

Like the others, I was desperate to talk about it, but all we could do was speculate. Stanley's suggestion was probably very wise. We decided to call it a day, and Harold escorted Audrey over to her apartment, while I said goodnight and walked back alone.

-oOo-

The next morning, I was awake early and thought I would go straight over for breakfast, just in case anyone else was there.

To my surprise, I found I was the last to arrive again, all except Lizzy. We quickly sat down in the lounge.

Stanley asked, "Has anyone slept well?"

We agreed that none of us had been able to stop thinking about last night's revelations. Stanley went through his ritual of settling into his chair and adjusting his buttons while drawing a deep breath in preparation for giving us his summation.

For our part, we sat awkwardly in the sure knowledge that Stanley had command of the floor, despite not having said a word. Sure enough, the moment came.

"Now my friends, allow me to just summarise the situation. Lizzy says she met and married four men. Our problem is to reconcile the circumstances. Each one was wealthy, each one met Lizzy at the nursing home, and each one employed Lizzy to nurse their mother at home. Each one married Lizzy and subsequently died after one year, and they all died of a heart attack. The question we need to ask is whether these apparent similarities are a coincidence? If not, there's only one other conclusion!"

We all knew what that other conclusion was, but no-one wanted to mouth the words.

Harold said, "There might actually be even more to this. Think what Lizzy said about Tom and Edward; she said their mothers died shortly after they got married, but she didn't mention the other two mothers."

"I hadn't thought of that, Harold." Audrey said. "If this is all as bad as we're thinking, then the mothers would have been an obstacle."

For the first time, Stanley had possibly missed a vital thread; he did look a little crestfallen for a moment.

"I can't understand how I missed that," he said, "but let's concentrate on the husbands."

Stanley continued his summation saying that Tom was the first husband and he was the civil servant who worked for Mr. Macmillan. We must assume that this was when Harold Macmillan was Prime Minister, which was 1957–1963, so Lizzy would probably have been in her late twenties. If Tom was in the habit of calling him Mac, Stanley's guess was that he must have been a very high-level civil servant, possibly even Permanent Under-Secretary. So, Tom was someone of considerable stature and some wealth.

Then there was Edward, the banker. Stanley asked if we'd noticed that the bank was not on the High Street, and that Edward worked in an old building in London. This sounded like a private bank to him. So, we could assume Edward wasn't your average bank manager.

Lizzy said that husband number three, Oliver, 'did very little'. He was obviously a part of the Underwood Department Store chain and, as such, he obviously had access to considerable wealth. Then finally, we came to Arthur who, thanks to Audrey, we knew was a shipping magnate.

Stanley asked if we saw the likely sequence between these

men? He suspected each one was even more wealthy than the previous.

"This is all well and good," said Harold, "but can we explain how all these men died so conveniently after just one year, without raising any suspicions?"

Stanley pondered that question and admitted that it did sound fanciful.

"Don't forget Lizzy was a nurse, with access to drugs and the knowledge of how to use them," Bill said. "There's one possibility; insulin."

Bill explained that an overdose of insulin causes hypoglycaemia or insulin shock and, if it's left untreated, it can be fatal. What's more, it can look exactly like cardiac arrest and, because insulin is naturally found in the body, it wouldn't necessarily raise suspicion at post-mortem.

Another consideration, Bill suggested, would be that if by any chance one or all the husbands was diabetic, then it would be even less likely to be traced. I think we almost didn't want to know that, but once Bill had told us, there was no putting it back in the box. We could all see the obvious connections, but the consequences were so serious, I doubted any of us wanted to really consider it.

Finally, Bill shared a sensible thought with us.

"We all know that Lizzy's dementia is progressive. Is it possible she met these people in the nursing home and her memories are now confused? Perhaps what she now recalls as memories are simply a re-enactment of her fanciful imagination at the time?"

Harold responded with, "What you're suggesting is that Lizzy's story is a figment of her imagination?"

Stanley seized upon the possibility.

"Exactly so. It's not impossible, and it means we can just ignore it."

Audrey, as sensible as ever, said, "You're all overlooking one thing. The marriage and death certificates will confirm it either way. Fiona could find those certificates for us in five minutes."

Once again silence descended upon the gathering. No-one said a thing for several minutes.

Eventually Stanley said, "If we're right about our worst-case scenario, then we have a civic duty to report it. The families of those deceased husbands would expect no less."

No-one else was about to say anything, so I offered a comment.

"I can see your point, Stanley, about the deceased husbands' families, but presumably they're at peace with the memory of what they think is a natural death. We might only cause more grief, and with Lizzy's advancing dementia, would it serve any purpose?"

"If we were to obtain the certificates and they confirmed our worst fears, we really would be duty-bound to report our suspicions but, without the certificates, we're only speculating," Audrey said.

We sat in silence again, thinking, until Stanley made a suggestion.

"Let's have a vote. All those in favour of obtaining the certificates, raise your hand."

No-one raised a hand.

"All those in favour of assuming that Lizzy's story is a figment of her imagination, raise your hand."

We all held up our hands.

Just at that moment Lizzy came staggering into the lounge.

"Why aren't you having breakfast?" she asked.

I made some flimsy excuse, and we all set off for the breakfast restaurant. Lizzy appeared to have completely forgotten our conversation of last night, and it was never mentioned again.

Everything continued as if nothing had happened, but of course something had happened, and it could never be the same again. I had the distinct feeling that our dear, sweet Lizzy had left the building.

Trouble was, I wasn't quite sure about the replacement!

Chapter Sixteen
CHARLIE'S STORY

For the rest of that day, and indeed for many days, the spectre of Lizzy's story hung over us like the sword of Damocles. I found myself one afternoon dozing off in an armchair thinking of dear, sweet Lizzy. Had we really become a bunch of co-conspirators in a dastardly cover-up, or was Stanley really Alec Guinness in *The Ladykillers* and Lizzy really Mrs. Wilberforce?

Just at that moment Harold said, "Wake up, Charles. I need to talk to you."

"Not about Lizzy, I hope?"

"No, we agreed not to mention that. No, this is closer to home."

"Okay, what's the problem?" I muttered, still half asleep.

Harold looked thoughtful. "It's about Audrey. I know you and Audrey are quite close and I don't want to do the wrong thing, but do you think there's any room there for me?"

I was well and truly caught off guard and simply said the first thing that sprang into my mind, saying, "Oh! No. I've no claim upon Audrey."

Harold seemed to be delighted with my response.

"Sorry to wake you," and he was off!

I just sat there, suddenly aware that my pathetic response

might have been a disaster. Just how serious was Harold? Had I just made one of those life-changing decisions without even realising it? Why did I say that? But just as I was reaffirming the depth of my stupidity, Lizzy appeared with a cup of tea.

"I thought you looked as if you needed a cup of tea, dear," she said.

The contents of the saucer poured into my lap. Just as I was thanking Lizzy for what she'd done for me, Bill and Stanley appeared. They took one look at me and burst into laughter. I had to admit that my situation was farcical, as indeed it often is, and so I soon saw the funny side of it, and we all laughed together. We chatted and laughed some more before setting off to prepare for dinner.

Stanley was on top form that evening, devouring his Glenmorangie 10-year-old with more than his usual relish while entertaining us with another of his anecdotes.

On this occasion, it was one from his long list of convent disasters. His order of nuns had called him out in great urgency when their roof started leaking. Stanley had previously inspected the roof and had pronounced it to be in admirable condition. For the nuns, he was second only to the Pope in terms of infallibility and so, to them, the water cascading down from the ceiling could only have been some perverse act of God. Stanley agreed with them, saying that he would have a word! The evening was off to a great start, as we made our way to the restaurant in high spirits except, that is, for Harold, who appeared rather preoccupied.

Unfortunately, Stanley chose the mediocre house red again, and indicated that Bill should order it. My heart sank a little at the prospect of yet another house red.

However, I managed somehow to say, "Good choice, Stanley."

Our meal was a delight, as was our conversation, again except for Harold, who remained preoccupied. We finished our main courses and were contemplating the arrival of our desserts when he rose to his feet. He tapped on his glass to gain our attention, which in turn gained the attention of everyone else in the restaurant.

"I've got something I need to say, and I think I need to say it to all of you," he said.

Audrey however, thought differently.

"Don't be ridiculous, Harold, sit down, everyone's looking at you!"

Harold did indeed look a little silly, so he sat back down. The restaurant fell silent in anticipation.

He composed himself, saying, "I've got a bit of a problem, and I've been to see the MO."

Lizzy piped up, "Oh dear, I hope it's nothing serious."

"No, it's nothing like that. I just keep getting these obsessive thoughts."

Bill stopped Harold in full flow.

"Sounds like PTSD Harold. I'm not surprised, with all you've been through."

Harold was clearly getting frustrated with all the interruptions but tried again.

"No, you've got it all wrong. The thing is, I wake up in the morning and it's the first thing on my mind, and when I go to sleep, it's always the last thing on my mind, and to be honest it's the same thing on my mind for most of the day. As you know, I'm not usually very sensitive about these things, but the MO seemed to know what it is."

We were still thinking along the lines of PTSD and so Stanley asked, "Is it the young lad in Uganda haunting you?"

Lizzy said, "Very serious, this STD."

I was trying to explain to Lizzy that STD was a sexually transmitted disease when Harold's frustration boiled over. He raised his voice and thumped his glass down on the table, spilling some of its contents.

"For God's sake, let me get on with it! It's Audrey!" he blurted out in a loud voice. "If you would all just stop interrupting me, I'm trying to tell you I wake up thinking about Audrey, I go to sleep thinking about Audrey. I can't bloody well stop thinking about Audrey!"

Normally the restaurant has a background clatter of cutlery on plates mixed with conversation, but not so now; it was silent. I think Lizzy was still concerned about the sexually transmitted disease and asked what the Doc had said. Harold looked very serious.

"I told the MO, and he said it was an easy diagnosis. I'm in love."

Audrey said, "Oh Harold!"

I said, "Oh my God!"

Someone in the restaurant said, "Well done, Harold!" Then she started clapping, which of course prompted everyone else to do the same, even I ended up clapping. It was a surreal moment. Audrey had her arms around Harold, and I was sitting there applauding! How on earth had things come to this?

We managed to calm down and gradually the restaurant came back to life, somewhat helped by the arrival of our desserts. It was a kind of normality, but this was a new normality. Audrey didn't say very much. I suspected she was bowled over but, just as we were leaving the table, I heard her say to Harold.

"That was the most romantic speech I've ever heard, thank you."

They left hand in hand, and Harold quite rightly had a broad smile on his face. We made our way into the lounge.

"First round is on me," Harold said.

"I'll have a single malt." Stanley replied.

"I'll have what he's having. Stanley, I mean." There was a smile from Bill who'd spotted my Freudian slip.

Harold returned with the drinks and sat next to Audrey. Stanley sat in his usual chair with Bill and Lizzy to his left, so this left me in the middle.

Stanley raised his glass of Highland Park 12-year-old to his lips and offered a toast to Audrey and Harold. For my part, I wasn't quite sure that Audrey had yet committed to this arrangement, but I wouldn't be the one to spoil the occasion.

"Well done, Harold, here's to both of you!" I said.

Stanley then took command of the gathering simply by sniffing his glass. We all knew this procedure would be followed by a pronouncement about the whisky, and dutifully sat waiting for his verdict.

"Ah yes, I can feel the waves gently lapping against the shoreline of Orkney and smell the peat from the island water. Now, tell me about your early upbringing, Charles."

Audrey then said, "Yes, come on, Charles, do tell us."

The others looked on expectantly, as I tried to make excuses, telling them they would find my life extremely uninteresting and that I would be a huge disappointment to them, but they were having none of it. I found myself trapped like a sacrificial lamb.

"Okay," I said. "I was born in Bristol, and I lived on an estate there."

Lizzy immediately asked, "Oh how nice; was it like Audrey's estate in Oxfordshire?"

"Very similar, except it was owned by the council and we didn't have a gamekeeper!"

Everyone thought that was very funny, which seemed to take a bit of the pressure off me.

"What about education, Charles?" asked Stanley.

"What about it?"

Stanley was obviously not content with that comment and I wished that I hadn't said it. I explained that I went to a secondary modern school, leaving there when I was sixteen to get a job as an apprentice bricklayer. I thought everyone would think the worse of me for not having had much of an education but, if they thought it, they certainly didn't show it.

Stanley seemed content with that and asked where my career in bricklaying progressed. I had a sneaky idea that no-one in this place had the remotest interest in bricklaying, so I tried to brush over that. I just explained how I ended up working for a small building firm in Bristol. The company did extensions, garages, loft conversions, that kind of thing.

At this point I told them again that they would find my life uninteresting, and it was likely to be more of the same, but they seemed to want me to continue.

"Now dear boy, tell me about the next important milestone in your life."

"Well, I suppose the next milestone was meeting my wife, but that was more of a millstone!"

My attempt at light-hearted banter failed miserably, so I continued, describing how I met Ann at the local bowling alley, and it was at a time when all my mates had steady girl-friends and wives. I suspect that subconsciously I was feeling pressure to do the same.

We went out together for a few months and I decided that it was probably not a good idea, so we split up. Annie was not content with this and insisted upon going to the places where I'd be, and generally not letting it go. I didn't find anyone else and eventually I suppose I was beginning to think that it might be Annie or nothing, so we ended up getting back together.

It was all quite ridiculous really. We were both only twenty-four years old, hardly the age for me to be thinking that my life chances had passed me by.

The next thing I knew, we were getting married, and to this day I can't explain how that happened. Even on the wedding day I had serious doubts, but inexplicably I went ahead.

Stanley sipped his Highland Park 12-year old.

"You wouldn't be the first person to go into a marriage with doubts, dear boy."

His expression made it clear that he well understood my position. This reassured me to a degree; it isn't easy admitting your mistakes, especially enormous ones.

Stanley continued, "So when did you realise it was a mistake?"

I hadn't admitted yet that it was a mistake but, as always, Stanley seemed to be one step ahead. I answered him saying that there was a specific moment when I knew all was lost, but that was a few years into the future.

Stanley looked over his glasses directly at me with an expression that told me we had a common understanding.

"Tell me old boy, how did you arrive at that point?"

It hadn't taken long for me to realise that all was not well. Harold asked me how long.

"About five or six hours." I replied.

I knew I wasn't going to be able to leave it at that, so I explained. We had a blazing row at our wedding reception. It was perfectly true that I was drunk. Who doesn't drink too much at their wedding? But Annie's reaction was out of all proportion to the situation. I was also accused of making advances towards one of the female guests, which was a complete nonsense.

The disconcerting thing from my perspective was the depth of bitterness and loathing that was directed towards me. It was incomprehensible and frankly a bit frightening, especially on your wedding day.

Stanley sipped his Highland Park while gazing momentarily towards the heavens, drawing a deep intake of breath which he then exhaled as a sigh. The look on his face said it all as far as I was concerned.

"Tell me old boy, did that event set the scene for the rest of your marriage?"

I reached for my own glass of Highland Park, as I confirmed that the events at the wedding reception were to repeat themselves throughout the marriage.

Audrey looked quite shocked.

"Why did you continue with it? Surely you knew it was a mistake?"

I had to agree. and knew they would all want to know why I hadn't walked away. I also knew that if I didn't understand it myself, then it was obvious that they certainly wouldn't!

Stanley, however, seemed to intuitively understand because he diverted me away from the subject.

"Tell us about your career, old boy. I suspect you didn't spend the rest of your life laying bricks."

I was pleased to get away from talking about the marriage, if only for a moment. I said that after we'd been married for three years, we managed to buy our first house and, although financially it wasn't a good time, I decided to start my own building business. It was a little reckless because we immediately went six months into arrears with the mortgage repayments and, in order to remain solvent, I was working fifteen hours a day, seven days a week.

Stanley adopted one of his all-knowing looks.

"I suppose all that put a lot of extra strain on the marriage?"

I had to admit life at that time was incredibly difficult, but I was now learning first-hand how Stanley, having just turned the smallest corner of a page, would then go on to gradually prise the book open and reveal its contents.

"I think I can imagine how difficult that was but, tell me old boy, how did those problems manifest themselves?"

I described a typical day where I was trying to balance the need to speak to potential clients, provide them with estimates, supervise various tradesmen who were working for me, and deal with administration.

All the while I was doing that, I also had to carry out the bricklaying or carpentry or whatever else it was which required doing. Come the end of a fifteen-hour day, I was shattered. I had to admit that my first requirement when I got home was a glass of whisky.

It was a regular occurrence in situations like this that Annie would suddenly change character. She'd accuse me of being so late because I had been womanising, and that I was a drunk. It was desperately difficult to deal with; there were times when being a drunk sounded like an attractive alternative.

Stanley looked concerned for me.

"Charles needs another drink, Bill, and I'll have a single malt."

Everyone smiled, as we always did by now, and Bill dutifully set off in pursuit of another round.

While we waited, Stanley entertained us with another of his anecdotes.

On this occasion, it was his battle with and subsequent loss of what was probably the largest salmon ever hooked by an angler in the entire history of the River Wye.

Stanley's anecdotes usually made me smile, but this time I was more attentive to the body language between Audrey and Harold. Both were my wonderful friends, and I was genuinely pleased for them, although it would have been difficult for me to tell them that through my gritted teeth!

Bill returned with another round including two glasses of whisky.

Stanley nosed the glass, saying immediately, "You must know what this is, Charles?"

I took a sip and said I thought it must be an Islay whisky; so much peat.

Stanley was pleased with me.

"Absolutely right, dear boy; it can only be one of the 'Holy Trinity' from South East Islay. It must be the Lagavulin 16-year old."

I confess, although I was a lifelong whisky drinker, Stanley had opened a secret door for me, and I was enjoying my whisky more than ever, something which I could see Stanley was delighted about.

Despite the diversion, I was quickly brought back to the story in hand. Stanley was determined to find out more about my relationship with Annie. I'd no option but to admit that my marriage was by now a disaster.

I was working all hours and we both drank to excess. The difference was that I only drank in the evening, while Annie would already be drunk by the time I got home. I became more concerned about this when I found a huge pile of empty bottles by the bins. These were not wine or whisky bottles, they were bottles of cheap vodka.

The first problem with alcoholism is how to recognise it, and the second is to understand it. The difficulty is that all of one's initial perceptions will almost certainly be wrong. I'd obviously missed these obvious signs, but now I was becoming concerned.

It was about this time that Annie announced she was pregnant, which was a complete shock to me. As far as I was concerned, this must have been an immaculate conception because we had virtually no sex life.

However, we both dealt with the situation. Annie did control her drinking and, by the time Sally was born, I had expanded the business with a small team of full-time employees and, probably best of all, I now had a secretary, Sylvia, who was simply brilliant. My hours reduced a little and at least I didn't have to work every weekend.

I'd naturally hoped that the baby might bring us together, but it only made matters dramatically worse. Everyone seemed concerned for me at this revelation, but especially Audrey.

"You have to tell us, Charles. How did this all get worse?"

I had my suspicions that Annie was back on the bottle soon after Sally's birth, and this came to a head with an incident which I regarded as the real turning point. It was when I finally realised that Annie was an alcoholic.

It had been the first occasion after Sally was born when we had my parents over to babysit so we could go out to a friend's for dinner, along with some other guests. Annie had argued all evening, making me and everyone else feel very uncomfortable but, while she was obviously drunk, she didn't look any more drunk than usual. This, however, isn't an observation you can make of an alcoholic. During the meal, she was ranting on unintelligibly when suddenly she just passed out and flopped forward, face first into her meal.

"Can you imagine the reaction of our hosts and the other guests?" I said. "I'd never been so embarrassed and humiliated in my life!"

Audrey looked horrified, saying, "What on earth did you do?"

I did what I ended up doing on innumerable occasions after that night; I carried her to the car, got her home, carried her to the bathroom, washed and changed her like a baby, and put her to bed.

"Oh, my goodness!" Audrey said.

Stanley commented, "I understand alcoholics exist in a dark place. I suppose you came to understand that?"

I agreed with Stanley. I found myself in a world of unspeakable misery.

I described how the condition is so counterintuitive that nothing can prepare you for it. Perhaps the alcoholic brings a personality disorder to the alcohol, or perhaps the alcohol brings the personality disorder to the alcoholic. The result, however, is always the same. Alcoholics do suffer altered brain chemistry, and it's probably not by chance that they generally seem to share a very similar approach to the outside world.

The typical condition is denial, but it goes far beyond denial of their alcoholism. It essentially involves denial of blame. In other words, responsibility for their grotesque behaviour is always projected onto someone or something else. Nearly always, this will be the spouse or a parent.

This situation is far more sinister than it sounds because, to satisfy the needs of the alcoholic, they must create an alternative reality which for them is totally real. Within that alternative reality, roles are often reversed, and typically the spouse or parent is demonised as the cause of all wrongs.

Stanley adopted his sympathetic expression again.

"How did this affect your relationship with your child?"

"It was a disaster," I replied.

I knew from experience that it was difficult for people to

understand my situation, and tried to explain that, within Annie's alternative reality, I was a monster. I had driven her to drink. When I had to physically control her, I was being 'violent' towards her, and when I tried to prevent her from making a fool of herself, I was trying to 'mentally control and manipulate' her.

I suggested they try to see the situation from within Annie's alternative perspective. How can a violent, controlling man possibly be a loving father, when he has driven you to drink? Your baby would have to be protected from him. The problem with that situation is that you only really understand it at the end of the process, not at the beginning, so dealing with it had become my worst nightmare.

Stanley, and indeed everyone, looked quite concerned for me, but it was Stanley who asked the obvious question.

"How *did* you deal with it?"

It's probably quite impossible to convey to anyone else just what my life was like at that time. It was essentially like a roller-coaster, where rock bottom is an unbelievably dark place, but then we would slowly climb back up the gradient to something resembling normality, which was always followed by the sudden steep descent back to the bottom.

I was never quite sure if the mental torment came from the glimpse of normality at the top of the incline, or from the descent into hell on the other side. Typically, I would get home from work never knowing which stage of the roller-coaster I was entering. Annie might appear to be bright and cheerful; we would appear to an outsider to be a perfectly normal couple.

This situation could last for days or even weeks but then, with no obvious trigger, Annie's alter ego would simply take over in a second. I'd know without a word being spoken. There was a certain look in her eyes. The alternative reality was there inside, looking out.

Audrey appeared to be particularly concerned. "This sounds terrible Charles! When these changes occurred, what happened?"

The alter ego loathed me. I might go as far as to say it hated me. There was another significant occasion when we'd gone out for the day to a country fair with another couple, two of our diminishing number of friends. Annie had sniped at me all day about my advances towards the other woman, advances which didn't exist. She drank constantly from her water bottle, which no doubt contained vodka, not water, and eventually the situation exploded into a torrent of abuse directed towards me.

The other couple were horrified, especially the woman, who took the accusations all terribly personally. She slapped Annie around the face who then responded by punching her on the nose. We were standing by one of the display tents and the poor woman fell over and landed on one of the tent pegs. She had a bleeding nose and a badly bruised rib which we all assumed was broken. There was an ambulance and paramedics. The police were involved, it was a total disaster. Obviously, we didn't see that couple again! It was just as likely to be me on the receiving end of one of these attacks.

"How on earth did you put up with it?" Harold asked me.

It's very difficult to explain to an outsider why someone like me continues in such a role. It's partly due to a sense of responsibility, but strangely it's also the perverse hope which is generated while the roller-coaster is going up the incline. Those glimpses of normality are probably the most cruel aspect. The other significant reason was that Annie was pregnant again.

I'd been particularly shocked and annoyed at this news because, assuming the child was mine, which is the kind of thing you think when your wife is an alcoholic, it was either another immaculate conception or it could only be as a result of a deliberately timed seduction. To intentionally bring another child into our circumstances was more than just irresponsible.

Of course, my reaction only reinforced her belief that I was a ghastly father. There were two redeeming aspects to this. Annie did lay off the drink for a while, and Debbie is simply beautiful.

By now, I could see that I had single-handedly managed to depress everyone, but quite suddenly I could also understand what they had all been telling me about letting go of my burden. The sordid details of my life with an alcoholic were excruciatingly embarrassing.

It had taken all of Stanley's considerable powers to encourage me to turn that first page but, having done so, it did feel as if I was letting it go. They all sympathised with me, and so I decided I might as well tell them about the other side of the coin.

Chapter Seventeen
JOANNA

I reminded them again that they would find my life depressing and perhaps now they might believe me. Then I added that there was one all too brief but exciting interval during my marriage. Stanley, of course, jumped upon the suggestion.

"Oh, come along now, Charles, tell us all."

"Yes, Charles, do tell us," said Audrey.

And so the story about Joanna began. It was three years after Debbie was born, I was just at one of those periods when the roller-coaster was at the bottom of the dip. I had an estimate to do for a couple in Bath. The address was very prestigious, and they wanted an extension to what was already a very large house. I duly arrived at the address to be greeted by a pleasant enough chap who proceeded to show me what he wanted. As we were going over the details, I couldn't help but notice some professional photographs of a beautiful woman on some of the walls.

One particularly caught my eye, the front cover of Vogue magazine with this same woman wearing a red dress. As I gazed at the image, a woman came into the room. Despite the old jeans and gardening gloves, it was immediately obvious that she was the lady in the photographs. The chap, whose name I now completely forget, introduced me to his wife. This was the moment when I first met Joanna.

I turned to look at her as she walked across the room and it was as if time stood still. She was casually dressed in old jeans, trainers and a loose t-shirt, her long blonde hair tied back loosely to reveal every detail of her exquisitely beautiful face. Her lips were full and created a permanent broad smile framing her perfect teeth. She was still wearing sunglasses with a tiny heart engraved in the top corner.

As she approached me, she reached up and removed them. I followed her hand and momentarily noticed her delicate diamond earrings, but as soon as our eyes met, I could look nowhere else. She offered me her hand, but I was transfixed by those incredible eyes. It was perhaps several seconds before I reached for her outstretched hand.

Obviously, I should have shaken her hand in a business-like fashion, but I just stood there, with her hand in mine, motionless, staring into those hazel eyes. I observed every detail. The eyeliner which accentuated the shape, the eyelashes that seemed to brush against her cheek, but most of all it was the contrast with those hazel irises and the white of her eyes. The effect was mesmerising. I suddenly realised that I was in imminent danger of making a complete fool of myself. I simply couldn't take my eyes off her.

After what felt like an eternity, Joanna said, "Hello, Charlie."

Moments later she removed her hand from mine, and this was enough to encourage reality to seep back into my world. I was flustered for a moment. I felt like a competition ice skater who'd just had a nasty fall and now had to continue as if nothing had happened. I found myself blathering on about the extension, how wonderful it was going to be, and why we were exactly the right people to build it for them. All the while, my full concentration was focused upon Joanna and those eyes.

She turned away from me to place her sunglasses onto a

table, moving with the elegance of a ballet dancer. I noticed how she brushed aside a waft of blonde hair from her forehead with the graceful movement of a single finger, and still there was that broad smile.

Her husband suggested that she should go and make us a cup of tea. Perhaps he was aware of my drooling over his wife. In any event, it was a good idea. I had to try to concentrate upon the job in hand! I looked at the proposed extension and took all the measurements I needed. We discussed the details, and, for a while at least, I behaved as a builder should. Then Joanna returned carrying a tray, floating across the room as if she was balancing a book upon her head.

As she placed the tray on the side table, her t-shirt dropped off her shoulder to reveal the strap of her bra. What should have been an inconsequential moment immediately became a terribly erotic moment for me. I suddenly realised I was making a complete fool of myself. I needed to get out of there in order to salvage whatever vestige of credibility I might have left. I hastily drank my tea and left.

All the way back to the yard in the car, I relived the experience over and over. Sure, I was a sex-starved young man and sure, I was drooling over an incredibly attractive woman. What sex-starved young man wouldn't? I tried to normalise the situation in my mind. She was without doubt the most attractive woman I had ever seen up close and so, naturally, I had drooled. It might have been an unedifying spectacle but surely I could just blame it on the testosterone? Then I thought about the incredibly erotic bra strap; how pathetic was that? It wasn't as if I had a lingerie fetish; my experience of bras was one of scraping vomit off them! I arrived back at the yard and tried to put the incident behind me.

I sipped my whisky with a sense of urgency, which Stanley of course noticed immediately, asking if I needed another one. I said I really shouldn't for now, and I'd best just get on with it. I continued, admitting that I priced the extension at a ludicrously cheap price in order to guarantee that I would get the job!

Stanley leaped upon this admission.

"Why do I get the feeling, Charles, that you've just unveiled the tip of an iceberg?"

I didn't feel half as awkward talking about Joanna as I did about my marriage, and so I answered, "That's because like an iceberg, 90% of it is hidden from view!"

I continued the story and confirmed that I did indeed get the job. It was a few weeks before the actual job started but, when it did, I found myself rushing to the house on day one, only to discover to my profound disappointment that they'd gone on holiday while the work was being done! They didn't come back until the job was nearly finished.

I wasn't there when they arrived back, but when one of the painters came back to the office he said, "The owners are back; you should see that bloke's wife! Bloody hell, what a cracker she is!"

I tried to look uninterested. "Oh, yes," I said, but the next day, I was there first thing, on the pretence of a final inspection!

The husband answered the door and we went over the extension together. He was apparently delighted with the result but if truth be told I wasn't really listening. I wanted to see Joanna again, just to confirm that I hadn't been hallucinating! I waited for her to appear, but she didn't, and when I could think of nothing else to talk about in order to extend my visit, I left, totally crestfallen. Eventually I managed to put the whole ridiculous episode behind me, but I could never actually forget her. I tried to convince myself that she was an unobtainable figment of my imagination, so I considered it to be a harmless preoccupation.

Three months went by and we still hadn't received our final payment for the work. Sylvia had pushed the client to the point where alarm bells had now started to ring. She was sure there was a problem, and I always trusted her judgement. I decided to go and see them before we completely fell out over it. Joanna had apparently telephoned to make an appointment and I duly arrived as arranged, feeling pensive. There's nothing like someone refusing to pay an invoice to focus your attention! I was expecting the husband to answer the door, but it was the sight of Joanna which greeted me. She caught me completely by surprise and no doubt I started to blather.

She reached forward, taking hold of my arm.

"Come in, Charlie, I need to talk to you."

We went into the new extension. It was apparent that the husband wasn't there, and we sat down. She looked really upset and I asked what the problem was. I could see she was holding back tears, and this really distressed me as well.

"He's lost everything," she sobbed.

"When you say lost everything, do you really mean *everything?*" I asked.

"That's exactly what I mean, he's gambled it all away. I had no idea how bad it was until it had all gone."

She told me what had happened, in what amounted to a torrent of pent-up emotion. It seemed that she had indeed lost everything, including her marriage. I asked her what she intended to do, and she took me completely by surprise.

"I just need a nice man that I can talk to. You look like a nice man, Charlie; take me out to lunch."

I didn't know if I was coming or going! I simply agreed. We decided on the local Italian restaurant as it was only a short drive away. Joanna was dressed casually like the last time I had met her, but her hair was now down in a golden cascade that touched her shoulders. As we entered the restaurant, which apparently is popular with local business types, I couldn't help but notice that every man in there stopped in his tracks and gazed at Joanna. Such a beautiful woman must be used to this kind of reception wherever she went. What felt unreal was that she was with *me!*

We talked as if we'd known each other for forever, and she

told me the full story about her husband, who was obviously a blithering idiot. They had been very well off, supported by his family's business, but what Joanna hadn't realised was that he was a gambling addict. She had no idea exactly how he lost it all, but she suspected that it just disappeared, hundreds if not thousands of pounds at a time.

The final straw was when the family business disowned him. She gave up a successful career as a fashion model when they married, and now her career was gone, along with everything else. She was absolutely devastated by the experience, and the more she talked about it, the more distressed she became. I asked about her childhood, attempting to change the subject.

Joanna said her family were quite ordinary working-class, but they made great sacrifices to pay for her to have a private education. It was quite apparent to me that she had benefited greatly from that education, and I admired the fact that her parents' sacrifices were so appreciated. Despite her current problems, she was obviously well grounded.

She asked me about my childhood, and I said that I came from a not dissimilar background to her, but while she had metamorphosed into a beautiful and sophisticated butterfly, sadly I'd remained a caterpillar! She laughed, and I was pleased to see a smile return to her face. We talked endlessly while I hung on to her every word. Eventually I plucked up the courage to tell her that I was married. I had no idea why this required courage. I remember thinking Joanna would never look seriously upon me. What difference would a wife make? Her answer however, surprised me, as a cheeky smile appeared on her face.

"Thank heavens for that! I don't want to marry you, Charlie!"

It felt as though only five minutes had elapsed but we suddenly realised that the restaurant was empty, and we were being encouraged to leave. I drove her home in the realisation that it wouldn't be her home for very much longer. It seemed obvious that I wouldn't see the many thousands of pounds which they owed me, but at that moment I couldn't care less. In fact, the thought barely crossed my mind!

We arrived at the house and Joanna said she'd love to continue our conversation, but she was already two hours late with an arrangement to see her parents. I found myself in one of those awkward teenage moments. I'd only known this woman for a matter of hours, but somehow it didn't seem appropriate that we should just shake hands. Alternatively, I certainly shouldn't kiss her. I decided that the gesture of a momentary kiss on the cheek would be the appropriate course of action.

Joanna, however, had no such reservations, saying without the slightest hesitation, "I was right about you, Charlie, you're a nice man."

With that she put one hand behind my head and stared directly into my eyes as she drew me towards her. As our lips met, a sensation ran through my mind and body that I shall never forget. I wanted it to continue forever, but inevitably it had to end. Joanna reluctantly pulled back, her hazel eyes widening as she looked deeply into my eyes.

"Wow! Charlie Bartlett, where did that come from?"

I had no answer. I was literally dumbstruck. Joanna sat there for a few moments, as we just looked at each other. For my part, this was the only thing I was able to do, but she was apparently deep in thought.

Eventually she said, "I've got to go, Charlie. I've got to start a new life."

With that she stepped out of the car and just walked away.

Every fibre of my body wanted to shout after her, but what could I have said? 'Hey! Why not start a new life with me? I've got an alcoholic wife and two lovely daughters we could share.'

Perhaps not! Perhaps I should just get on with my own life instead.

I hadn't noticed that I was showing such emotion, but Audrey said, "Well done, Charles. I can see what Joanna still means to you."

Bill was much more concise, as he put his hand on my shoulder and simply said, "I know."

Lizzy was asleep. I had obviously bored her into submission.

Stanley looked at Lizzy and said, "I think we should all call it a night, especially you Charles; you need your sleep, so you can continue your story tomorrow!"

So, we all left together, Audrey and Harold hand in hand, while the rest of us each went off in our different directions.

Chapter Eighteen
POPPIES HOTEL

Once back in my apartment, I tried to put those memories from so long ago firmly back into their box. Inevitably the box leaked, as one by one they came tumbling back out. I found myself once again torn between the indescribable ecstasy of that first kiss, and the abject misery that I would probably never experience it ever again. It was the two sides of the Devil's coin.

Quite naturally, the music of the period formed the backdrop to my memories and *Three Times A Lady* drifted through my mind. I slept badly, inevitably rising early, almost welcoming the opportunity to continue my story with my friends. As the others had suggested, it had become like an exorcism and, although I needed to be free of my malevolent spirit, I knew I would never let her go!

We met for breakfast and chatted just as usual, but now that I'd taken the lid off the box, my mind had little room for anything else. It made me appreciate even more that this was the same process the others had gone through. I admired them all for their courage, and I knew they would help me. Stanley wound up the breakfast proceedings saying we should decant ourselves into the lounge without further ado, so that I could continue my story.

Just as we were leaving, Puffer got up from his table and we crossed paths heading for the lounge.

"How are you Puffer?" Harold asked.

Puffer did look a bit under the weather, but that's really a relative term. Puffer always looked under the weather. I guess sixty fags a day does that to a man! We waited for his passing joke and he did try, but the coughing was relentless, and we lost patience.

Harold quickly said, "Tell us that one next time," and we went on our way. As soon as we sat down, Stanley went through his customary preparations, and the conductor looked up towards the orchestra as if to say, 'Are we ready?'

Before he could raise his baton, Audrey said, "Carry on, Charles, you'd just left Joanna at her house."

I smiled at Stanley's slightly peeved expression and continued, saying that I drove back to the yard but had no memory of doing so. I just kept reliving that kiss. I simply couldn't fathom what had just happened to me, it was all so much more than just a kiss. Joanna was by far the most beautiful woman I had ever seen, let alone kissed. But there was something else, a kind of inexplicable connection.

When I arrived at the yard, I was still just as confused as when I set off. The only thing clear to me was that this woman filled my senses, and the memory of her was going nowhere. There were innumerable things which I needed to do, having been out for several hours, but again I have no memory of any of it. I told Sylvia that the debt was very unlikely ever to be paid. She was furious, saying she would instigate proceedings immediately. When I calmly said it was just water under the bridge and to forget it, she looked at me as if I had lost my mind. Perhaps I had!

I arrived home about 7.30 to find that Annie, or rather Annie's alter ego, was waiting for me. She was sure that I'd been with another woman but, then again, she was always sure I had been with another woman! For the first time, of course, she was right, and I was consumed with guilt. Did I smell of Joanna's perfume? Had I kept the restaurant bill? Did I have lipstick on my face? Had anyone seen me? I was the opposite of a seasoned philanderer and so these guilty fears filled my mind. I had no idea how to deal with this situation, but gradually I realised Annie was drunk and her accusations were just the norm. However, it opened my eyes to a whole new and hitherto unknown world of guilt, and it didn't rest easily with me.

Stanley was unmoved.

"Did you ever get to see Joanna again?"

I smiled because I knew that they'd all already made up their minds.

"Yes, I did," I said, and went on to tell them the story.

It was about a year later. I hadn't forgotten Joanna; how could I? But her memory was becoming pleasurable rather than tormenting and so, when Sylvia said she'd arranged an appointment with a Mr. Wilson to view a new development, the last person I expected to see was Joanna! I duly attended, to find an open building plot, and a couple sitting waiting in a Mercedes. Joanna stepped out of the car, and the shock of seeing her again so unexpectedly made my pulse race.

She introduced me to the man, George Wilson. He was considerably older than Joanna. He said he wanted a new house built on this plot and that Joanna had told him that I was the best builder for the job. We walked around the site and all the while Joanna had her arm in his. They were obviously a couple, but I guessed that they weren't married. A part of me was still thinking about that kiss in the car, but the other much more sensible part concentrated on the job.

We went over the architect's drawings. They were both excited at the prospect of what I assumed was going to be their new home together. After my last financial encounter with Joanna, I had the office check out Mr. Wilson. All seemed well, in fact this man turned out to be the MD of a multinational company, so I went ahead. My business had expanded quite a bit by now and when we did finally get the contract to build this house, most of it went ahead without my involvement.

I attended the site occasionally. On one of those visits, Joanna was there by herself, and we talked together for quite a while. She looked fabulous, and I had to consciously try not to drool! I think I largely succeeded, but every time she looked at me, she smiled, and her wonderful hazel eyes were saying something completely different to what her mouth was saying. Joanna could only ever look beautiful, but as our conversation about the house ended, her expression changed, her face suddenly lit up with a radiant smile.

"Take me out to lunch, Charlie. I still need a nice man to talk to."

I had desperately wanted to suggest the same thing, but I had convinced myself that it would be totally inappropriate. When she suggested it, my enthusiasm was probably embarrassingly obvious. I hastily directed her towards my car, and we were soon sitting in the local pub where I marvelled at every detail of her. I tried so hard not to look into her eyes, but it was hopeless, so I then tried hard instead to convince myself that it was Joanna who was staring into mine but, obviously, why would she do that?

We talked without a moment's silence. I was right that she wasn't married to Mr. Wilson, but she said that she intended to be, telling me about their plans. There appeared to be no great enthusiasm in her voice, or was it just that I didn't want to hear it? I can't remember anything about our lunch. I was only aware that time was running out and I desperately didn't want my second visit to paradise to end. Perhaps there might be one more dream to come true?

We looked at the time and reluctantly I drove her back to where her car was parked, my only thought being that just maybe I might get to kiss her one more time. I parked and found myself babbling nervously as we walked towards her car.

The moment we stopped next to the vehicle, Joanna placed a finger against my lips as if to say, 'Stop babbling, you fool,' which of course made me feel even more foolish. She looked at me and a wonderful smile slowly spread across her face.

"Kiss me, Charlie," she said softly.

My self-esteem probably demanded that I shouldn't broadcast quite so obviously that I was smitten by this woman, but it was a lost cause. I threw myself into her arms and we kissed. This was no ordinary kiss; for me this was an expression of something far more significant. This time I wasn't just the recipient, I held her tightly in my arms. I felt her body against mine, breathing in her perfume as if I was consuming her. After the most sublime few moments, she pulled away.

"Oh, Charlie. If only."

My mind was racing in all directions. Had I made a fool of myself leaping into her arms like that? Had I done the right thing? Said the right thing? Joanna stood for a moment looking into my eyes. She held my hand for a brief second, then opened the door and stepped into her car.

She looked almost sad as she said, "It's been lovely, Charlie," and with that she was gone.

I was left to wonder, 'if only' *what?* Once again, I had my journey back to the yard to relive every second of our brief encounter and, like last time, I could understand none of it. We had just kissed like two long separated lovers, and yet she was no more than a client who was just about to marry dreary old Mr Wilson. Try as I may, I couldn't rationalise any of it, but I couldn't stop trying.

I wasn't sure if Stanley and the others wanted to laugh or cry. I was besotted by her, that much at least was clear but, as I was telling my friends the story, I was only too aware how foolish it all must have sounded.

Stanley appeared to empathise with me.

"Did you have any real indication that Joanna felt the same as you did?"

I had to admit that she remained a total mystery. Perhaps I just imagined what those eyes were telling me. I could find no answers other than the unavoidable reality that exotic creatures like Joanna didn't exist in my world. I was a bricklayer, what possible appeal could I have for her?

The house development was completed, but I never saw Joanna there again. Even after several months, there wouldn't be a day when I didn't think about her. I used to occasionally drive past the new house in the hope of catching just a glimpse of her, but I never did.

Stanley gave me one of his understanding looks, as if to say 'You're not the first man to behave like an idiot!'

I suspected that they all felt I'd been a fool, but Audrey especially could see how significant it had been for me.

"I'm sorry it was never to be. I suppose you didn't see her again?"

I smiled and said, "Not exactly."

There was a little bit more to the story. I told them it must have been about nine or ten months later when Sylvia called through to me from her desk.

She said in her usual efficient voice, "There's a lady on the phone for you, says it's a personal call."

I immediately thought, as I often did, that just maybe this might be a call from Joanna, except that this time it was! I just knew instantly that she wanted to see me. She didn't have to ask, I just knew.

We talked pleasantries for a few minutes, and I astounded myself by saying, "It sounds to me as if you need a nice man to take you out to lunch."

"You're right, Charlie. That's why I called you."

We arranged to meet in two hours' time, as if that was perfectly normal. I had completely forgotten an important business lunch, which was why I was standing there in my best suit. Sylvia reminded me of the meeting and my heart sank. What a disaster! She could see the panic I was in and, bless her, she obviously knew it was all about the voice on the phone.

"Go on. I'll sort it out for you," she insisted.

I did something I had never done before. I rushed around her desk and kissed her on both cheeks.

She was very embarrassed.

"Oh, for goodness sake! I just hope you know what you're doing!"

As I drove away her words echoed in my mind. Did I know what I was doing?

I walked into the pub to see Joanna sitting alone at a corner table; she was clearly not her usual bubbly self, but the moment she saw me, her eyes lit up. Smiling, she looked me up and down, and it dawned on me that she'd never seen me dressed in anything smart before, let alone a suit.

"Wow, Charlie, you clean up well!" she said. "You look gorgeous!"

I hoped it was a compliment because nobody had ever said I looked gorgeous before! It didn't quite sound right! She started to tell me that the relationship with Wilson hadn't worked out, and she'd never actually moved into the new house we'd built. I said how terribly sorry I was to hear that, but all the while I was thinking, 'Thank God.' As if it had anything to do with me!

We talked non-stop for a couple of hours, but I began to feel that I'd taken up the role of a close girl-friend of hers, someone in whom she could confide without any embarrassment or repercussion. She was now living somewhere in Marlborough, though she didn't tell me where, and I rather got the impression that perhaps she had a new relationship, although she never actually said as much. I was never a part of Joanna's life; our worlds simply brushed together before she moved on again. This was always our reality but, in this situation, I felt she was more at arm's length than ever before.

It was as if she was standing on the deck of a cruise liner, flashing her beautiful eyes and confiding in me as I stood on the quayside. The mooring ropes were stowed, and she was about to embark on a cruise to some exotic place. I couldn't reach out for her even if I wanted too. I was no less besotted with her, but the hopelessness of my situation seemed more glaringly obvious than ever.

Joanna was quite unlike anyone I'd ever met before, both deeply mysterious and yet open and forthright at the same time. I'd no idea where she went or what she did outside those brief moments when our lives came together. Not only did I not know, I somehow knew that I wasn't supposed to know. What I could understand even less was how this apparently closed book could be so outgoing and vivacious. Her confidence seemed to know no bounds. She was deeply enigmatic, which only served to make her even more attractive.

I was sure of one thing; Joanna lived outside the usual social norms. If she wanted to be taken out for lunch, she wouldn't just wait to be asked. If she wanted to passionately kiss a man she hardly knew, she would simply do it. All this was so far removed from my world, it all conspired to make her the most exotic creature imaginable! As we sat at that table, I couldn't help but feel like the mouse drooling over the cheese in the trap. Despite all my fears and doubts, I still didn't want it to end and so, when it came time to leave, my heart sank. I knew she was about to walk out of my life again.

I stood in the car park next to her car with my heart racing. I hated my role as the trusted friend in whom she could only partially confide but, at the same time, I so desperately wanted to kiss her again. She opened her car door and dropped her shoulder bag onto the seat. For a moment I thought she was about to get in without that kiss, but then she turned back towards me as if it was an afterthought. Neither of us said a word. She put her arms around me, and we kissed. One moment, I was a trusted old friend to use and then discard. The next moment, we were passionate lovers, except that we'd never had a relationship! She left, asking if she could ring me again one day.

Every ounce of common sense and self-preservation was telling me not to do it, but I said, "Just don't leave it so long."

-oOo-

I spent the next weeks and months hating myself for the self-inflicted torment to which I was subjecting myself. There was no future with this woman, just exquisite peaks of joy along a path of despair. I reasoned that if I had the same feeling for Annie, then I wouldn't be doing this to myself, but then we both had our own addiction. Annie hated what the alcohol had done to her, but she couldn't give it up. I hated what my pointless relationship with Joanna was doing to me, but I couldn't give it up. The months turned into nearly a year and with no word from Joanna, I was finally beginning to appreciate how an alcoholic must feel after being dry for a year. Stanley and the others all looked as though they were feeling very sorry for me.

"Unrequited love. Can anything be more tragic?" Audrey said.

"I suppose you're right. It is all a bit tragic, looking back," I agreed.

Stanley sighed on my behalf and asked if she was finally gone for good, and I had to say, "Not quite," and told them what happened next.

I was certainly beginning to assume that, after nearly a year, I would never see her again, but then one morning Sylvia shouted out to me just as I was leaving the office.

"There's a woman on the phone for you."

I grabbed the phone in a rush saying, "Yes, can I help you?"

The voice on the other end said, "I need a nice man to take me out to dinner. Are you still that nice man, Charlie Bartlett?"

My heart as always leaped in my chest. I could feel my

pulse beating in my throat, and there was a brief silence before I managed to answer.

"I think you know the answer to that."

We spoke only briefly but decided to meet for dinner at a pretty country hotel which by all accounts had a very highly rated restaurant. I vaguely knew the place; it was called Poppies. My immediate concern was how I would explain to Annie my not being at home that evening. I had a couple of days to think about it, and eventually I settled upon a plausible story about meeting a group of developers regarding a proposed housing development. There was an element of truth in the story, which helped, but I wasn't used to this subterfuge and felt riddled with guilt before I'd even done anything!

The evening finally arrived. Not having been to this hotel before, I had no idea what to expect and it proved to be incredibly upmarket for a country hotel. All the staff wore uniforms, and I was immediately escorted to a table in the lounge bar. I was quite taken aback by the grandeur of the place. I'd been nervous to start with, but now I was beginning to feel a bit out of my depth as well. A member of staff asked me what I would like to drink, and I instinctively asked for a pint of draught beer, only to be told there was no draught beer, so I ordered a bottle of German lager that I had never heard of.

As I sat there at the bar, waiting for Joanna to appear, I realised I should probably be drinking one of the fancy cocktails which I suddenly noticed everyone else was drinking. This made me feel even more ill at ease. The decor gave me the impression of a gentleman's club, with an abundance of oak panelling and leather furniture.

The maître d' stood in the corner of the room, scanning every detail. When a waiter left the bar with a tray of drinks, he spotted immediately that the decoration protruding from one of the cocktails was not quite at the right angle, pouncing on it as if the waiter had committed a cardinal sin. It then occurred to me that Joanna had specifically chosen this place. It was her world that I had entered.

I glanced at my watch just to confirm that time had not stood still. I had become so aware of my heart beating, it seemed to drown out the sounds around me. This, however, was nothing compared to my reaction when Joanna appeared. She was a vision to behold. Her golden hair was styled up and partly pulled back from her face, her diamond earrings and necklace flashed in the dim light as she looked around the room. Even her high heels looked amazing. I hadn't seen her looking so tall, but above all it was the low-cut red dress she was wearing which took my breath away. I recognised it immediately from the front cover of the Vogue magazine which had made such an impression on me when I saw it on the wall of Joanna's house, that first time I met her.

As she walked towards me, every contour of her body shimmered as the fabric caught the light, and where the dress did not hug her figure, it seemed to flow effortlessly in time with her every step. She was utterly breath-taking. Not only had I never seen such a vision before, I was quite sure that no-one else in this place had either. She absolutely filled the room with her presence. I felt sure that every single person, male and female alike, was mesmerised by her. I needed to pinch myself. Was this unbelievably gorgeous creature *really* here to dine with *me?*

The moment our eyes met, her face lit up with that wonderful broad smile. As I stood up to greet her, I felt incapable of doing or saying anything, but I needn't have worried. Joanna simply threw her arms around me and we kissed. This was not an appropriate kiss on the cheek; this was a full-on passionate kiss. We stood there in each other's arms, in full view of the entire room, initially oblivious to the fact that every single person present was looking at us, but as soon as that realisation dawned, we both sat down smiling. Mine was a decidedly embarrassed smile, but it was obvious that Joanna was not remotely concerned what other people might be thinking.

We immediately started talking as if we had seen each other

yesterday, not many months ago and, all the while, I simply couldn't take my eyes off her. She was simply exquisite in every detail. I couldn't begin to explain what it was about that dress that made it so sensational. I obviously knew nothing about such things, apart from, of course, the fact that it was Joanna wearing it. I had to comment upon it. She said with enormous pride that it was created especially for her by Sally Cumming, seeming momentarily bemused when I said that I hadn't heard of her. Apparently, she was one of the world's most sought-after designers and it was this red dress that appeared on the front cover of Vogue which had launched her career.

Audrey momentarily interrupted me at that point.

"Typical man not to know who Sally Cummings was! That dress would be worth an absolute fortune today, but do carry on, Charles."

I said that when I'd calmed down a little, I asked Joanna where she was living but she was, as always, vague about that. She said she was still struggling to recover financially after what had happened with the idiot husband. I made a joke that she may be poor, but she certainly didn't look it!

"Oh don't be deceived by this stuff, Charlie. The dress is worth far more than I am, and the diamonds aren't real."

That calm comment was typically Joanna, incredibly open and frank, with no pretence, provided it didn't involve her other relationships. I hadn't much cared for my role as the old friend to confide in, but tonight she seemed totally different. Perhaps I was just being seduced by her beautiful eyes and her wonderful smile. Perhaps it was the captivating red dress. Whatever it was, she was simply radiant and for the first time in our tortured relationship, I felt I was sitting with the real Joanna.

The maître d' came over to us saying that our table was ready, and he led us toward the restaurant.

As we walked together hand in hand, I was trying to make sense of this strange but wonderful situation in which I found myself. This was so unlike any of our previous meetings. This suddenly felt like a real relationship. I was assuming as always that, at some point, Joanna would say it was time for her to go and I would have no idea when or indeed if I might see her again. I was trying to prepare myself.

My concentration was broken as we entered the restaurant together. There was immediately an audible murmur from some of the diners as they caught sight of Joanna and the dress. By the time we reached our table, it felt as if every head had turned in our direction. Joanna seemed to take all this attention in her stride, but I confess, from my perspective, it was an unforgettable experience.

Joanna spoke during our meal more openly than she had ever done before. I felt she needed to somehow justify this strange and painful relationship that we had. She went back over her childhood and all the sacrifices her parents had made for her, and how determined she was to repay them. She explained that when she was married, she thought she was both wealthy and secure. Her modelling career had been quite successful, but having given it up when they married, she now had nothing. She could never describe her devastation at losing it all. It was clear what her goal in life was. She was bubbly and vivacious, but beneath it all, she was utterly determined to get where she wanted to be, which was undoubtedly the top of the tree. She wanted it all: status, position, wealth and security.

I asked her the obvious question, how she intended to achieve all this. Once again, the answer was not remotely what I had expected. She smiled at me.

"Look at me, Charlie, do you think I don't know what my attributes are?"

I smiled back and answered.

"You've got the best attributes I've ever seen!"

We laughed, and she spoke in a very matter-of-fact way.

"I am what I am, Charlie, and I'm not going to be poor again."

"I believe you."

Joanna looked quite serious for a moment, before she spoke again.

"We lead different lives, Charlie, you and me. We're on separate paths to the future, but I don't want to worry about the future right now. I just need to be with you, Charlie Bartlett. Is that okay?"

I didn't know where to turn or what to say. I had no idea what she was proposing. I simply said what I was thinking.

"Need is so much more than wanting; I need you too."

We looked at each other as I reached with some urgency for my glass of wine. Then everything changed abruptly.

Without a moment's hesitation she said, "Let's not drink too much if you're going to make love to me tonight."

Audrey choked a little on her gin and tonic, coughing. Stanley swallowed deeply. Nobody said a word. I had felt the same that evening. One of those life-changing moments had suddenly thrust itself into my life. What on earth was I going to say? My heart was now in danger of bursting out of my chest. This sort of thing simply didn't happen to me! I'd been out of my depth and paddling furiously all evening. Once those words had been spoken, nothing else existed.

Joanna really was a truly exotic creature, and in a way, it was like being in a room with a tame tiger! I so much wanted to touch, but who wouldn't be a little afraid? I think, with hindsight, Joanna obviously knew that I was in over my head, and simply took control. We didn't say another word, which from my perspective was probably just as well. She rose up from the table, and I simply followed her through to the hotel reception.

"Call your wife and tell her you can't get home tonight. I'll book a room."

I really don't remember calling Annie, but I must have done. It was as if I was caught up in a whirlwind. I had no idea where this storm would deposit me, but I found myself outside one of the hotel suites. I opened the door and stepped inside. As the door closed behind us, we spontaneously fell into each other's arms and kissed passionately. We held each other so tightly, she must have been able to feel my heart racing.

Eventually she moved away from me, and turned her back towards me.

"Get me out of this dress, Charlie."

I found myself unfastening Joanna's red dress and slipping it off her shoulders until it dropped to the floor. Then she turned around and we kissed again as I ran my hands down her body. It would be fair to say that she took me to a place that night which I didn't even know existed! If there is such a place as heaven on earth, then it was in that room on that night!

The following morning, I awoke to find Joanna asleep in my arms, her head on my chest. I didn't want to wake her. I didn't want the moment to end. As carefully as possible, I moved to one side and cupped her face in my hands. Slowly and deliberately, I laid her head down upon the pillow. Gradually she stirred and the first thing her eyes focused upon were my eyes looking into hers. A wonderful smile radiated across her face. She opened her mouth as if to speak but instead we kissed; a kiss which just went on and on.

I felt, through that kiss, I was exploring every aspect of her being, and she mine. We were two people, but we seemed to occupy the space of just one. We made love again. This time it was less frenetic, more considered, more sublime. Eventually and with some reluctance our thoughts turned to breakfast. Joanna became aware of the red dress.

"I can't wear this for breakfast." she said. "There's an overnight bag in my car; can you get it for me?"

I suddenly realised she had come prepared. Finally, as we were gazing at each other across the breakfast table, I asked when I would see her again.

"I'll ring you," she said.

Normally I would have assumed that 'I'll ring you' meant perhaps, or maybe, or possibly in a year's time. After this unimaginably wonderful night that we had shared together 'maybe' really didn't sound like an option. For the first time, I *did* expect her to ring me.

When the time came to leave, she said, "Don't forget to pay the bill with cash; don't use a card."

Our final goodbye left me feeling empty and abandoned. Joanna had become a part of my life. I felt incomplete without her. Stanley smiled, and I noticed they were all smiling.

"Hang on," I said, "I've just admitted to committing adultery here. You shouldn't all be smiling!"

"My dear Charles, in today's circumstances, do you feel guilty about that night? Do you wish it had never happened?" asked Stanley.

I fell for Stanley's little trap, hook, line and sinker. Indignantly I replied, "Certainly not, it was the most wonderful day of my life!"

Audrey looked quite emotional.

"You're an idiot, Charlie Bartlett! Can't you see why we're all smiling, we're all so happy for you!"

I hesitated a moment as I realised that this wonderful group of friends really did care for me! I felt a bit awkward and wasn't quite sure what to say, but my embarrassment was saved by Charlotte who came rushing through the lounge. We could see from her expression that something was up, so Harold called after her, asking what the problem was.

She came back over to us.

"I'm sorry to tell you that we've just found Mr. Routledge. I'm afraid he's dead."

Harold appeared nonplussed.

"Sorry to hear that," he said.

I wasn't sure that any of us knew who Mr. Routledge was, but it was obviously sad news, nonetheless.

"Yes. I suppose you didn't see much of him; he was always

outside having a smoke. In fact, that's where we've just found him."

"You don't mean Puffer, do you, Charlotte?" I asked.

"Yes, I do. I forgot you all call him Puffer," she replied.

We looked at each other for a moment in silence. Eventually I said, "I can't believe old Puffer has gone. I know we tried to avoid him, but he was a good old boy."

"One of the best, old Puffer, especially his jokes," said Harold.

Audrey said, "Oh how terribly sad, I really will miss him."

All the while this was going on, Lizzy quietly looked on until eventually she offered an observation.

"I don't know what you're all on about. He was a ghastly old man. He reeked of fags and used to cough all over us!"

"Of course, I didn't know him as well as you all did, but I agree with Lizzy, I found him to be pretty ghastly," commented Stanley.

Harold thought for a moment.

"Actually, he was pretty awful, wasn't he?"

Audrey now reconsidered her position.

"Absolutely right. I've never met such a loathsome man."

It seems that we all agreed about Puffer, but we would certainly miss him and his jokes. I raised my cup of coffee in a toast to Puffer.

"Here's to you, Puffer, ashes to ashes!"

We were just in the middle of sharing again some of Puffer's more memorable jokes when Stanley spoke.

"Now, Charles, after what we've just learned, there are two things you need to tell us. What happened to your relationships with Joanna, and with your wife?"

As usual, Stanley had gone straight to the point. He was quite right; I couldn't think about the one without the other. When I got home after that wonderful night, I immediately entered a whole new world of subterfuge. I had to lie, of course. I had to consider every detail which might expose me, suddenly becoming aware of why Joanna had said to pay the hotel bill with cash.

It must take a singular type of person, to be both married and a philanderer. The two situations don't make natural bed-fellows. I could justify my adultery to myself on the grounds that I had no proper sex life with Annie and, as they say, needs must. I could also justify it on the grounds of the emotional necessity, but of course if I could really justify all these things, I wouldn't have felt the crushing burden of guilt which haunted me. From that day on, the constant fear of discovery was not the fear that my behaviour was beneath contempt. For me, it was the simple necessity of not emotionally destroying another person.

I had the feeling Stanley empathised with me, but Bill struggled to understand, and I admit that I thought it could only really make sense to someone who'd had a similar experience.

"I'm not sure people like us can really understand, Charles. Were there moments when your guilt was especially difficult to deal with?" commented Audrey.

I said that it was often little things while I was with Annie, such as waking up next to a brunette when, in my half sleep, I expected to see a blonde. Then there were those moments when I found myself smiling and singing along to a favourite song that I had shared with Joanna. I wrestled with my conscience for months. I always knew that if, or when, Joanna telephoned me, I would have to be there in an instant. I would go no matter what I might be doing at that moment with Annie, the girls or at work. My guilt was difficult to reconcile.

Stanley intervened at that point.

"If you knew that you wanted to be with another woman, why did you not leave your wife?"

I knew this question was bound to be asked and I answered it as honestly as I could.

"I made a commitment through our marriage vows.

My sense of duty and honour is not flexible, and of course there were the girls, Sally and Debbie. As the daughters of an alcoholic, there would always be the possibility that they could end up in care as the result of a broken marriage. I just couldn't allow that to happen."

Everyone sat glum-faced, until Stanley eventually made a comment.

"I think you'll have to tell us more about Joanna, now we know that there's more to tell."

Just a few days later, Joanna phoned me again and this time Sylvia recognised the voice. She buzzed my phone.

"It's the same lady on the phone. Be careful, Charlie".

Sylvia's words rang in my ears. She knew me so well, but I grabbed the phone, and the second I heard Joanna's voice, I knew I was powerless.

"Hello, Charlie."

That was all she said, but as with all things, she had her way of saying it. I could see her lips forming the words. We chatted for a while and we agreed that our night at Poppies was simply sublime.

"Do you know, Charlie, I think we've achieved a rare thing. We've created one of those special memories that will stay with us right up to our last breath."

It was a wonderful thing to say and I couldn't have agreed more.

"Do you think we could ever top it?"

Joanna seemed to understand these things so well, and quickly replied.

"We shouldn't even try Charlie, that was so special. It will be different next time. It will be even more special but in a different way. When can you go back to Poppies?"

I didn't want to imagine for a moment that our relationship had ended that night, but it was such a relief to hear her say that! We arranged to go back to the same little hotel. Joanna was, of course, quite right. It was indeed different the next time, every bit as intense as before, and even more special. We seemed to be incapable of being together without being in each other's arms; saying goodbye the next morning became a painfully protracted torment.

-o0o-

A pattern developed where, most weeks, we would be together at least once, either at our little hotel or another that we had found, but never where Joanna lived. In fact, she never really told me where she lived, and I sensed that, if I were to ask, she'd find some way of changing the subject, and I'd end up being none the wiser.

We ended up having a strange association with our little hotel. It was the most glorious and perfect place for our relationship to evolve. Obviously, we became well-known there from the moment Joanna made her entrance that first night. They obviously realised what our relationship was, but their protocol did not slip for a second.

I never went to Poppies without Joanna, but if I ever arrived there first, the maître d' would ask, "Will Madam be joining you this evening, sir?"

I would complete the ritual by saying, "Yes, I believe she will be here later."

He would then say, "Shall I prepare Madam's usual cocktail?"

I think I fell in love with Poppies nearly as much as I fell in love with Joanna. It was Audrey rather than Stanley who asked the next question.

"You said, Charles, that Joanna was determined never to be poor again. So, what happened?"

Once again, I'd been waiting for someone to ask me that. It was a difficult one to answer, but now I had no option; I had to try. I told them that Joanna's goal in life was to marry a very wealthy man, and she had set about finding one. She would never ever give me any details, but I always knew when she was seeing someone. I found it utterly unbearable to think that she was with another man, but she treated the exercise in a totally matter-of-fact way, and of course how could I criticise, when I was going home to my wife?

I found myself in the most surreal situation imaginable, and it was really tormenting me. This strangest of situations lasted for many months. She would give me the vaguest hints that the last 'beau' was unsuitable, and I would breathe a sigh of relief that I hadn't lost her. A long break between our liaisons presumably meant that she was seeing someone; a short break meant that she wasn't. When we met, Joanna would always throw herself into my arms. I assumed when that initial embrace lasted even longer than usual, it was because her other life had somehow gone badly. On those occasions, her kiss told me everything.

All the while, it was perfectly obvious to me that we loved each other, but she was adamant that the word must never be spoken. On one or two occasions, she would place her fingers against my lips when it looked as if I might say the word. I think it was clear, if only I had the eyes to see, Joanna struggled with her feelings for me. Her obsessive pursuit of wealth and position meant that eventually she would have to give up the one she loved. I've no doubt her denial of that situation was her way of coping with it.

"You must have been under so much mental pressure to leave your wife and put an end to such torment," Bill said.

He was judging me from his own experience of love which could hardly apply to my situation, but he did have a point. Joanna had created her own image of the future, but sadly for me I was not the image of wealth and position she had in mind. I was Charlie the bricklayer. I knew Joanna was resolute in her determination and, if that meant giving me up, I knew she would.

I had now realised that being married was probably one of my attractions for Joanna, since it enabled her to label me as unattainable. I admitted that I often wonder now what might have happened if I had left Annie.

At the time I was convinced it would make no difference. Today, with the aid of hindsight, I suspect it could have changed everything. Stanley's expression was difficult to fathom. I doubted that any of my friends were able to fully empathise with my position. It was undoubtedly a strange situation to be in, but somehow it had become my norm.

However bizarre and unsatisfactory our relationship now appears, the unspoken love that we shared seemed to grow more intense with each meeting. I was not proficient at the clandestine aspect of the relationship; it was Joanna who understood those things. It was always necessary for Joanna to meet me somewhere. In the case of Poppies Hotel, it was ideally placed.

Occasionally, we would go somewhere else where it was easier for her to meet with me first before we travelled together. Increasingly this was my builder's yard. A more seasoned philanderer would have intuitively known not to do that but, for whatever reason, I was naive and becoming rather reckless.

Chapter Nineteen
BAD DAY AT THE OFFICE

I was gradually learning, albeit far too late, that one of the subconscious allures of the extra-marital affair was the risk. Perhaps it was a secret desire to be found out and to precipitate the end of the marriage. For some inexplicable reason I was taking risks. One morning, after we arrived back at the yard from an overnight stay at another hotel, I asked Joanna to come up to my office for a cup of coffee. She tried to refuse by saying it was too risky, but I insisted. I know why I did it. Joanna only existed in our alternative world, and nothing we did together touched our other lives. I wanted our two separate worlds to meet.

It was perfectly obvious that my staff would see her, but I pretended to myself that it would appear to be innocent. We went in and I tried to ignore everyone. My secretary, Sylvia, was away from her desk, which I thought was fortuitous, because I had no doubt that she would realise immediately Joanna was the voice on the phone. Little did I know that Sylvia was with Annie in my office.

Stanley looked aghast, and Audrey said, "Oh no!"

Oh no indeed! It was one of those excruciating life-changing moments that remains with you forever, every ghastly detail. The trap was set, and I fell straight into it. I opened the door and Joanna stepped in ahead of me. Initially, I only saw Sylvia but then there was that moment of realisation, a moment of abject horror and disbelief. The body, when faced with circumstances of downright terror, initiates your fight-or-flight response. Your body floods with stress hormones. Your blood rushes to your major muscle groups, your heart races and your blood pressure goes through the roof. The brain is sent into overdrive, and my first involuntary reaction was to step back outside and run. I momentarily turned back towards the door but of course a glimmer of rationality remained, and I realised I had to deal with it.

I knew immediately that this was my nemesis. My initial reaction had already said it all; when you're guilty as charged, you find it difficult to pretend otherwise. I said to Joanna that this was my wife Annie, and my secretary Sylvia, then as calmly as I could, with my fist in my throat, I said to Annie that this was Joanna. Sylvia instantly assessed the situation and looked extremely embarrassed. She almost ran out of the room, and of course any modicum of credibility that I might have been able to salvage went out with her.

Joanna remained amazingly calm, taking a moment to collect herself, and obviously thinking she might be able to bluff her way out of it.

"Hello Annie. I'm a colleague of Charlie's," she said, while offering Annie her hand.

It was a surreal moment. I so desperately hoped it was a straw that might float, but Annie's alter ego was staring out from behind her eyes, projecting a terrifying unspoken torrent of vitriol. She stormed out of the room, knocking Joanna aside, slamming the door such that the building shook.

Stanley and the others looked nearly as shocked as I'd been at the time.

"This appears to be one of those worst possible moments when one's destiny is decided in a split second."

I nodded in agreement. It was indeed one of those moments.

Joanna and I had taken some time to collect ourselves. She asked me what I would do, but of course I had no idea. I just knew the worst was yet to come. We hastily said goodbye and I was left to contemplate. I was incapable of decision-making, but the fact that I had to face Annie again was inescapable

Sylvia brought me a cup of coffee. She was fighting back tears, very concerned for me.

"It's all my fault. When Annie turned up, I just didn't know what else to do with her."

I assured her that this was entirely a problem of my own creation, and it had nothing to do with her. Eventually when my heart rate had slowed down to only about twice normal rate, I knew what I had to do. So, I drove home.

The confrontation was instant. Annie was both drunk and violent. She hated me with every fibre of her being. There was no possibility of discussion until she had slept it off, so I spent the night on the sofa.

The following morning it started all over again. Annie's obsession with me and the other illusory women had finally been vindicated. I had reinforced her alternative reality. It confirmed she was right to hate me. It was an awful situation. I knew I had to get out of there for my own safety. I tried to persuade her to let me take the girls to my parents but, as they were three hours' drive away, it wasn't entirely practical, and any discussion was impossible anyway. Annie wanted me gone permanently. I'm still not sure if I left of my own volition or if I was thrown out, but I certainly left.

Part of me still cared for Annie, but all those feelings had now been subsumed into this new desire to just leave it all behind. Of course, I couldn't, because of Debbie and Sally, and I couldn't take the girls with me, because I had no home to go to. I just had to rely on Annie's normally overriding mothering instinct, for her to stay sober while the girls were in her care. I went straight to my office.

One of the first lessons a philanderer learns is to have

several changes of clothes available at work. Sylvia booked me into a local hotel for an indeterminate period. I was relieved to finally get away from work that evening and sit in one of my favourite restaurants.

It was a cold, miserable night which mirrored my disposition perfectly. The good food and wine didn't offer a solution, but it did ease a little of my pain. My relationship with these two women was suddenly brought into stark contrast. I loved one so passionately that I couldn't see how I could live without her. I was inextricably tied to the other, but I couldn't see how I could live with her.

That evening in the restaurant my mind was racing around in circles. Inevitably, as I kept passing the same signposts, one of those signs was not only the most attractive. It was also the most obvious. Why was I sitting here alone? I should be in the arms of the woman I loved, planning our future together! I tried desperately to dismiss the not-inconsiderable reasons against reaching this logical outcome, namely an alcoholic wife and two beautiful girls. My epiphany came when I realised that, had our roles been reversed, I would have found a way to be with Joanna in her hour of need.

I knew I filled Joanna's senses to overflowing, but it was to no avail. Her driving ambition for wealth and status controlled her to no lesser an extent than Annie's addiction to alcohol controlled her. It's strange how one moment the elephant in the room is invisible; the next moment, its enormity leaves you with little air to breathe. I'd always known, but now, finally, I accepted it. I was never going to spend my life with Joanna, which was why she wasn't here with me, during *my* hour of need.

I finished my glass of wine, even more depressed than when I started it. I asked to use the restaurant's telephone just to check that my girls were asleep. I hung on for an eternity but there was no answer. Hearing an alarm bell ring in my head, despite being well over the drink-drive limit, I ran to get to my car.

It was a short drive and I was home within 15 minutes. Debbie was asleep, but Sally was wandering around, distressed and crying. I looked everywhere. Annie's bed hadn't been slept in and there was no sign of her, other than an empty vodka bottle that had rolled under a chair, and a glass on the coffee table. I calmed Sally and finally got her to bed and asleep.

Clearly Annie had gone out somewhere but, even for her, this was unusual. Then a thought sprang into my mind; the garden shed. This was where she kept her vodka stash, about which, unbelievably, I wasn't supposed to know. It supposedly gave her control. I jumped up, rushing outdoors into the dark. The outside light came on and I could see Annie lying on the ground. She was alive but incredibly cold. The night was wet and not far above freezing.

Annie didn't respond at all. I had no idea how serious her condition was, but I did realise that if I left her there in the cold, she would most certainly die. I admit that a thought occurred to me. Would it have been my fault if I hadn't found her for another 15 minutes? Well, yes, it would. I carried her indoors, turned up the heating and wrapped her in everything I could find, but she remained unconscious. Having done everything that I could think of to help her, I dialled 999. Within ten minutes, an ambulance arrived, and they rushed her to hospital while I stayed with the children.

Although it was past midnight by now, I phoned my parents and asked them to come over in the morning. It was a long, sleepless night and I had never been so pleased to see my dependable Mum and Dad walk through the door the following morning. Quite obviously they had questions to ask and I needed to come up with some answers, but I managed to postpone that difficult conversation for another time. I was in the hospital by 10am to be told that Annie had alcohol poisoning and severe hypothermia. The doctor said she had been within minutes of dying.

It was five days before Annie was allowed home, still in a

poor state. She hadn't been in the house five minutes before she broke down in floods of tears. The full impact of what she'd done really hit her, and there was more, much more. Social workers needed to assess us, to see if they could risk leaving the girls in our custody. That process turned out to be a harrowing experience, but I managed eventually to convince them that Annie was off the alcohol and that I, as the responsible parent, would ensure the girls' safety. Annie had not actually stopped drinking, not permanently anyway, but the shock of that incident did have a powerful sobering effect.

Our life together entered a new period. Her alter ego still loathed and despised me, probably even more, but she realised for the first time that she and the girls could not function without me. We had no option but to form an unhappy alliance. Joanna was never mentioned again, although I suspected that, for Annie, this was regarded as the price she had to pay. We were locked together around a centre of gravity that was our two wonderful girls.

Stanley and the others looked as depressed as I'd been at the time.

"What a terrible situation to find yourself in, Charles. How did you cope with it?" Stanley queried.

It was one of my unhappiest times but, despite my painful recognition of the fact that I would eventually lose Joanna, I felt I needed her, now more than ever. As always, I had to wait to hear from her, and as the days went by my anguish grew steadily stronger. Finally, she rang, sounding remote, not her usual self.

"Can we meet at Poppies?"

"Of course, when?"

We met in the car park at Poppies. Joanna had obviously thought that perhaps our relationship was over. The moment we met, she threw herself into my arms. I had never known her to be so distressed. I assumed the worst and instantly over-reacted. We were both in tears, standing in silence, clinging to one another. I thought every second was our last together. Joanna had never once shown that she was vulnerable. I had seen her upset, even in tears before, but always she protected her vulnerability.

This was different. She didn't think to hide the tears running down her face and didn't try to protect herself in any way.

"Have I lost you, Charlie?"

"Oh God, I hope not."

It took a few seconds for those words to sink in. In some respects, I didn't know her at all, but in this regard, we were as one person. We didn't need to confirm anything, it wasn't over. In the space of a minute, our emotional journey had descended into deepest despair, only to re-emerge in exquisite joy. Our mutual reaction was the same, we ran from the car park directly to our room. It was the most intense experience of my life. For now, at least, I couldn't live without Joanna, and finally she admitted she couldn't live without me. We formed a triangle with Annie, each with our own addiction.

Our relationship continued for several more months. That one display of vulnerability, the admission that she needed me as much as I needed her somehow drew us even closer, something I wouldn't have ever thought possible.

Despite the intensity of our unspoken love for one another, gradually the breaks between our liaisons were getting longer. I just had the most appalling realisation that our relationship was heading toward the edge of a cliff. I felt every nuance of Joanna's mood.

There were days when she was distracted; I assumed these were those days when her 'other' life encroached upon ours. Then there were days when her need for me was almost desperate. I knew nothing was going to deviate her from the path she had chosen, but I also knew she was torn between her two worlds. I silently shared her anguish, though it was never discussed. There was no need; never was so much said, with so few words. There were times when her unspoken torment was palpable. Leaving me was breaking her heart.

I finally plucked up the courage to suggest to Joanna that we should have a long weekend away. My plan was to finally admit to her that I knew she had to go, and perhaps this was that time. I was by now heavily involved with quite large-scale property developments and was genuinely spending more and more time away when the developments were quite distant, so a long weekend wouldn't have looked out of place. Although Annie probably assumed the relationship had continued, it seemed to be imperative that the subterfuge also continued.

Joanna said she would love a long weekend away but would have to let me know nearer the time. I knew why. I was like a condemned prisoner. I saw colours in the sunrise that I'd never seen before, heard sounds in our favourite music I'd never heard. I smelt fragrances I'd never noticed before but, like a condemned prisoner, I knew the end was approaching.

When the time came, I sensed it was going to be our last time together, although it was difficult to accept the reality of the situation. The conventional wisdom is that couples break up when they fall out of love; not when they are still in love. This was going to be the most exquisitely painful experience of my life.

Recklessly I met Joanna at my yard again where she could leave her car, and we drove down to Bournemouth together. It may have been unimaginative, but it really didn't matter where the hotel was. As soon as we walked into the room, we rushed into each other's arms, and we were making love within ten minutes of arriving. As passionate as our lovemaking was, it was always the long lingering kiss which communicated even more.

I wanted to be a part of that woman's very soul. Every kiss confirmed that she felt the same about me. I now sensed a desperation in her, as if she needed to extract every sensation from every moment that we had left. The hotel, the food, the resort; in fact, everything. We were oblivious to it all. We were consumed by one another.

We talked as incessantly as we always did, and absolutely nothing was said about ending the relationship. I tried to talk about it, but it proved to be impossible. The prospect of it hung over me like a cloud. Come the end of that weekend, I knew the drive home was going to be an excruciating experience.

We loaded the car and set off as usual, except that this was anything but usual. We spoke less and less as the miles ticked by. I desperately wanted to say something, anything, but if I tried to say a single word, I would break down. Despite not a single mention that our relationship was over, we both seemed to have an unspoken understanding. I welcomed every momentary delay in the traffic, anything that might give me a little longer.

Inevitably we arrived back at the yard. I simply couldn't speak, knowing that if she said goodbye, I would collapse in tears, and she obviously felt the same. We kissed for the final time, the most passionate lingering kiss of our relationship. Through that kiss we said everything we needed to say without a single word being spoken. I felt every contour of her lips, the smell and taste of her, I felt her body pressed to mine. We were as close as two people could possibly be.

Then it was over. Joanna looked at me with those beautiful eyes of hers; they were full of tears. She tried to speak but it was all too much for her.

Finally, after an agonising silence and with her voice trembling, she whispered to me.

"Charlie, I must go."

It was time for her to move on. She picked up her overnight bag from the back seat and she was gone. I sat there long enough to watch her drive away.

The moment her car disappeared, it hit me like a suffocating anaesthetic. I felt powerless to do anything. My whole body was shaking, tears were streaming down my face. I was utterly distraught. There was a large part of me which was hers to keep, it seemed impossible that I could ever be a whole person again. I couldn't possibly go home. I just drove around incapable of any thoughts other than of Joanna.

We had many pieces of music which were significant to us, mostly uplifting songs, but for me *I will always love you* will always be Joanna's song. I pressed the cassette into the car's player and played it over and over, as I slowly drove back toward my other life.

Chapter Twenty
CHINESE RESTAURANT REUNION

Talking about that harrowing experience had brought it all back to me! I really hadn't appreciated how deeply affected I still was. Even after all the intervening years, it was as if I was sitting in the car again, playing the cassette. Talk about bittersweet memories, that really was all I took with me. I found my voice was trembling and I was holding back tears. Audrey flung her arms around me and that was it; we were both in tears. The others all rushed forward in a group hug. I wish I could say that the spectre of Joanna had left the building, but she hadn't, not quite.

It seemed that I'd occupied the entire morning relating my story. We were now late for lunch and frankly I felt drained. I needed the break! We just headed straight into the restaurant. No sooner were we sitting down than Audrey checked her diary for something and suddenly spoke with some alarm.

"Oh, my goodness! It's tonight when those dreadful people from the Chinese restaurant are coming!"

"Oh no!" said Harold, looking depressed.

It was a sentiment which was universally echoed by us all. Three generations of them were coming. What could possibly be worse?

"Do you remember that awful man with his broken glasses? Didn't he look ridiculous!" said Audrey.

Stanley said he thought the deplorable young girl with the tattoo and the pierced nose was his favourite.

Lizzy thought it was totally outrageous that the middle-aged man was wearing trainers and a t-shirt in a restaurant!

"It's just not good enough," she said.

Bill was the most charitable of us.

"Not the sort of people you'd *choose* to dine with."

We needed a plan to get rid of them as quickly as possible.

"What a shame we've lost Puffer," I said. "We could have got him to cough over them!"

Bill said we needed to see what the kitchen was preparing, perhaps it wasn't too late for them to have fish fingers or something. We agreed this was a good idea, as they mustn't be encouraged to stay any longer than was necessary. Sadly, the kitchen staff said it was too late for special orders, and they could only be given what we were having.

This was a setback, but Stanley had an idea.

"How about separate tables?"

We all agreed that was a masterstroke. By the time we'd finished our lunch, it was four o'clock.

"Oh dear. Where has the day gone?" asked Lizzy. "Have I been asleep?"

We then decided we should just go back to our apartments and prepare for the evening. As we left, we asked Alan the barman to have ready a separate table for six. I had a leisurely shower and tried to wash Joanna out of my hair.

The whole experience had quite drained me, but perhaps this fiasco tonight would cheer me up. Soon enough, it was time to meet the others in the bar.

We needed to be there before the ghastly people arrived, so I made my way over. I could see Harold was busy ringing Audrey's doorbell, so I thought it best to leave them to it.

"Who's buying? I'll have a single malt." Stanley said.

Bill did the honours with the usual round, and we sat down to contemplate the unappealing prospect ahead. Stanley nosed his whisky and then swirled it around in his mouth.

"Difficult one this; not exactly sure what it is," he said.

Just at that moment, the Munster Family appeared.

"Oh, my goodness! They're here!" said Audrey.

To our surprise, they were all extraordinarily well-dressed. Both the senior and middle-aged women wore rather elegant dresses.

"Oh, my goodness!" said Audrey again. "If I'd known, I would have put on something smarter!"

Both the older gentlemen were well turned out. The middle-aged chap was in a suit and the elderly gentleman was wearing a blazer with a military badge on the breast pocket. They were carrying two bunches of flowers, one each for Audrey and Lizzy, plus a bottle of wine for the table. I glanced at the wine to see it was a bottle of Leoville Las Cases, a 1995 vintage.

"Get this man a chair!" I said to Alan. This was going to be the finest bottle of wine I had drunk in ages!

Harold immediately noticed the older man's pocket badge and they were instantly deep in conversation. Our ladies were so surprised by the flowers, they too immediately started up a conversation with the guests.

The young brother and sister were casually dressed but smart. She didn't have the ring through her nose, indeed she looked very attractive. We began to organise drinks. The middle-aged chap said he was a whisky drinker.

"Take my single malt," I said. "I haven't touched it yet; I'll get myself another one."

Eventually we each had a drink and they proposed a toast to us and thanked us for our kind generosity this evening.

The middle-aged chap took one sip of his whisky and I could see that he was deliberating. Stanley looked on with a wry smile on his face. He was obviously thinking the poor man would have no idea what it was. The man swirled it around the glass.

"What am I drinking?" he asked.

Stanley, having failed to identify the whisky, mischievously posed a question.

"Perhaps you can tell us?"

He swirled it again, looking closely at his glass.

"Classic Speyside obviously, but which one? Very clean and fresh, a little apple and berry. I'd say perhaps the Glenlivet 15- year-old or maybe the 18-year-old?"

Alan stood nearby and nodded in acknowledgement. Stanley had made a new friend!

We went into the restaurant to sit down, but of course we had separate tables! Stanley was brilliant.

"Oh! How stupid of you, Alan. I asked you to prepare a table for twelve!"

Alan was equally brilliant.

"Of course you did!" he said. "How silly of me. Just give me two minutes."

We finally sat down and enjoyed a wonderful starter course with sparkling conversation, but the time was approaching for the bottle of Leoville. Alan decanted it and our new best friend tasted it. There was a long silence as he considered it.

"Perfect!" was his pronouncement.

When I finally tasted it, I agreed, it was glorious. What an evening we had! The ladies chatted non-stop, the gentlemen had so much in common, and the two teenagers were both sharp and intelligent; wonderful company!

I think we were all sorry to see the evening coming to an end, and they insisted on being given the opportunity to reciprocate our generosity with a trip to their favourite restaurant. Audrey said she would be delighted to organise a date.

They finally left after enjoying a cup of coffee in the lounge, and our disgraceful behaviour in the Chinese restaurant was never mentioned!

I turned to Audrey when they'd gone.

"I said they looked like fine people, didn't I?" I said.

"I immediately got that impression of them in the Chinese restaurant," Audrey agreed.

"As soon as I fell into the older gentleman, I could see they were a lovely family," Lizzy stated.

"I knew they were fine people the moment I saw them." Bill said.

Stanley was more impressed than any of us.

"I knew the second I saw the middle-aged chap pour his wine in the Chinese restaurant. I can just tell the quality of a man the moment he pours a glass of wine, you know."

We retired for the night delighted that our unerring ability to make an accurate appraisal of people had lost none of its prowess!

Chapter Twenty-One
THE LAST GOODBYE

We met for breakfast the next morning, full of our wonderful evening with those delightful people. The flowers were wonderful, and the wine was out of this world. It wasn't long, however, before Audrey felt the need to say something.

"I know you weren't keen to tell us your story, Charles, but I have to tell you, however sad, it's a truly wonderful story. Do please tell us how it all ends?"

In fact, I was keen to share the remainder of my story with them; it had become something that I needed to do.

After that weekend together, I found myself in a perpetual state of what amounted to grief and endless introspection. Every time the telephone rang, I would hope it was Joanna, but of course it wasn't, and my heart would sink. I even found myself driving over to our little hotel, just so I could feel her presence again.

There was one occasion when I went in for a drink and the maître d' said, "Will Madam be joining you this evening, sir?"

I answered in a very depressed voice, "No, I'm afraid not."

The maître d's name was John, he was a lovely chap. We had a kind of understanding together.

He looked at my distressed face. "Will Madam be joining you on another occasion, sir?"

"No, I'm afraid not."

In a totally out-of-character gesture, he put his hand on my shoulder.

"I'm so terribly sorry. May I say sir, I think Madam was the loveliest lady to ever grace our hotel. You both brought such joy and happiness to this establishment. All the staff will miss her. I hope you don't mind me saying sir, but I will greatly miss you both."

Somewhat taken aback, I thanked him for all his kind attention, and we shook hands. We both knew we wouldn't see each other again. In a strange way, saying goodbye to Poppies was a great sadness in its own right. I had fallen in love with Poppies nearly as much as I had Joanna.

The grieving process went on for weeks. I had never felt so depressed. It must have been about three months later when Sylvia completely took my breath away as she put her head around my office door.

"Joanna's on the phone for you," she said.

The conversation was a little awkward while we wasted precious time talking about anything other than the purpose of her call. Eventually she said, "I'm getting married in three weeks' time."

I felt flustered, not really knowing what to say.

"Do you expect me to buy you a wedding present?" after which there was a momentary silence.

"No, of course not," she said. "I just thought you should know, that's all. Also, I just wondered if you'd thought any more about leaving your wife?"

I remember those words as if it were yesterday. Now, in the cold light of day, it was perfectly obvious what Joanna was asking, but at the time for some inexplicable reason, it wasn't.

If she'd said, 'Will you think about leaving your wife?' then I wouldn't have been so slow. What she said was: had I thought any more about it? I said that I hadn't. The conversation ended soon after that, and her last words were simple.

"Goodbye, Charlie."

Some moments after the call, I realised what she was asking, and I thought of my two lovely daughters and how dependent on me Annie was. Could I leave them all? My sense of honour, duty and compassion combined with the love I had for my daughters meant that I could never leave them. But equally, could I possibly live with the knowledge that just maybe I might have spent the rest of my life with Joanna?

"You must tell me dear boy," Stanley said. "If you could go back in time knowing what you know today, what would your reply be to Joanna's question?"

I'd asked myself that question a thousand times, and of course hindsight is a wonderful thing but, given my time again, I knew exactly what I would say. I waited for Stanley to ask again, as I knew he would.

"Will you share that with us?"

"Despite everything, and knowing what I know today, I would say yes. I would have left my family if Joanna said she would marry me."

"For what it's worth Charles," Stanley said. "I think that would have been the right answer, but I assume that you never heard from her again?"

I hesitated for a moment.

"Not quite."

It was the 18th of June 1982. I only remember that because the date was written in my diary. There had been a request for me to personally view a development property in North London. The owner had been very specific, it was important, and it must be me. I had other developments in London so, rather intrigued, I agreed.

I arrived to find a very substantial five-story townhouse and rang the doorbell. The door opened and there was Joanna, looking more beautiful than ever. Even after the intervening years, my heart leaped in my chest as it always did the instant she appeared! It was as if we'd never been apart. We went inside to a fabulously palatial home where Joanna had a bottle of champagne waiting.

My obvious thought was, 'What the hell is going on? Why am I here?'

Somehow, we just pretended for half an hour that this was perfectly normal, drinking champagne together. Eventually Joanna began to tell me why I was there. Her husband had to move to America for his work, and so they were selling this house and moving to the States permanently; the husband had already gone. For one absurd moment, I allowed myself to think perhaps she was leaving her husband and wanted me back. The sudden realisation that this was just another page in the agonising saga of our long goodbye really annoyed me. I said that she'd hurt me enough without having to say goodbye again; what more did she want of me?

Joanna's eyes welled up.

"I'm so sorry, Charlie," she said tearfully. "When you refused to leave your wife that last time, you hurt me too. I was so hoping that perhaps you might. I've never wanted to hurt you."

She wiped away a tear.

"I don't know what I was thinking. I'm moving to America permanently, and I just couldn't bear the thought of not being in the same country as you, Charlie. I just had to see you one more time. It was stupid. I've made such a terrible mistake. I'm so sorry."

The sight of Joanna crying reduced me to jelly and so, perhaps foolishly, I held her close to me. The chemistry was still very much there.

I drew a deep breath before I could speak.

"Oh, JoJo, where did it all go wrong for us?" I said with a long sigh.

She pulled back from me and the expression on her face

changed. Her tearful eyes widened. I had clearly asked the right question.

"I know exactly when it went wrong Charlie. That's why I asked you here, there's something I can't leave without telling you. Do you remember that first morning at Poppies when you laid my head on the pillow, and I woke looking into your eyes? I desperately wanted to say I loved you, it was all I could think of. I *do* love you, Charlie, but I wouldn't allow myself to say it. I didn't say it, Charlie. That was the moment when I lost you."

The meaning of what she had just said was written across her face. Tears were rolling down her cheeks, she didn't need to say anything else. Joanna had never once used the 'L-word' before. She wouldn't even allow me to say the word. What she had just said was a revelation. Of course, I knew she loved me, but somehow her saying it made our relationship complete.

What happened next was a dangerously absurd thing to do. We looked into each other's eyes and we just automatically kissed. Everything else was inevitable. We made love with a passion that equalled our first night together. I left there several hours later, torn apart once again, and I've never seen nor heard from Joanna again.

No-one said a word. Stanley sat glum-faced while Audrey wiped tears from her face. Eventually she smiled.

"Well done, Charles," she said. "You do know that you're a fraud, don't you? You said your life was uninteresting!"

Stanley agreed. "Your modesty becomes you, Charles, but you've been to the top of the highest mountain. Most of us only get to the foothills!"

I guess he was right. I'd never seen it as a cherished memory, and much less as a privilege. In fact, there have been times when I considered it to be a curse, but Joanna did take me to a place where the air was rarefied, a place that I would have never otherwise known existed. Stanley really had made me think, and I offered one final thought.

"Your mountain analogy is a good one, Stanley, but you've made me realise that it's not all about standing on the summit. It's about how far it is to the valley below. I came from a very low point, and it was a hell of a long way up to the summit. No wonder she took my breath away!"

"What a wonderful way to look at it, Charles," Audrey said. "In my opinion, she was a fool. I would never have let you go."

Harold wasn't quite sure what to make of her comment, and neither did I. Stanley asked if I'd ever thought about trying to find Joanna again. That was a complicated question, but the simple answer was no.

For me, my journey from despair to ecstasy was always likely to be my longest journey. Joanna was such an exotic creature. She breathed the same rarefied air as I did, but she always had her own separate journey. The difference between us was that, when it was over, I had to go back to the place where I'd come from. Joanna moved on to a new place. I still needed her, but she no longer needed me.

Stanley was justifiably pleased with himself. Once again, he'd opened a book that I would have instinctively wanted to remain closed and, to my surprise, I was grateful to him. He sat in his chair looking extremely contented, though his expression changed slightly as he thought of yet another question to ask.

"Can I ask about your two daughters, Charles? We can't but help notice that you've never had a visit from either of them."

I suppose that question was inevitable at some time. My girls spent their entire childhood being told their father didn't love them or even want them. When you add to that the fact that Annie's version of reality was that their father was the cause of all their mother's problems, then it's inevitable that this would shape their personalities for life. Annie suffered a long period of dementia before she died of Alzheimer's. I had a horrible feeling that the girls see that as the final torment I had caused her. Stanley asked how I coped with that situation.

"Not very well," I replied.

Bill tried to change the subject because he could see I was uncomfortable.

"Tell us about your building business. How did that progress?"

I was grateful for this diversion. I devoted a large part of my life to the business. We gradually went from general construction into specialist house building, and through a process of expansion, combined with a few takeovers, ended up as one of the country's biggest house builders. I probably relied on Sylvia more than I had a right to but, bless her, she has stayed with me right to the end. She still deals with my personal stuff and the little bit of consultancy that I get asked to do.

I assumed they had heard of Bartlett Homes?

"We're a FTSE 250 company," I said.

Audrey, ever the financial analyst, knew all about Bartlett Homes.

"You never cease to surprise me, Charlie Bartlett!" she said. "I did wonder, but you never actually said!"

I could see Audrey was thinking.

"Oh! My goodness! You know what this means? Joanna gave you up in her pursuit of wealth and position, and you were that person all along!"

Lying in bed that night, unable to sleep, I quietly smiled to myself; a part of me 'left the building' that day. I could hardly believe I had shared those most personal aspects of my life, but I was so pleased I had.

Our little group was now intimately close. We had finally laid to rest that thorny question of why we had each decided to come here, to a retirement community. I had given up on life, I realise that now. I went there to leave my past behind, only to find that life has not given up on me.

My friends are the same, they each had their own demons.

I realise that by lowering our guard, we each expelled those demons, and of course, if you lower your guard, you do invite others in. Here was the key to our new-found close bond.

Above all, we had Stanley to thank for that. In so many ways, he himself remained a mystery. Did he intentionally orchestrate this bond that we now share between ourselves? I think he did. I had no idea what the future held for me in that place. Should I even have been there?

For the first time in ages, I was looking forward to tomorrow.

Chapter Twenty-Two
THE GREATER LOVE

We all sat down for breakfast the next morning and I immediately sensed an air of expectation.

"What are you lot up to?" I asked.

Audrey was smiling mischievously.

"We've been discussing you and Harold."

I looked at Harold in surprise.

"We'd like to ask you both something," Bill said.

Obviously intrigued, Harold asked Audrey to continue.

"Both of you have shared your former lives with us, and you were both known by a different name. So, Charlie when did you become Charles? And Harry when did you become Harold?"

I looked at Harold. We both laughed.

"I was christened Charles, but everyone always called me Charlie until I became the CEO of a FTSE 250 company and suddenly, I was 'Charles'!"

"I was christened Harold, but I was always called Harry, that is, until I came here. The whole point was to start afresh, so suddenly I was 'Harold'!"

"I was christened William, but I've only ever been called 'Bill'," laughed Bill.

"It was Charlie not Charles who told us his story yesterday,"

Audrey said. "And it was Harry not Harold who told us his story last week, so we've decided that we would like you both back!"

Harold smiled at me and I smiled at Audrey. It seemed that we had squared the circle.

The following weeks were uneventful, which means they were wonderfully enjoyable! We all did our own thing and enjoyed our own space, but we came even more alive when we were together. Our conversation had no boundaries. We would discuss politics, religion, philosophy, nothing was off limits, though it was interesting that our health issues now required little discussion.

An interesting recurring theme gradually emerged, often attaching itself to whatever the previous subject was, namely happiness.

A particularly in-depth discussion developed one evening before dinner. It started between Harry and me before the others arrived.

Harry obviously had something that was troubling him, and I guessed that it would concern Audrey. He'd taken an incredibly brave step when he publicly declared his love for her, but things did appear to have stalled. He said he had two concerns, the first being his age and the second being me.

He freely admitted to being very inexperienced with women, and that my relationship with Joanna had really made him realise there were things in life that he'd never experienced. We agreed that the early physical intensity of a relationship was not sustainable, but Harry had experienced that. What he was concerned about was emotional intensity.

Basically, he was asking me if I thought the intensity of love which existed between me and Joanna was possible at his age. I understood exactly what Harry was saying but struggled for words to express what I was trying to say. How do you describe the love between two people? All I could say was that, when I had been with Joanna, it was as if we were one being; nothing else existed.

"Bill would no doubt be able to explain it all away as a natural function of brain chemistry," I said, "but, if it was real for us, why did we need to question it? As for any connection with age, I can't see one. We both see the world in the same way today that we always did."

Harry agreed and said that perhaps he was just worrying about conforming to a social stereotype.

"Exactly! You should know better at your age, but better than what? There *is* nothing better."

Harry smiled. I think he was reassured, but I did add a caveat about emotional intensity and physical intensity not being quite the same thing. If he was thinking about making love to Audrey twice after dinner and again before breakfast, then he might do well to refine his schedule!

We laughed and chatted some more before Harry said there was another problem, namely me! It was obvious where this was going, but there wasn't the slightest tension or embarrassment between us. I knew Audrey had a flame burning for me. I knew that, because I had one that burned for her.

Harry didn't blame or despise me for that, which was remarkable. He simply wanted to know precisely where he stood, not the first time he'd asked me that! This was a long-standing issue which needed resolving, I knew that only too well. I had a distinct feeling of déjà vu.

Had I really lost Audrey? Was I letting her go simply due to my own inaction? I didn't know what to say but promised to talk to Audrey about it soon. The only thing abundantly clear was that Harry was head over heels about Audrey. I would need a first-rate reason to deny him.

The others joined us and asked what we had been deep in conversation about.

"Oh, just trivial stuff," Harry said, "Love, romance and those intense emotions, nothing serious!"

We all laughed but inevitably it sparked interest and we had to go over it all again. We had a wonderful discussion about happiness, approaching it from all angles from Socrates to Nietzsche.

Bill was inclined to agree with Socrates. You can't buy it and you won't find it by chasing after it. It did require personal effort, however. I agreed with him. I thought happiness and contentment ran a parallel course.

Stanley reminded us that Socrates was executed for corrupting the youth, so we all agreed that he must have been on to something. Bill liked the concept of "flow" meaning those moments when our minds are so focused that we become unaware of the passage of time.

He quoted something from Henry David Thoreau.

"Happiness is like a butterfly; the more you chase it, the more it will elude you, but if you turn your attention to other things, it will come and sit softly on your shoulder."

We all smiled. What made us all happy was simply being together and discussing things like this. We decided to head off to the restaurant.

"Brush that butterfly off your shoulder, Bill! Lead the way!" I said.

We had a delightful meal and talked some more about happiness. All the while I was thinking about Audrey. In so many ways, she too was an exotic creature, like Joanna. Why on earth did I not claim her for my own? I suddenly realised that Stanley was saying something to me.

"Another glass of wine, Charlie?"

I simply hadn't heard him, I was so far away in my thoughts! In my own way, I had no doubt that I loved Audrey, so why prevaricate? There was one possibility which was so ridiculous that I had pushed it out of my mind. Audrey couldn't erode my memory of Joanna, so it wasn't fair to ask her. I rationalised that a thirty-year-old memory had long ceased to represent reality. I should live in the present, not in the past.

I had now decided what I would say to Audrey, and that moment came much quicker than I expected. I suspect Harry had something to do with that!

-oOo-

That same evening Audrey asked me to walk her back to her apartment, and invited me in for a night cap. I spent my entire life avoiding situations like that! It would normally terrify me but, with the help of Stanley and the others, I now had a new confidence which amazed me! I took a deep breath, managing to come straight out with it.

"Audrey, neither of us has actually admitted it, but we both know in our own way that we love each other. I think I fell in love with you the first day we met. Do you remember? I glanced at you across the room, and your face lit up with a smile. Well, the thing is, what I'm trying to say is that, much as I love you, I can't ignore the fact that there is someone who loves you even more than I do."

Audrey gasped but I didn't allow her the time to respond, as I continued.

"I've experienced love once before, and I can never replace that, but you can. What you feel for me is preventing you from seeing what you have with Harry. He loves you with every fibre of his being. Reach out to him. For goodness sake, don't do what I did. Don't let it slip away."

Audrey burst into tears, which started me off too.

"That's the most wonderful and selfless thing I've ever heard. I can't believe you said that, Charlie."

"I can't believe I managed to say it either!"

We laughed and held each other. It had always seemed absurd to me that, considering what we felt for each other, that I'd never really kissed Audrey, not like I would kiss Joanna. Somehow that felt very wrong. I took a deep breath.

"If I kissed you now, one more time, could it always remain our secret?" Audrey had that wonderful smile; she didn't need to reply.

I spent the next several days absolutely tormented with

doubt, hoping that I'd made the correct decision. I knew from experience that I had form in that department; I allowed Joanna to slip away.

When I told Harry what I had told Audrey, I thought he was going to kiss me, so that helped to convince me! It took a little time, but we could all see the relationship between them blossoming into something that made us all smile.

Audrey and I kept our little secret and whenever the time is right, I wink at her and she smiles back, affirming that we would always keep our secret safe. It provides us with an invisible bond. I cherish them both. They're my dearest friends. And when Harry asked me to be his best man, I nearly kissed him!

Chapter Twenty-Three

THE WEDDING

They wanted a low-key affair at the local registry office. They considered all kinds of other exotic locations and venues, but eventually decided that they wanted a simple wedding, with the reception here in the Village. We obviously needed to add something to that; we weren't about to let them get away without something special! We knew Harry had organised the most amazing honeymoon, which Audrey was unaware of. A chauffeur-driven limousine was on standby to drive them to the airport where they would fly off to the Seychelles. We had to work hard to compete with that, but we came up with one or two ideas.

We knew where Audrey's nanny and lifelong friend Pam was living, but she was very elderly now and not in the best of health. Even though Pam was in a nursing home in Yorkshire, we decided we would get her here, even if it meant a private ambulance and nursing staff. Our other idea was Harry's old army buddy, Jim, but we didn't know where he was without asking Harry. However, Fiona was brilliant at this kind of research, so we quickly had her on the job. Armed with his Christian name, rank and his service in the Falklands, combined with his military award, not to mention his prosthetic leg, Fiona said it shouldn't take her more than a few minutes to find him.

I approached Pam and Jim initially by phone, and they were delighted at the prospect. Bill and I decided that we wouldn't send a car for Pam. We resolved to drive up to Yorkshire and bring her back ourselves. That proved to be a good decision, as it gave us plenty of time to get to know her, and to put her at ease. She was very frail and had lost her confidence to leave the nursing home, and this applied even more to her husband who really wasn't up to it. Bill and I stayed overnight beforehand, allowing her some time to get to know us two handsome young men before the journey back. Audrey was very suspicious that we were up to something, but we hoped we'd got away with it. Our plan was to get Pam to the Village on the day before the wedding, and Charlotte was going to see that she was well cared for in one of the vacant apartments.

Corporal Jim was no problem. He said that he and his wife would turn up on the day, so we planned exactly how we could keep them under wraps. Everything was going well so far, but we did have a recent history of our good intentions turning into fiasco! Fiona was insisting that we must remain on our very best behaviour. After we'd returned with Pam on the day before the wedding, Fiona and Sylvia were there taking care of last-minute arrangements, and Fiona took me to one side.

"I know all about you and Mum," she said. "She's doing the right thing, isn't she?"

I had adopted Fiona to some degree, I had even started to think of her as 'our' daughter, although I had only just realised that.

"You do know that she still has a thing for you?" Fiona said.

I didn't really want to hear that at this stage, so I tried to bluff my way out of it, but Fiona was having none of it. We talked about it in the most astonishingly frank way! Fiona just wanted to be sure that everyone was doing the right thing. She said that if she had to decide upon a father-in-law between Harry and myself, she wouldn't know which way to turn. She obviously adored Harry, but that wasn't her concern.

"The fact is, Charlie, if you ended up doing a 'Mrs. Robinson' on my Mum, I think she might turn and run down the aisle towards you."

As she left, she turned and said, "Don't do it, Charlie!"

Unsurprisingly, I had a tormented night, but the big day dawned, nevertheless. Everything was going like clockwork. It would be too much for Pam to go to the registry office, so the plan was for Pam and Jim to be the surprise special guests at the reception. Our first surprise arrived courtesy of half a dozen of Harry's recent PMC comrades. They turned up in two armoured personnel carriers, kitted out to transport everyone to and from the registry office. What a masterstroke! Everyone was wide eyed. They had steps at the rear for us lot to climb in, and when Lizzy said she wouldn't be able to make it, she was picked up and placed inside. It was a triumph, though it was not what Audrey had in mind, but she joined in with the spirit of it immediately.

It all happened so quickly, I didn't have time to worry about it. Before I had time to think, we were standing in front of the registrar and I had the ring in my hand. Audrey looked fabulous; she wore a wonderful powder blue silk shift dress and matching jacket with three-quarter-length sleeves. The whole outfit was finished off with an impressive hat which would have turned heads at Ascot, let alone at the Village. Harry looked like an advert for Giorgio Armani, and in every respect, they looked like the perfect couple. The registrar went through the service and as she approached the crucial part, Audrey turned to me and smiled. I winked at her, our secret signal, and she winked back. I offered Harry the ring and, in the blink of an eye, I had lost her.

Everyone was elated, and I was lost among the hand-shaking, the kissing and the hugging. Fiona was the first to kiss and hug me, and then I shook hands and put my arms around Harry.

"Well done, mate! You've just won the star prize! Take care of her."

Harry wanted to say something, but he was quickly overtaken by hand-shaking. Eventually it was my turn to hug Audrey. Neither of us said anything for quite a while. I'd re-hearsed what I intended to say, something about reaching the summit with Harry and never looking back. Although I tried, nothing came out. I couldn't say a damn word! Fortunately, I was overtaken by other well-wishers.

We made our way back to the wedding reception in the personnel carriers, feeling for all the world like a triumphant army marching into Rome. We were greeted by more friends and the Village staff who were waiting for us. There were more of Harry's army comrades who had formed a guard of honour, all standing to attention and saluting the happy couple. Harry was elated. His military pals, combined with the personnel carriers, had neatly managed to combine his past with the present. He was completely in his element.

He stepped out of the vehicle with all the swagger of an Emperor. I could almost hear the crowd chanting 'Hail Caesar,' as the Emperor unveiled his exotic treasure, offering his hand as Audrey stepped out of the vehicle. As they made their way inside past the guard of honour, we sprang our surprise in the shape of Pam and Jim, and the reaction from the newlyweds was quite something to behold! Audrey was immediately overcome with tears, her joy at being reunited with Pam was a very special moment. However, as soon as Harry saw Jim, it was immediately obvious that we had little understanding of the bond which existed between those two soldiers. Harry is the toughest character I know, but the reunion was too much for them both. Fiona, as always, was brilliant. She saw the situation and ushered the pair of them into a side room to give them some time in private.

The wedding lunch was the perfect occasion. The restaurant was beautifully decorated with flowers, the staff had excelled, and the meal was exceptional. When it came to Harry's speech, he also excelled. He said how he had come to the Village not knowing what to expect but hoping to simply turn a page in his life and leave the previous chapters behind him. He joked how he thought he would even leave 'Harry' behind. He said that not even in his wildest imagination did he ever think that he would meet someone like Audrey. When he did, he simply looked from afar, never daring to think that one day she might be his. He went on to say that even now, when he looks at Audrey, he still had to pinch himself to see if he was dreaming!

He thanked me as the best man and gave me all sorts of praise, none of which I deserved. He improvised the end of his speech which he finished by saying that, after the ceremony, I told him that he'd won the star prize and he agreed. He ended by saying that there was no greater prize than sharing his future life with Audrey. He did so well, and received a rapturous applause.

As for my speech, I'd been rather cowardly. I prepared two: one where I would wax lyrical about how wonderful these two people were, especially Audrey, of course, and how they were at the start of a road which would take them to ever greater happiness; my other speech thanked everyone, made a joke about Harry and then proposed a toast. I opted for the latter.

The afternoon merged into the evening. It was a splendid day; everything ran like clockwork, there wasn't a single fiasco. Lizzy did fall over, dragging down one of the tables of flowers, but that was brushed aside as an everyday occurrence. This had been Audrey's day and she was truly magnificent. It had all been a fairy-tale and she was the queen of the ball, which she so richly deserved. I found myself thinking back to when she described her big function where Freddy and his friends had disgraced themselves by humiliating her. I knew Audrey hadn't forgotten that awful day; perhaps she thought about it today. In any event, today had been perfect and it had surely drawn a veil over those shadows from her past.

All too soon it became time for the happy couple to depart and we all started to initiate our goodbyes. Harry was in such high spirits, he was irrepressible. He was busy shaking hands and hugging everyone in sight! Audrey maintained her usual elegance, as she flitted among the guests. I think I was probably the very last person she turned to as she stood by the door. Harry was putting their luggage in the limousine when I reached out my hands toward her.

She took my hands in hers.

"Thank you for everything." Then she kissed me on the lips, saying, "Bye, Charlie."

I winked our secret signal, but she had already turned away.

I went back toward my favourite chair in the lounge to find Fiona heading in the same direction.

"I was looking for you, Charlie, are you okay?" she asked.

We sat down and discussed the day. I thanked her again for organising so much of it, but she dismissed her efforts, and asked me to thank Sylvia for the help she'd given her.

"I don't know what you'd do without Sylvia." she said. "It was a lovely day, wasn't it? And seeing them together like they were today, I think she's made the right decision Charlie. I really think they're going to be very happy together."

I smiled through the alcoholic haze that surrounded me.

"Don't worry about your mum. She's made the right decision. She's got a lot of catching up to do with her life and she's well on the way to doing it."

We chatted some more until she said she needed to check on everyone else. Then she kissed me on the cheek and said she'd see me before she left.

"Now that you won't be my stepdaughter," I said through the haze, "can you be my adopted stepdaughter?"

"Don't be silly, Charlie. I already am!"

Sylvia came into the room just as Fiona was leaving, and the two of them hugged each other. I hadn't realised that they had become so close.

I asked Sylvia to sit with me, but she said she had a taxi waiting and had just come to say goodnight. We agreed the day had gone incredibly well, and she made the comment that Harry and Audrey really did make the perfect couple.

"I know you might have thought otherwise, Charlie, but Audrey *has* made the right decision, you know. She will be happier with Harry."

With that she kissed me, albeit briefly, which was something she had never done before.

"I'm sorry, Charlie, you've lost another of the women in your life. We all seem to go the same way."

She then left, saying she would see me next week when she had some draft proposals the Board wanted me to look at.

I sat there wondering why it was that my life was surrounded by women who seemed to know more about me than I did. Even my PA apparently knows me better than I know myself!

Chapter Twenty-Four
LIZZY'S FINAL SURPRISE

Audrey and Harry came back from their honeymoon like a couple of teenagers. They seemed to light up the entire Village. Happiness is apparently contagious; everyone enjoyed just being around them. One evening when we were all together in the bar, there was a song playing, *Why must I be a teenager in love?* Bill and I started singing it aloud and soon others were joining in, directing it towards Audrey and Harry. In no time at all, everyone was singing. Rather than being embarrassed, they hugged each other and sang along; it was a special moment. Then of course the inevitable happened.

"Oh, isn't it silly? I just can't think who sang that," Stanley said.

This was an old song, even for us lot! Of course, none of us could remember who was singing it, and so the torment began; was it so-and-so or was it someone else?

We were just getting to the point where our brains were beginning to ache when Fiona arrived; Audrey had invited her to dinner. She hugged her mother. It was the first time she'd seen her since the wedding, and she had an equally enthusiastic hug for Harry. She turned towards the rest of us.

"Hello, you lot," she said and blew me a kiss.

We immediately asked her if she knew who was singing the song, whereupon she produced her mobile and, in a few seconds, she came up with the answer.

"Dion and the Belmonts."

Lizzy was dumbstruck. How could this be?

"Oh, it's called Shazam," Fiona said. "I just point my phone at it, and it tells me what the song is."

We couldn't believe it! We needed another demonstration, but it worked again! In no time at all, Fiona had somehow enabled all our phones to carry out this trick, and it suddenly dawned on me that perhaps we might miss those endless hours of torment. Life was never going to be quite the same again!

We went through to the restaurant.

"We need to talk to you about where we're going to live," said Harry.

A discussion ensued, and it soon became evident that they were considering buying a house outside the Village.

"You mean you would leave us here?" asked Lizzy.

Audrey looked upset and said this was the problem. They needed a bigger house because they were living in her single apartment, and when they really thought about it, they didn't *need* to be in a retirement community.

Stanley suddenly took command of the gathering by swirling his wine glass as if he was about to make a pronouncement. Everyone fell silent, which had been Stanley's intention!

"If I might be allowed to say something, my dear, you overlook one thing. You may not need the Village, but the Village certainly needs you."

I agreed with Stanley, and said that if they left, we'd have no option but to go with them! They did indeed need a bigger apartment but unfortunately there were none available in the Village.

Now, if there was one thing that I understood well, it was acquiring land and building houses, so I suggested they leave the whole thing to me. I'd have a think about it. The rest of the evening was wonderful, with one of our usual in-depth discussions. On this occasion it was about the current world-wide financial disaster.

It was all a bit too much for Lizzy who said she was feeling under the weather and was going to retire for the evening. She staggered off with a wave goodbye. She was barely out of sight when there was a loud crash.

"She's walked into the hall table again," Harry said.

We all agreed that's what had happened. I went to check, just to be sure she was on her way again. When I rounded the corner, Lizzy was still lying on the floor. I hastened towards her, seeing no movement.

"Lizzy?" I said, bending over her and patting her hand.

I looked closely and checked her pulse. I couldn't find one, so shouted out for help and everyone came running, including Charlotte. She quickly took command of the situation, instructing one of the assistants to call an ambulance as she began CPR. She continued with it for five or ten minutes.

Finally, she said, "I'm so sorry. Lizzy's dead."

We stood around her in silence; it wasn't possible! Lizzy was indestructible! Charlotte was wonderful, telling us all to go back to the lounge. She would take care of Lizzy. We all realised that the Grim Reaper stalked the corridors of a place like this, and that, heaven forbid, Charlotte was of course used to it. I can't imagine what we would have done without her. The shock was delayed, and none of it seemed quite real. We discussed every aspect of Lizzy's health looking for some clue as to what might have caused it.

"Whatever it was that has taken her, she's gone," Harry said. "Let's raise our glasses to Lizzy!"

We all realised he was right, and a terrible sadness fell over us. The time between that difficult moment and the funeral felt like a strange hinterland between life and death. Lizzy was gone but not yet completely gone. We were the only people to attend the funeral. Charlotte said she had no record of any next of kin, not even any documentation in her apartment, and so it was a quiet but dignified send-off. When we returned, I took Charlotte to one side to ask about the funeral expenses as there were no next of kin. I was thinking I would cover the cost. Charlotte looked a little embarrassed.

"I had to promise not to mention it, but Stanley has paid for everything," she said.

It wasn't until that evening that we really felt Lizzy had truly left us. Our conversation was naturally about her, and it didn't take long for Audrey to mention that maybe we should now think about obtaining the marriage and death certificates for her four husbands. We debated it at length, but our eventual decision was to let sleeping dogs lie; perhaps it was better if Lizzy's secrets died with her.

-oOo-

This was how the situation was left until a month later when, one afternoon, a gentleman arrived at reception, asking for each one of us by name. We sat down with him and he introduced himself as a local solicitor. He had just read about Lizzy's death in the local paper; did we know that we were all beneficiaries in her Will? We said we didn't even know that she had a Will. The solicitor asked us if we had any idea about Lizzy's affairs, and so we said again that we had no idea at all.

"In that case," he said, "I think you're going to be surprised."

Then he told us that Lizzy had left an estate of over fifteen million pounds! Stanley was the first to break the silence.

"Good God!" he exclaimed, a sentiment we all echoed.

The solicitor continued, saying that although we five were named as her closest friends, she didn't feel we needed all the money, so she was leaving us £100,000 each, the rest to go to the various charities that she supported.

It was a long, long time before this news really sank in. The solicitor finally took his leave after no end of paperwork, and we were left alone in our dumbstruck condition.

"I'll have a single malt. Make it a large one," Stanley said.

"I'll have what he's having," I said.

Everyone else said to 'make it a large one'. Harry returned from the bar with our drinks and five minutes later, I went back for the same again!

Lizzy was right, we didn't need any of this money, but that wasn't the point. The point was that this seemed to confirm our worst suspicions!

"What do we do now?" Audrey said. "If we accept the money, are we not a part of the problem? I can't possibly accept it!"

Just at this point I said that I had something important to say to Audrey and Harry, and that, although I'd been keeping it as a surprise, recent developments meant this was probably a good time to mention it. I then drew their attention to some open farmland adjacent to the far corner of the Village.

"No secret there, Charlie," Harry said. "The landowner refuses to sell".

"Indeed, until I made him an offer he couldn't refuse!"

Then I went on to explain that I'd been in several long negotiations, and now had an agreement with the retirement community proprietors and the local planning department. That wasn't all! Would they like to see the plans for the apartment which I proposed we build? The look on their faces was priceless! I could never describe my satisfaction! Socrates was quite right, you just need to make a little bit of an effort.

When they were over the shock and had stopped hugging me, I mentioned the obvious. What would Lizzy say if she knew that she had the opportunity to pay for their house? Audrey smiled; we all knew what Lizzy would have said! Stanley said he'd give his share to his son and daughter. Bill said he'd give it to his children too, and I said that was exactly what I had in mind. I said everyone could rest in peace, knowing that the money was all going to good causes. We raised our glasses to Lizzy in a toast.

"Well! She definitely wasn't Mrs. Wilberforce, was she!" I said.

Chapter Twenty-Five
THE APARTMENT

The next few months were exciting times. It was as if the entire Village was involved with the design and build of Audrey and Harry's apartment. If the truth be told, we had little scope with the design. My agreement with the Village proprietors meant that we had to conform to the rest of the architecture, and it had to be the standard two-bedroom apartment design. However, this left us with some leeway regarding the internal layout and the fixtures and fittings, all of which had Audrey's full attention.

Harry attempted to offer some suggestions in the initial phase, but he soon accepted that he had better leave the decisions to Audrey and to everyone else. We had endless hours of debate over room layouts, the size of this or that, and then the colour of this or that, but Sylvia had it all under control.

For my part, I was in my element. I must admit, I would have much preferred a free hand with this building. As soon as the machines turned up to begin the ground works and I had donned my hard hat, I felt ten years younger!

All the Bartlett Homes staff were more than aware that they were working for the ex-CEO and largest shareholder. I couldn't help but think how easy it would have been if all my developments had progressed so smoothly!

I made one thing abundantly clear, especially to the site manager. I told him that as far as he was concerned, Audrey was the Queen of England. If she walked over the site and there was a puddle, then he was Sir Francis Drake, and if Audrey wanted anything, it was already hers.

I think perhaps I must have put the fear of God into the entire construction team because they literally took me at my word! I knew that, for the crew, this had started out as a bit of fun. Audrey did have a regal presence and although she continued to treat it in good humour, I noticed how quickly it ceased to be just fun for the crew. They genuinely wanted to be helpful and to show respect. It's interesting when you realise that respect is only ever earned.

November slipped into December as the final finishing touches were added, and our hopes for the apartment to be finished for Christmas were obviously on target.

We had a ribbon-cutting ceremony, an abundance of tears from Audrey and Fiona, a very un-manly hug from Harry, not to mention a ridiculously long speech from him, heaping another load of undeserved praise upon me.

Everything had gone so well, except for one significant exception. Stanley had suffered a stroke. It was relatively mild, so he was out of hospital and back among us within a week.

For Audrey, especially, it was devastating. The reminder of what had happened to her father was just too strong, and I felt so very sorry for her; this was supposed to be her moment.

Stanley returned to us just before Christmas, and while he put a brave face on it, he wasn't the Stanley of old. However, the main thing was that he was with us for the festive period.

The fact that Audrey was in her new home with Harry raised her morale enormously, and we all joined in with the spirit of the occasion. We had Christmas lunch in the restaurant followed by an evening of champagne and mince pies in the new apartment.

It certainly raised Stanley's spirits which, of course, added to ours; it was a wonderful day.

Unknown to us, the entire Village and staff had arranged to come out carrying torches, surrounding the apartment as they started to sing *Noel*. We'd had no idea about this, and it was just the most perfect moment!

Stanley's stroke hit me very hard. I hadn't realised how attached to the old boy I'd become. Everyone pampered him with attention.

He'd been told not to drink but as far as his whisky was concerned, this was like asking a bird not to fly! I instructed Alan to select his very finest single malts from the bar's comprehensive collection, and Stanley revelled in giving me tasting instructions on each one.

Two days after Boxing Day, I pushed him back to his apartment in a wheelchair and got him into bed. He didn't want me to go, so we chatted for some considerable time.

I asked him the question that I had always wanted to ask.

"Why does it seem to be your mission to get people to reveal their life stories?"

He smiled broadly, his kind smile making his cheeks even more rosy.

"Look at you, Charlie. Are you not a happier person, now that you've shared your life with us?" I had to agree.

"Look at the others, are they not happier, and are we not all closer together now?"

Once again, I agreed.

"Why you, though, Stanley? Why is it your mission?"

"I suppose I'm just a selfish old sod," he said. "You know me, Charlie. I've got the gift of the gab but, if I can share that gift with someone and leave them happier than when I found them, then for me that's my gift well shared. It gives me a lot of pleasure in return."

I realised he was quite right. Everyone left Stanley's company a little happier for the experience. I still wasn't quite clear how he managed to do it, but what a wonderful gift to have! Even better that it gave him such pleasure in return.

I asked him if it wasn't about time that he told us his story, sensing that it was more interesting than all of ours combined.

He smiled and said it would take a long time, and he wasn't sure he had that much time left. We joked about that, and I said he had at least another cask of whisky to sample yet; the prospect brought a smile to his face.

Then he said something rather strange.

"Did you see that miserable bugger today, wearing a black cloak with a hood, and carrying a scythe? I'm not sure I can evade him much longer."

I said he was talking nonsense and I would see him in the morning. Whenever bidding Stanley goodnight and saying you would see him tomorrow, he would always respond in just the same way

"If I'm spared, dear boy, if I'm spared."

Well, that night, Stanley wasn't spared.

-oOo-

Stanley's departure hit me like a runaway train. I had only known the man for a little less than a year, but I had a bond with him which was difficult to describe. My father had died when I was relatively young. Although Stanley was not old enough to be my father, I suspected that in some ways he'd become a father-figure to me. We were all devastated, but none more than me; it was an awful time.

We all went to the funeral which was organised by his family, none of whom we had ever seen before. It was an unforgettable experience. We knew so little about Stanley other than the fact that he appeared to have been everywhere, done everything, and seemed to personally have known most of the world's population! It was not so long ago that we had attended Lizzy's funeral where we were the only attendees. I somehow expected something similar.

Within moments of arriving at the church, this was decidedly not what we found. The church was already full, with people lined up outside. There were hundreds of mourners. We couldn't hear the service, which was such a shame, though I'm not sure that we needed to. Later at the gathering, we spoke to various other mourners, each with their unlikely tales of Stanley, but each story familiar to us. We introduced ourselves to Stanley's son and daughter, who said their father had spoken so kindly about us, and they were pleased to finally meet us. We left the gathering realising that, in so many ways, we were just one small part of the incredible story known as 'Stanley'.

The story, however, wasn't quite over. That evening in the bar, we were trying to enjoy a drink but even the thought of a single malt was more than I could cope with. I had a gin and tonic, the same as Audrey. Personally, I loathe the stuff, but I needed the alcohol.

At that point, Alan came into the bar and we told him about the day's events.

"I'm really going to miss him, but it must be terrible for you, especially you, Charlie. You were always so close," he said. "Hang on a moment, he left something behind the bar the other week. He said I'd know when to give it to you. I guess he meant now."

He produced an envelope. On the front it said, "This round is on me. I'll have a single malt."

Inside there was £1000 in cash together with a note. The writing was extremely shaky, and it said:

"   *Thank you, my friends, for the wonderful but brief time we have shared together.*

Thank you for the whisky you all so generously shared with me.

A single malt whisky given in generosity and friendship has so much more to say for itself than one you buy yourself. The act of giving sets the whisky free.

Think of me when I buy the next round and listen to what the whisky tells you.

Let that be my gift to you.   Stanley.   "

Chapter Twenty-Six
AN UNEXPECTED VISITOR

The New Year was, as always, a time to reflect and to look forward to a clean sheet. Audrey and Harry were living the dream, and when I needed cheering up, all I had to do was to be in their company. Audrey had left behind her misguided love for me, but what remains between us is a very special and unique relationship. We never talk about it, but our little secret sign endures, and it epitomises our relationship. We were never lovers, but we are so very much more than friends. Fiona did indeed adopt me as a kind of stepfather and whenever we are together as a group, she walks with her arms around both Harry and me. She is everything to me that I have lost in my own girls.

Bill will never really stop grieving for his beloved Sarah, certainly not if it would mean diminishing the memory of her, but time has replaced some of the pain with happy memories. The New Year gave us all the opportunity for a fresh start, and even Bill decided that he would go on a diet. I was delighted, doing everything I could to encourage him. Not only would this be good for his health. I knew it meant that he was once again thinking about the future.

Stanley had left a gift out of all proportion to the brief time we shared together. I read Stanley's note over and over, and he was so right. Every subsequent glass of single malt whisky that Stanley generously buys me has something of him in it. Sometimes he adds great joy, or perhaps great sadness, but every single glass really does have so much more to say for itself. Finally, I understand that, when Stanley spoke of the peat, or citrus and berry fruits, or the smell of sherry or vanilla, it really was because his glass spoke to him, just as mine now speaks to me. Thank you, Stanley.

As for me, I tread a difficult path between despair and happiness. Often great happiness, and seldom deep despair, but I need to watch my step along that path. The good times with the others are always wonderful but it's those times alone, lost in my own thoughts when the 'what might have been' moments come back to haunt me. If I allow myself to enter that dark place, I might even end up finding Joanna. So it was that afternoon.

It was an afternoon much like any other. Audrey and Harry had gone out somewhere together, and Bill was out for the day with his daughter. They all very politely asked if I'd like to go with them, but of course these are occasions for them to share together. They didn't need me, and so I thought I'd relax with a good book in the lounge.

As always, my concentration was limited, and I read a little and then let my mind drift off. It was a bit like letting go of the string of a helium balloon; my thoughts would bob around in the wind. One moment I was thinking about Stanley, dear Stanley, and how much I miss him. The next moment, I dived into my life with Annie and my girls. Then I was pondering what might have been with Audrey, when I found I had been blown into the branches of a tree and my trailing string was snagged in numerous places. I decided to get back to my book. Just at that moment, Charlotte came over to me.

"There you are, Charlie. I've been looking for you. There's a woman in reception asking for you. She says she would like to talk to you."

I was obviously intrigued.

"It's been a while since a woman came looking for me, did she say what it was about?"

"No, she says it's a personal matter."

Even more intriguing! I asked what sort of woman we were talking about.

"She's a young woman, early thirties, extremely pretty girl, an American, I think. Said her name is Molly Wright".

I was even more intrigued. An American. Molly Wright. I had no idea! I said I couldn't wait to see this mysterious woman, and Charlotte said she would bring her through to me.

I sat waiting for my mystery woman to appear and, when she did, my heart jumped into my throat! It was Joanna! Except of course, it *wasn't* Joanna. This was a young woman! I immediately pulled myself together, telling myself I was an idiot for imagining things, but the resemblance was remarkable! Then I realised that my memory was playing tricks with me. This young lady was about the age Joanna was the last time I saw her thirty years ago.

She introduced herself and sat opposite me. She was obviously ill at ease, and it all felt a little awkward. However, after initial pleasantries, she paused and looked at me with a serious expression.

"You are Charlie Bartlett?"

"Yes, my dear, what can I do for you?"

"Can I ask you just three questions?" I was really hooked!

"Ask me anything, my dear."

She sat back in her chair and brushed a waft of blonde hair away from her forehead with the single stroke of a finger. I could see that, whatever these three questions were, they were extremely important to her, such that she was struggling to utter the words.

I tried to help her get started.

"Whatever it is, my dear, just say it. I won't bite!"

Molly drew a long deep breath.

"Is the Poppies Hotel near Clifton a significant place for you?"

Once again, my heart leaped into my throat.

"Yes," I answered.

Molly drew another very deep and slightly shaky breath.

"Does the name Joanna mean anything to you?"

Not only was my heart racing, I felt my hands shaking as well.

"Yes, I loved her."

Molly's eyes welled up with emotion, and I noticed her hands were also trembling. Then she said that Joanna was her mother.

"Do you remember the date 18th of June 1982?"

"Yes," was all I could say.

"What I'm about to tell you, Charlie, is going to be a shock but I promise you it's true."

She paused for a long moment, but then finally said what she had come to tell me.

"I am your daughter."

There can be few times in life when just a few words have the power to hit you like a bolt of lightning, but this was one such time. Molly sat silently waiting for my response. For my part, my mental circuitry had tripped a fuse. I looked at her and raised my hand a little as if to say hang on a second, give me a moment to regroup.

I managed to compose myself sufficiently to reply.

"I don't doubt it for a second."

I'm not sure what reaction Molly had expected, but mine was obviously at the top end of her scale. She leaped out of her chair and hugged me, her tears running down my neck.

"We have an awful lot of catching up to do," I eventually managed to say.

Molly smiled that same broad smile of her mother's.

"I've got one more thing that I've been told to say, and you must think about it before you answer."

In truth, I wasn't sure I could cope with any more surprises, but I answered.

"Go ahead."

Molly took another deep breath.

"The message is 'I need a nice man to talk to. Are you still that nice man, Charlie'?"

Molly could see my reaction.

She glanced over her shoulder towards the car park.

"She's in the car, Charlie."

THE END

A Final Word from the Author

As I wrote those final dramatic words, "She's in the car, Charlie", I have to confess I had to wipe a tear from my laptop!

I knew immediately that it couldn't end there. I had inadvertently ended the story by beginning another. It had never been my intention to continue the story; it simply became inevitable.

It continues as Joanna's story in Autumn Daffodils, where both their lives are taken to a final conclusion.

An introduction to the first chapter follows.

I hope you have enjoyed this book, and I would really love a nice review! Thank you!

Peter Turnham

AUTUMN DAFFODILS

JOANNA'S STORY

Chapter One
THE DOOR OPENS

My decision to wait in the car had been an easy one to make. This was Molly and Charlie's moment. However difficult, this was something they both had to confront. I was quite another matter. Charlie didn't have to confront me again; it would have to be his choice. I had always known this moment would come. Having Molly reminded me of it every day. I acquired Charlie along the way, but Molly was born attached to him. It was inevitable that the thread joining us would eventually draw us together.

After what felt like an eternity, the door suddenly opened, and Molly stepped through it. For a brief second, I thought she was alone. Perhaps Charlie really had refused to see me. Then I saw that he was following close behind her, his hand clasped in hers! They took a few steps into the light. Charlie stopped in his tracks the second he saw me. Molly stepped back, putting her arm around him. This was the moment I had spent so long both dreading and longing for, in equal measure. I stepped out of the car and stood in that moment.

Continued.........

About the Author

Peter Turnham describes himself as an accidental novelist. As a semi-retired businessman, Peter's life was very active, until an injury incapacitated him for several months. Unable to be active, he turned to writing.

The result was his first novel, 'Autumn Daffodils'. Inspired by the success of 'Daffodils', he has written a second novel, 'Autumn Daffodils – Joanna's Story'.

He lives in the English Cotswold hills with Carol, his wife and collaborator. They have three adult children and four young grandchildren. They manage a holiday cottage, as well as fishing interests.

Peter is a passionate fly fisherman, and amateur cabinet maker. He has a keen interest in many aspects of science and is particularly interested in the environment and climate change.

www.peterturnhamauthor.com
peterturnham.author@gmail.com

Made in the USA
Las Vegas, NV
25 May 2022